Praise for the Jaded Gentleman Series

Seduction Wears Sapphires

"An amazing read. I enjoyed it immensely . . . Ashe and Caroline are wonderful characters that made me fall in love with them from the beginning of the story."
—*Night Owl Reviews*

"A fine book, well crafted, well researched, and an entertaining romantic novel . . . Historical romance fans will be delighted, I have no doubt." —*The Book Binge*

"What a refreshing new take on two people who from first sight are determined to detest each other . . . I was immediately engrossed with the fiery, witty dialogue and the curiosity of how this couple, who loathed each other upon their meeting, would come full circle to a beautifully shared love in the end." —*Fiction Vixen*

Revenge Wears Rubies

"Sensuality fairly steams from Bernard's writing. This luscious tale will enthrall you. Enjoy!"
—Sabrina Jeffries, *New York Times* bestselling author

"If you're a fan of spicy hot romances mixed with a bit of intrigue and set in Victorian London, don't miss this one!" —*The Romance Dish*

"Galen's journey from emotional cripple to ability to love is a captivating, er...

Ecstasy
Wears Emeralds

RENEE BERNARD

BERKLEY SENSATION, NEW YORK

THE BERKLEY PUBLISHING GROUP
Published by the Penguin Group
Penguin Group (USA) Inc.
375 Hudson Street, New York, New York 10014, USA

Penguin Group (Canada), 90 Eglinton Avenue East, Suite 700, Toronto, Ontario M4P 2Y3, Canada
(a division of Pearson Penguin Canada Inc.)
Penguin Books Ltd., 80 Strand, London WC2R 0RL, England
Penguin Group Ireland, 25 St. Stephen's Green, Dublin 2, Ireland (a division of Penguin Books Ltd.)
Penguin Group (Australia), 250 Camberwell Road, Camberwell, Victoria 3124, Australia
(a division of Pearson Australia Group Pty. Ltd.)
Penguin Books India Pvt. Ltd., 11 Community Centre, Panchsheel Park, New Delhi—110 017, India
Penguin Group (NZ), 67 Apollo Drive, Rosedale, Auckland 0632, New Zealand
(a division of Pearson New Zealand Ltd.)
Penguin Books (South Africa) (Pty.) Ltd., 24 Sturdee Avenue, Rosebank, Johannesburg 2196,
South Africa

Penguin Books Ltd., Registered Offices: 80 Strand, London WC2R 0RL, England

This is a work of fiction. Names, characters, places, and incidents either are the product of the author's imagination or are used fictitiously, and any resemblance to actual persons, living or dead, business establishments, events, or locales is entirely coincidental. The publisher does not have any control over and does not assume any responsibility for author or third-party websites or their content.

ECSTASY WEARS EMERALDS

A Berkley Sensation Book / published by arrangement with the author

PRINTING HISTORY
Berkley Sensation mass-market paperback edition / September 2011

ISBN: 978-0-425-24372-5

BERKLEY SENSATION®
Berkley Sensation Books are published by The Berkley Publishing Group,
a division of Penguin Group (USA) Inc.,
375 Hudson Street, New York, New York 10014.
BERKLEY SENSATION® and the "B" design are trademarks of Penguin Group (USA) Inc.

PRINTED IN THE UNITED STATES OF AMERICA

10 9 8 7 6 5 4 3 2 1

For the real Rowan we lost. If the universe holds any logic or beauty, somewhere out there, you are laughing and chasing the stars. When the wheel turns again, I hope you get to be a spoiled, fat, and happy prince.

For Geoffrey and my beautiful girls. There are no words for how much I love you. None.

Acknowledgments

How is it that with every book the list of people I need to thank just gets longer and longer? I'm hoping it's a sign of a life well lived and the blessings that come with knowing so many wonderful people. (And not the reverse, which would be that I'm losing my ability to keep it together unless there are more and more hands on deck.)

I want to thank my incredible editor, Kate Seaver, and the fantastic team at Berkley. It's been a dream to work with all of you, and I'm continually surprised with how easy you make it for me.

Thank you again also to Readers Entertainment/COS Productions and Sheila English for having me on board and giving me an excuse to laugh at least once a week on *Canned Laughter and Coffee*. You've created such a warm community for readers and authors to find each other, and I'm grateful to be a part of it.

We lost Geoffrey's father while I was working on this book, and for anyone facing the decline of a parent due to Lewy body dementia, you know what it was like. But I wanted to take this chance to thank the wonderful people at the care home Sunshine Manor, as well as Partners in Care and Hospice. Through it all, we were lucky enough to have stronger, wiser, loving shoulders to lean on . . .

My eldest is now the official darling of the ER at Marshall Hospital, so I can't forget to include all the nurses and doctors who are doing their best to keep me sane and convince my five-year-old that she should be more careful. (The free teddy bears they give out seem to be working as an incentive in the wrong direction, if you ask me.)

My thanks to Lisa Richardson, who has become part of the family, for everything you do so gracefully and selflessly to keep us afloat and organized. The girls adore you, but I'm right behind them. You're beautiful inside and out, m'lady. Thank you for your friendship and support.

To my author friends, near and far, *thank you* just doesn't cover it. If I list you all, it will look like shameless name-dropping, but you help me to feel less isolated as I battle it out with my keyboard. You know who you are. I'm just eternally amazed that you answer my emails and take my calls and even pretend to know who *I* am. Thank you.

And just in case she feels left out, I want to thank my mom. I seem to be one fan of many when it comes to everything she's doing these days, volunteering at her local hospital, participating in social clubs, caring for others, and being the consummate friend; I'm breathless with fatigue just listening to her schedule. When I grow up, I want to be just like her.

And to all the readers who have continued to send emails and notes from all over the world—thank you! You literally make this all worthwhile, and I'm endlessly cheered and motivated to improve when I think of you. Thank you for picking up the books and for keeping romance alive!

What is the body? That shadow of a shadow
of your love, that somehow contains
the entire universe.

—RUMI

Ecstasy
Wears Emeralds

Chapter
1

Winter 1859
London

"Bless you, Dr. West." The woman's hands gripped his arm through his white shirtsleeve, desperation and grief giving her fingers an icy strength that guaranteed bruises would bloom later. "Thank you for staying so late!"

Rowan shook his head. "No need to say any of that, Mrs. Blythe. Jackson's resting comfortably now, and I'll be by in another day or two to see how he's coming along." He reached up to cover her fingers with his gloved hand. "Send for me if he worsens. Ignore the hour and just send for me, Mrs. Blythe."

Her son was dying. And Rowan was little more than a witness to the young man's gradual demise. At sixteen, Jackson was one of his favorite patients—all fire and bravado, all adolescent manly swagger interspersed with quiet moments when he and Rowan would talk about everything and nothing without his mother's anxious presence.

Jackson had never recovered from a terrible fever he'd suffered at twelve, and his heart and lungs had failed to work as they should ever since. Each winter took its toll, and now it was a matter of days or weeks before the widowed Mrs. Blythe lost the love of her only child and draped her house in black crepe.

And she's standing there thanking me.

"I will," she replied, the vow making her eyes darken with emotion. "Any hour, and I will send for you. Bless y—"

"Please, Mrs. Blythe. Save your blessings for yourself and your beautiful boy. I am . . . in your service. If I could do more . . ." *Damn.* His professional façade was crumbling fast, and it was all he could do to retreat out her front door and down the steps to his waiting carriage. *What kind of physician waters up like a fool?*

I'm tired. Too many long nights and my emotions are too frayed to fend off a woman like Mrs. Blythe. She'd wanted him to lie, and he knew the game. He was supposed to reassure her that Jackson looked better, that this rest would do him a world of good, and that she should see about some new books for him to read while he recovered so that he would be prepared for the university exams in the spring.

How hard was it to lie?

Harder and harder. I've lost my knack for it since India. Hell, I've lost my knack for a lot of things. . . .

"Home, Theo." He climbed into the carriage unassisted, throwing his leather physician's bag unceremoniously onto the seat next to him. He slammed the door behind him and leaned back, a man without the energy for sighs or self-pity, and stretched out his long legs to rest them on the upholstered seat across from him.

The carriage pulled away and his loyal driver skillfully navigated the fog-choked streets to make their way to Rowan's brownstone in fashionable West London. The dark streets of London echoed with eerie noises of horses and the few brave souls with business afoot at that ungodly hour. Dulled sounds of a city in restless slumber, like a play heard through a wall, serenaded him as he ran his hands through his hair, mussing his dark auburn curls.

I am bone tired and soul weary, as my father used to say. He was still a relatively young man, having just turned thirty-three, but Rowan felt a hundred and thirty-three tonight. He was useless in the face of Jackson's illness and dreaded his inevitable failure to save the boy's life.

His mother's anguish will be punishment enough, I suspect. And there's a bitter tonic to take . . . too soon. Poor Jackson! What a man you'd have made! Not a whisker on your face and you're already better than most, if it's any comfort to your mother to know.

The trip went quickly, as Theo was able to drive smoothly through the emptier streets. Most of the wealthier London residents had retreated to their country estates at the end of the summer season to enjoy the hunt and the fresh brisk air of autumn. Rumor held that the city was notorious for breeding disease in the damp and cold of the wintry months, and it was easy to understand how anyone with means would flee the soot-covered streets and gloom.

But this was when Dr. Rowan West was needed most, and everything in him balked at the idea of putting his feet up by the fire in some quiet country cottage when he had so many patients in need. As for rumors and wives' tales, he also knew that the irony was that the warmer months were far deadlier in the city, though no one in his profession yet agreed why.

His head pounded in rhythm with the horse's hooves on the cobbled lane, and Rowan shut his eyes for a few minutes to try to keep the sensation of gray sand filling his skull at bay. *Fatigue. It's just fatigue, but I swear if I look, there will be grit on my coat from this ground glass that's leaking out of my ears.*

The carriage slowed to a halt, and Rowan opened his eyes in relief. "Home, at last."

Once again, he didn't wait for Theo, but simply climbed out with his doctor's bag as was his custom. His stubborn independence was a long-standing joke amidst the Jaded—the name given to his closest circle of friends—but it was a point of pride for Rowan. Those in the Jaded who had grown up with wealth, and even his friends who hadn't, marveled at his reluctance to be waited on. Rowan had never seen a good cause not to treat all men as his equals, and in his imprisonment in India during the Troubles it didn't seem very revolutionary to accept that brotherhood could transcend bloodlines.

The small society known as the Jaded had taken root in the worst of circumstances, but Rowan was sure the experience had made them all better men.

If not better men, then perhaps in my case, simply more aware of how another person's discomfort or hard work shouldn't be taken for granted.

He resolutely failed to see why a gentleman couldn't take care of himself whenever it was warranted. Not that he could imagine his life without his dear staff, but they were more like family than employees, and their care eased the demands of his profession.

He frowned as he entered the foyer, instantly concerned by the lit tapers and by Carter's presence. The older man should have been in bed hours ago, but he was at the ready as if he'd been waiting for Rowan's return.

"Carter? A bout of insomnia or did I miss something?"

"We've a guest, Dr. West." Carter gestured toward the receiving room off the foyer on the other side of the main staircase.

"At this hour? What kind of guest?" Rowan dropped his bag on the table by the door. The men of the Jaded often called at strange hours, but they'd have just gone to his library and made themselves at home—and Carter had long given up paying them any attention. But from the older man's stance, Rowan knew that this was a situation that defied protocol and had poor Carter rattled.

"It's a woman. Or rather, a lady, Dr. West. Came alone in a hired carriage and insisted on waiting for you." Carter looked sufficiently miserable at the admission, as if all his usual starch had been drained away. "I . . . I thought it best to put her in the salon."

"How long has she been waiting?"

"Since eight," Carter supplied. "I've checked on her regularly and she is . . . unchanged."

Even eight at night is scandalously late for a call. And now it's well after midnight! What the hell drives a woman to sit in my parlor for almost five hours?

"Did she give her name?" he asked.

Carter shook his head. "Refused to do so, but insisted that her business with you was critical and highly personal. I had no idea when she first appeared that it would become such a strange siege."

"No worries, Carter. I'll see her and have this matter squared away as quickly as possible." He started for the receiving room, then hesitated. "Wait here, if you can, Carter, in case something is required?"

"Yes, of course!" Carter's relief was palpable and Rowan took another deep breath to try to banish the grinding pain behind his eyes before he opened the door. He wasn't sure what to expect from his butler's expression. But a lady on his doorstep at such a late hour, alone and unexpected, didn't bode well. Even so, he knew she wasn't a bawd, or Carter would never have allowed her in the house. *It might simply be that the lady was too embarrassed to make an appointment. Although—*

His speculation ground to a halt as he found the female in question. She was like an exotic young bird perched on one of the carved wooden chairs in a beautifully tailored traveling dress that only added to his impression of a swan. Her dark hair was pulled back into a sleek little nest of curls that trailed down to accent the graceful lines of her face and neck. She was an aristocratic creature with balanced and symmetrical features, and the look she cast in his direction was one of mild impatience and cold calm. She stood as he came through the door, a porcelain cameo brought to life, and Rowan had to remind himself to breathe as eyes the color of violets came to bear upon him.

"May I help you? Miss?" His nerves were jangling as the small details that weren't meshing began to press into his awareness. *She's still wearing her gloves. And—are those pieces of baggage?*

"Dr. West! I am pleased to, at last, make your acquaintance. It's Renshaw. Gayle Renshaw."

Except she didn't look pleased.

From Rowan's vantage, she looked as if she wasn't entirely sure that she was in the right house or that he was the right Dr. West. She was openly assessing him, and he couldn't help but feel that he was falling short in her measurements.

Gayle Renshaw. Renshaw. That sounds vaguely familiar but I'm sure I'd have remembered this woman—even if I do have a ripping migraine.

He nodded but didn't drop his gaze. God help him, he didn't think he could stop staring at her under the very threat of death. *I think I'll just cling to what protocol I can, since I'm not sure what one says to women who come calling with luggage.* "While I'm always pleased at new referrals, I find I'm at a bit of a loss. It's late for a call, but if there was some emergency—"

She shook her head, her brow furrowing a bit as if his words frustrated her.

Rowan took a deep breath and tried again. "I apologize if I've misunderstood, but Carter was sure you needed assistance in some way, and I assumed . . ."

"No need to apologize, Dr. West. I've come without a word of warning, but when I received your favorable response to my letter, I decided that there was no time like the present to commence."

"Your letter?" *Renshaw. No, it wasn't possible!* "I responded after I'd received a letter from a Mr. G. L. Renshaw but—"

"No, you received a letter from me inquiring about an apprenticeship." She put one gloved hand into the deep pocket of her skirts and pulled out the folded vellum of his response. "You were very candid in your need for an extra pair of hands."

"I may have been, but I was under the impression that you were . . . male."

Her spine stiffened and the color in her cheeks changed to betray that the lady may not be as coolly disconnected as she'd pretended. "An intentional deception I'm not proud of, but an unimportant detail for a man of your character. You set a price and I've come with my apprentice's fee in hand."

Rowan was sure he'd misheard her. "I beg your pardon? You confess to fraud, yet expect me to happily ignore it and enter into some kind of insane contract?"

"You do take apprentices, do you not?"

Ah, here's a moment of surreal departures in conversation. . . . "I have in the past, but—"

"I mean to become a physician, Dr. West, and I have come with the sole purpose of securing an apprenticeship with you. I have heard much of you, and while I realize that this arrangement is somewhat unconventional, I was sure you'd agree."

He shook his head slowly, the dreamlike elements of the encounter getting the better of him. "Did you just say you'd heard much of me? How is it that I am famous enough to warrant this absurd petition?"

"There is nothing absurd about seeking to be a physician!"

Rowan put a hand over his eyes, pressing gently against his eyelids to ease the ache. "I'm sure I never said there was, but meant to describe this particular instance. It's late, Miss Renshaw."

"If I'd meant to commit fraud, I'd have completed the negotiations by letter and sent payment in advance of my arrival, Dr. West. But I'd convinced myself that you were open-minded enough to respect a more direct approach." She put his letter back into her pocket, as if to prevent him from taking it from her.

"You are nothing if not direct, Miss Renshaw." He walked over to the side bar and poured himself a much-needed drink. "Let's try again."

"Yes, once more." She sat back down as calmly as if he'd asked her to tea. "Once I've completed a successful apprenticeship, I am hopeful that a university will have difficulty arguing against my qualifications. Naturally, an apprenticeship with a country doctor would be easier to obtain, but just as easy to disregard. But as you are a London man, certified by the Royal Academy and a graduate of Oxford, they may take my training and dedication more seriously, and since I have no intention of allowing them to dismiss me simply because I'm a woman—it seemed a good plan."

It seemed a good plan.

A part of his brain was actually in agreement, chiming in that if you ignored reality and the horrible power of entrenched old men and traditional thinking, the lovely bird might have a chance. But reason intervened as the throb behind his eyes began to keep pace with an ache in his neck. *Damn it, what was it she was saying before?* "Miss Renshaw, what exactly have you heard that would convince you of my *open-mindedness*?"

"I came from Standish Crossing."

There's a cold wind from my past. Damn! A single winter spent in Standish Crossing and I'll be an old man before I'm allowed to forget it. "And there's talk in the village, is there, of my secret desire to take on a female apprentice?"

"I don't think you'd enjoy hearing any of it repeated, Dr. West. Suffice it to say, I understood you weren't afraid to break the rules."

He took a long sip of brandy before he answered her. "Really? I can't imagine being described in those terms. You misunderstood the gossips, Miss Renshaw, and have traveled a long way for nothing."

She didn't move, and for a moment, Rowan wondered if she'd heard him. But then she replied as she casually readjusted her gloves and smoothed out her skirts, and he almost dropped the glass in his hands.

"An odd thing about gossip, Dr. West. It can travel long

distances with a single whisper. Refreshing to think that no one in London seems to have heard anything of your life in the village, wouldn't you agree?"

I don't care how beautiful you are, Miss Renshaw—you vicious little thing! "Are you attempting some subtle threat to my reputation?"

"Not at all. There was nothing subtle about it. But let me start again, Dr. West. What I propose is mutually beneficial. You need help and I am bound and determined to do whatever it takes to gain the knowledge and experience I need to become a true physician. I have the money and the means. My gender is irrelevant, but no one else will even talk to me on the subject. . . . When I learned certain details of your past from an involved source, I seized on the chance. It occurred to me that a man of your skill, with a reputation to protect, might be willing to risk bending the rules once you knew how set on this I am."

"It's one o'clock in the morning, Miss Renshaw."

"Perhaps you should have your man show me to my room, then?" She stood up and bent down to retrieve her bags. "We can come to terms in the morning."

We could if you weren't insane.

"By morning, your reputation is forfeit, Miss Renshaw."

"My reputation is already forfeit, Dr. West. I have traveled unescorted into Town and called on an unmarried man at an inappropriate hour, and whatever you think, I am none the worse for it." She waved off the matter as if it were of no consequence. "But I agree that it's far too late to worry about the finer points of my current social standing. My room?"

"I'm agreeing to nothing, Miss Renshaw, but I honestly don't think I have the strength to debate your ethics or lack of them until I've gotten a few hours of sleep. This headache is crippling my ability to reason." He set down his glass and walked to the door to open it and signal the waiting Carter.

"Have you tried feverfew with an infusion of rosemary? I prefer ginger, myself."

Rowan turned back to look at her, a bit surprised. "That was too easy. Any housewife would say the same. Have you a remedy for kidney stones?"

She hesitated for a single breath before answering coldly, "Cinnamon. Or celery seed and stone root. But if the pain is acute, perhaps corn silk. I know the use of herbs is deemed quaint, but I was a quick study of the apothecary in the village—at least, when the man wasn't looking."

Carter appeared before he could think of a ready response, and Rowan decided he'd had enough for one night. "Carter, show Miss Renshaw to the first-floor guest room, if you please, and let Mrs. Evans know of her presence so that a breakfast can be provided before she leaves us."

"I'm not leaving, Dr. West."

Carter gave him a look of alarm at the protest, but Rowan held up a hand to smooth his butler's ruffled feathers. "That's to be determined, Miss Renshaw. We'll talk more in the morning and see if we can't reach a compromise or if I'm better at holding my ground when I'm not exhausted and in agony. But if you change your mind in the next few hours and come to your senses, I wouldn't wish to see you return home on an empty stomach."

A nice hearty breakfast and a nice debate about your sanity, and you'll voluntarily march back to Standish Crossing—because whatever lies you've heard, I'm not going to let you dictate anything to me.

Carter cleared his throat. "This way, miss." He held out a hand for her suitcase, but Rowan stopped him.

"Miss Renshaw prefers to carry her own things, Carter. She is a forward-thinking creature who would probably claim insult."

The color on her cheeks returned at the petty gesture, but she didn't argue as she readjusted the apparently heavy leather satchels to carry them more easily. "Thank you, Dr. West."

"Good night, Miss Renshaw."

He watched her ascend the stairs, as graceful as a duchess despite the awkward load she carried, and he marveled

that anyone could be that beautiful and still manage to
make a man dedicated to healing consider poisoning her
poached eggs in the morning.

* * *

Carter made brisk work of seeing her to the guest room,
openly rattled by her disregard for the rules of decency and
decorum. "There's no coal, as we weren't expecting anyone, but if you insist, I can have some brought up to warm
the room."

"That won't be necessary, Carter. I have no desire to
impose on the staff any more than I already have. The
room is lovely, and only a simpleton would think to complain about its comforts." She set her bags down at the foot
of the bed, careful not to groan at the relief in her shoulders. "Thank you."

The compliment did its work, and Carter bowed briefly
and retreated with a minimal amount of grumbling under
his breath about houseguests in the middle of the night and
misguided ladies.

Once the door closed behind him, she sat on the edge of
the bed with a shaky sigh. It had worked. She'd brazened
her way into his home and made her first arguments toward
convincing him to take her on as an apprentice. Her impul-
sive plan had carried her along on the journey and her day-
dreams of easy success had bolstered her spirits—until
she'd actually found herself sitting in his parlor.

The mail coach had arrived later than she'd anticipated,
and by the time she'd reached his brownstone, Gayle had
been shaking with nerves. The brilliant proposals she'd
crafted to dazzle him into agreement in the afternoon light
sounded like nothing short of bedlam after dark.

His poor butler had borne the brunt of her unorthodox
invasion, and amidst other things occupying her thoughts
in the long hours of waiting, she'd begun to prepare arguments to spare the man just in case his employer proved to
be an unreasonable man and threatened his butler's livelihood.

But Dr. Rowan West had been nothing she'd anticipated. The brilliant demon that her aunt had cursed and spit vague invectives over for the last year had seemed the perfect candidate for her plans. What difference would it make to a man like that if he had a unique apprentice? And if his reputation were bruised slightly, who would care? There had been a twisted justice to making a villain play the role of her savior and become the means to her noble end of becoming one of the first female physicians in England.

She would turn the tragedy of her family's past into triumph, and the evil man who had played a part in her cousin's death would provide her with the tools she needed.

Except he hadn't looked very evil.

Nothing like a demon, at all.

She'd overheard her aunt, Mrs. Jane Hamilton, say that the doctor was far too old for her delicate daughter, Charlotte, and that only a colder soul could have destroyed such a tender young flower without a single backward glance. Mrs. Hamilton had then lowered her voice, and Gayle wasn't sure about the method of destruction, but the point was made.

"Why did you allow the engagement, then?" Mrs. Smythe had asked over her teacup.

"Because he has an unparalleled reputation as a physician, of course! My brother assured me he had a future ahead of him and had inherited a fashionable practice in London that would give my little nightingale nothing but the best that life had to offer! If only I'd known what a vile, vile heart could hide behind such talent! To destroy my darling and skip off without a nod!" Aunt Jane had cried.

And suddenly the daring plan had taken shape.

All her inquiries to the physicians in her aunt's acquaintance had been firmly rejected and, worse, had alerted Mrs. Jane Hamilton to the strange designs of her wayward charge. She'd spent weeks locked in the house afterward and learned that the direct approach was going to end her up in bedlam.

So when the specter of Dr. Rowan West was invoked,

the solution was simple. If a good man who was a doctor was too worried about his social standing to take on a female assistant, then a bad man who was a very good doctor might not even blink. And if he did balk, well, he wouldn't want the world to know just how evil he was—and if she could be ruthless, she would possess the lever to move her own world.

In Gayle's imagination, Dr. Rowan West had taken shape as a wicked genius who would do anything to further his practice—or protect it. She would make a generous offer from her inheritance to acquire a position in his service, and with hard work and study, she would receive her own certifications and take London by storm as one of the first women to venture into the medical profession.

But where was the vile man she'd envisioned? Gayle wondered. Where was the pockmarked, icy soul who would growl about ethics, but bend to greed at the promise of her money?

The real Dr. Rowan West was a man to be reckoned with, well seated in his prime and radiating masculine power and authority. There was nothing wizened about him, and even exhausted and in pain, his gaze radiated experience and intelligence. He hadn't shouted or threatened to throw her out. He hadn't even chastised his butler for allowing her to wait. Instead, he'd appeared to be every inch the gentleman, even expressing concern for her reputation and well-being.

Worst of all, Dr. Rowan West was a bit too handsome for a woman to recall contempt and keep her wits about her.

She pushed away the sensation instantly.

How am I to prove that a woman has the disciplined mind necessary to become a doctor if I turn into a giggling pool of idiocy the first time I see my teacher's rugged good looks? Who cares if the man has broad shoulders or if he's tall? He's a skilled physician and possesses what I need to move forward. Who's to say the devil wasn't the most attractive angel of all before he revealed his wicked heart and fell from heaven?

Gayle nodded, letting out a longer sigh as her hands finally stopped shaking, although the tears came at last. Quiet trails slipped down her cheeks and betrayed her true nature. Gayle retrieved her handkerchief from her reticule and purposefully wiped her eyes. She had the tiger by the tail and couldn't let her conscience weaken her grip now. She had hinted that not even blackmail was beneath her, and there would be no backing down.

If Dr. Rowan West was half the villain her aunt believed him to be, then there was nothing unjustified in pressing him into this contract against his will. She didn't require him to be a decent human being. She just needed a decent teacher.

And if he hated her for it, so be it.

She only prayed that she didn't end up hating herself as well.

Chapter
2

By dawn, she had unpacked her dresses, organized her things, and even polished all her shoes. She'd brought only what she considered her most practical clothes, though Gayle's vanity didn't preclude that a practical and professional wardrobe should not also be as flattering and fashionable as possible. It was London, after all! Whatever obstacles and prejudice she was going to face, she'd decided that no one was going to look down on her and mistake her for a woman without means or proper feminine sensibilities.

He'd failed to appear for breakfast, but Gayle wasn't going to retreat. She ignored the pinched looks from Mrs. Evans, his housekeeper, and ate alone in the small downstairs dining room. Her nervousness had returned in full force, but she did her best to hide it behind a façade of complete confidence that there was nothing out of the ordinary in an unmarried woman arriving unannounced and inviting herself to stay.

I'm his apprentice and he sent a letter of invitation, so

Mrs. Evans can stew in her own juices for the moment. At least, until he comes downstairs and we put the worst of it behind us.

Because the worst was surely to come. The argument they'd begun last night was hardly finished, and conscience or no, Gayle was determined to use every cruel weapon in her arsenal until he agreed to take on her education.

Forgive me, Charlotte! But if I have to invoke your name, I will. I can't go home now! Your mother will see to it that I'm locked up until I turn gray if I'm forced back to Standish Crossing.

Carter came into the room and made a quick bow. "Dr. West should be down in a few minutes. You can wait in the library next to the salon, but I must ask you not to wander the house, Miss Renshaw."

"Of course not." She folded her napkin and followed him to the library, hiding her trembling hands in the pockets of her morning dress. "Thank you, Carter."

The butler left her without another word, clearly unwilling to align himself too closely with a guest whose status was yet to be determined. She smiled as she began to circle the room to assess the doctor's library selections, happy to be distracted from the impending meeting that would decide her fate.

The books ranged from literary classics to an astonishing selection of rare texts from Italy. Her Latin was passable enough to discern that his collection included tomes on ancient poultices and surgery in the field of war.

The long, slender blades of her fingers traced the spines of the medical reference books she found as she was silently admiring the wealth of knowledge beneath her touch. She pulled a volume on the study of human anatomy and opened it to a detailed plate on the musculature of a corpse. The color drawing was fascinating, offering a glimpse of what lay beneath the skin and powered human movement.

"Enjoying a quick study of the mechanics of a man, Miss Renshaw?" Rowan appeared behind her as if by magic, startling her as he reflexively reached out to press the book safely back into its slot and out of her hands. "Or were you looking for my weak points?"

"I wasn't able to secure much in the way of medical texts back home. I look forward to studying yours."

"While I admire your curiosity, and may I say, your perseverance, that may be a bit premature of you."

"Only if you've already made up your mind to refuse me, Dr. West." She squared her shoulders. "Have you?"

"I haven't completely made up my mind, but I think that's only because a part of me is still in shock. It was a long day, yesterday, and you . . . were more than a little surprising. Surely you can understand that even if I am the devil himself and dance naked on rooftops without a care for convention, the odds are against you."

"Why?"

Why? He'd braced himself for a snippish little argument from her, a squeak of insult or a feminine pout of protest. But this—this cheeky question and the openly defiant look on her face were extremely disarming. Rowan wasn't fooled for an instant into thinking that the impossible Miss Gayle Renshaw was actually awaiting his words of wisdom. *This is where I hang myself.* "There are so many arguments against it, I'm not sure where to begin."

"Choose one."

"Where is your family, Miss Renshaw? Are they native to the village of Standish Crossing? I don't remember hearing of the Renshaws when I was visiting there."

"I have relatives in the village and only just arrived over a year ago after my parents died. But I turned twenty-four a few weeks ago and I came into my trust money, so there is no one in authority over me."

"Twenty-four is young to have your independence. There is no chance you can convince me that your family had approved of you seeking to train for a profession, miss." He indicated that they should sit, guiding her to a pair of chairs facing the fireplace. "Who exactly are these relatives, Miss Renshaw? I'm asking because, for some reason, I have a sinking feeling it's very much part of this tangle."

She had the courtesy to blush. "My aunt is Mrs. Jane Hamilton. Charlotte Hamilton is, or rather, *was* my cousin."

Charlotte. Beautiful, mesmerizing Charlotte. Cold and dead and the source of more misery for me than I can measure. Didn't I once wish I'd been buried with her?

He looked at his petitioner with new eyes. She'd hinted at blackmail and brought the worst of his past squarely into the room, and had the audacity to look lovely while she did it. Charlotte Hamilton had been his fiancée when he'd left for India, and when he'd received word of her death just after his arrival, he'd been devastated. But the aftermath of her death had involved more guilt and blame than he'd ever dreamt—and Rowan knew that the black brush he'd been smeared with had cemented Miss Renshaw's opinion of his character, like so many others. The question was, how much did she really know and why was she still here?

"My parents never approved of my dreams, but I don't see that that is relevant now. I have my own money, almost eighteen thousand pounds, and it is for me to decide how to dispose of it."

"You have money enough for a decent dowry and . . ." He was unwilling to blurt out nonsense about how she was too beautiful to be a doctor. "You cannot deny you had marriage prospects aplenty. No woman *chooses* to live the life of a servant spinster. Not if she has a chance at any reasonable alternative."

"Is independence such a surprising choice? I have the resources to secure my freedom but you seem to think a woman would naturally prefer to be confined. I *choose* to make my life more meaningful than to play the role of one man's wife."

"Then why not simply be free, as you put it? Why not travel or paint tea cups or buy a racehorse? There are women who spend more days than they like in the sickroom, hovering over their dearest ones—women who dread those hours. But you—you are seeking it out. Their nightmare is your quest."

"I don't seek out suffering or relish the sickroom, any more than you do."

"What do you want, Miss Renshaw?"

"I want to know if you had to undergo this kind of scrutiny when you professed a desire to become a doctor."

He took a deep breath and a new calm overtook him. "Tell me, Miss Renshaw. Tell me why you want to become a physician."

"My reasons are my own. I'll not reveal them to you for mockery or dissection. You'll either accept me for my skills, by giving me a chance to demonstrate them, or not."

"And your threats from last night? Should I include them in my decision making or dismiss them as the idle rant of a desperate child bent on getting her way?"

She lifted her chin defiantly but said nothing.

She doesn't know what she's asking. But I will say one thing, there's no denying that she'll never accept a simple, merciful no. I'm afraid Miss Renshaw is the sort of person who can only learn things the hard way.

And as for the ghosts of Standish Crossing, let them come.

Rowan also held his ground. "I'll dismiss your threats for now and confess that if I had had a fortune and an absence of family, I would have been sorely tempted to seek another life. It's not a calling for everyone. No matter how lofty my professional goals may be to heal the sick or make some grand discovery, it's still a trade. There's not a peer in the land that doesn't put me in the same column as their solicitor or their gardener. I'm a glorified servant, Miss Renshaw."

"It is a calling for me."

"You're too fair and too young to heed such a calling."

"My reasons are as sound as yours. It's not as if you're some lifeless old prune! Or do you really view it as just a trade, Dr. West? Is it profit alone that drives you so that you're incapable of imagining why anyone would want this?"

"You cut me to the quick. But why don't we set aside the

fact that this course of action will destroy your chances for a decent match? I'll even try to set aside the distinct possibility that Mrs. Hamilton has even now called for the guard and declared me a criminal for engineering your presence on my doorstep—"

She interrupted him. "Aunt Jane has no idea that I've sought you out!"

"Where, precisely, does Mrs. Hamilton believe you to be?"

She hesitated, finally displaying a bit of uncertainty that made him wonder what else she was keeping from him. "I may have led her to believe that I was determined to make a tour of the Continent to gain a bit of worldly polish before agreeing to marriage."

"Alone?"

She crossed her arms defensively but said nothing.

"Shopping for an imaginary trousseau, are we? Did you remember your invisible chaperone and send Mrs. Hamilton a pretend itinerary?"

The look she gave him was pure disdain. "I could correct her misconceptions about my travels, but I don't see the advantage. Besides, weren't you saying something about setting aside an argument based on Mrs. Hamilton's potential alarm at my departure? Or was that the last of your protests and you were going to agree to take me on?"

This woman has a mind that tracks like a falcon and is probably just as deadly. Still, let's try another more traditional tactic.

"Frankly, Miss Renshaw, medicine is not for the faint of heart. There are . . . indelicate subjects a physician must be familiar with that a lady can't . . ." He tried again, hoping the moral high ground wasn't about to give way beneath his feet. "Society's rules of etiquette and decency dictate that you maintain a certain ignorance when it comes to the human condition." Even as he said it, the words sounded pompous and inane in his ears.

"How is that possible?" she asked, completely nonplussed.

He couldn't even muster the energy to answer her.

She recrossed her arms, shifting her stance defiantly. "Women bear the brunt of childbirth, do they not? A most *indelicate* experience, by all accounts, and yet you would prefer to believe that we are blithely, as a gender, oblivious to life's messier and more painful aspects? How exactly does society expect me to shield myself from the human condition—whether I'm a doctor or a milkmaid?"

"Good question. But I'm sure that since women commonly faint at the very prospect of seeing blood, it's hard for most men to imagine them drawing it out of a patient or cutting into the flesh to withdraw a tumor or remove a limb. Ideally, you are seen as the weaker vessel and—"

"I have never fainted, Dr. West, and I see no reason to wobble at the mechanisms or fluids that sustain a human being's existence. Do not make the mistake of describing *me* as a weak vessel or a fragile angel! I'll not—" She stopped herself, as if the very passion of the argument that overtook her was now the greater threat. She turned her back on him, openly fighting for composure before she turned around again, the icy mask back in place. "If you can bear a thing, I don't see that I am any less capable of bearing the same! I am less experienced, granted, but *not* less capable."

"That's a claim you cannot make so confidently, Miss Renshaw. You haven't been exposed to the worst."

"Precisely! I haven't been exposed to anything! And until you stop lecturing and agree to give me the chance, then we can bark at each other from now until the end of time and you'll never know what I can do!" She pressed her lips together, and Rowan wished she hadn't. The simple gesture was a distraction that drew his attention to her full pink lips just when he needed his wits most. Thankfully, she didn't notice and continued speaking. "If you mean to be right in this argument, Dr. West, then you will have to prove me wrong."

And there it was. The answer to his problems.

She'll quit after a fortnight of training and limp from the house with her baggage—and then she can find an-

*other use for her fortunes and a better dream to pursue.
Instead of coddling her and begging her to see reason, I'll
treat her like I would a man, and it will be Miss Gayle
Renshaw who will realize that there are some lines not
worth crossing.*

"I cannot believe I'm saying this, Miss Renshaw, but it
seems I am going to have to prove that you are wrong and
accept this insane proposal of yours."

For a single second, her mouth fell open in shocked surprise before she caught herself and gave him a wary look of
suspicion. "You're accepting me? Just like that?"

"What do you mean *just like that*? You've almost brow-
beaten me into another headache, woman. It's either bend
to your arguments and take you on as an apprentice, or toss
you out kicking and screaming onto my doorstep, and
truthfully, I cannot have insane women throwing fits on my
steps. It is very bad for business and almost impossible to
explain to my neighbors."

Suspicion flowed into warm gratitude that melted the
ice in her violet eyes, and when she smiled, Rowan had to
remind himself to breathe. His new apprentice's charms
were undeniable, but only a fool would forget that desire in
this instance was tantamount to suicide.

"Thank you, Dr. West! You won't regret this decision! I
won't disappoint y—"

"Wait! Since we've established that I do in fact care
about my reputation, we proceed only so long as you are
discreet about the arrangement. No grand announcements
of your training and no formal titles given until I give the
word."

"And what should I tell people when asked why I reside
in your home or why I am here?"

"You can tell them that you are assisting me or learning
to be a nurse."

She hesitated and he could almost hear the wheels in her
beautiful head grinding out the details of his request and
digesting its meaning. "Is that what you will tell people?"

"Probably. Beyond a very few close friends and my

household staff, the fewer people aware of our true arrangement the better for you. After all, word will spread like wildfire if you're foolish enough to fan about the existence of a woman attempting to become a doctor—a fire hot enough to draw the attention of your aunt in Standish Crossing, and then where will you be?"

She bit her lower lip and crossed her arms defensively, but he could see that he'd scored a few points of logic. While he might not want Mrs. Jane Hamilton on his doorstep, neither did she, and for the first time, he felt a certain kinship with Miss Gayle Renshaw.

At last, she nodded. "I will be the soul of discretion, Dr. West."

"Then I'll have my solicitor draw up the usual documentation for your signature this afternoon. You'll occupy the room I have set aside for my assistant, and I will require all the work and study of you that I would have from any man in your position, if not more." Rowan paused, and then went on to the practicalities. "As for the master's fee, keep it. I don't need your money, Miss Renshaw, and I think I'll sleep better at night knowing that you have something to fall back on, in case—"

"I. Won't. Fail." She bit off each word, her hands clenched at her sides. "And every decent apprenticeship has its price, Dr. West. I'll pay you, because when this is over, I want no one questioning the legitimacy of our agreement or the nature of our relationship and the education I shall receive."

"Are you going to argue against everything I say, Miss Renshaw?"

The ghost of a smile crossed her lips before she recovered and crossed her arms. "Not after I win this point, Dr. West. After this, I shall be the very soul of conciliation and contrite obedience."

"Very well." He kept his voice level, wanting to convey to her that this was no game. "I'm not hiring a chaperone. You are not in London for social pleasures or to make any new acquaintances. You are officially in my employ and will obey me without question. Are we clear?"

She nodded, once again all prim business and calm control. "We are clear."

"Mrs. Evans will fill you in on the rest of the rules for the house, and while you report directly to me, I'll terminate this in an instant if she reports to me that you're causing her any trouble."

"As you say," Gayle replied, undaunted.

"Your self-directed studies were undoubtedly limited. We'll see how far behind you are, and since I cannot send you to lectures at the Academy, you'll have to work twice as hard to make up for lost ground and demonstrate your worth. I'll tutor you personally and provide as much practical knowledge as I can. And when the time comes, I'll do my best to see to it that you are given the medical examinations that any male surgeon or doctor would take, but I'm not in a position to say that anyone will accept the results."

"They'll have to! All I need is the chance."

He had to swallow a cynical groan in the face of her unwavering faith. The men he knew would rather jump off London Bridge than see a woman anywhere near the medical profession, and he feared that even if she passed a hundred exams, they would never let her step foot inside their "hallowed" halls or give her the certification she wanted. *Hell, they'll try to stone her first.* "Because you're a woman, you're expected to fail."

"I understand. I won't fail."

He looked at her for a moment and questioned his own judgment. *What if she doesn't quit? What if this insane creature really does have the tenacity and intelligence to stay the course? What in God's name am I going to do with a female apprentice? And am I forgetting that I will have Charlotte's cousin under my roof?*

Months and months of avoidance and resignation to the strange half-life he had led evaporated as Rowan marveled at the lovely and stubborn manifestation of Fate that had landed on his doorstep. Miss Gayle Renshaw would receive her money's worth, and Rowan had the feeling that he would never be the same.

A line from the Oath of Maimonides came into his mind. *"May the love for my art actuate me at all time; may neither . . . the thirst for glory or for a great reputation engage my mind."*

I've worried for so long about my reputation ever since I returned from India and learned the truth of her death. All this time wasted, waiting for those months in Standish Crossing and my engagement to Charlotte Hamilton to boil to the surface and either end my career or prove to be paper tigers.

But now, the wait is over.

He held out his hand. "Then, there is no time like the present to begin."

Chapter
3

She'd shaken his hand when he'd offered it to her, and a small shiver ran through her at the gesture. Gayle told herself that it was because he'd held out his fingers as he would to an equal, not to gently uphold her hand for a dance floor turn or for a gloved touch in a formal introduction at a park. He'd held out his strong bare hand and she'd taken it with her own bare fingers, marveling at how warm and firm his grasp was and how quickly the business of a hand-shake could be accomplished.

I didn't want him to let go.

She ignored the nonsensical thought and turned her attention back to the business at hand. Dr. Rowan West was giving her a tour of the house and her new working environment. The ground floor was taken up by the entry way and receiving area, the waiting room, a small exam room (though most of his patients preferred to be seen at their own homes) and doctor's office, a library, and Mr. Carter's quarters. The first floor provided for bedrooms and an extremely interesting private study and library that she caught only a fleeting glimpse of through a partially opened door as they strolled past. The second floor was more utilitarian, though the hallway she caught a glimpse of was still wonderfully appointed with antiques, and Gayle tried not to wonder what else was in store.

"This is where you will be spending most of your time, on the third floor." Rowan answered her unspoken question. "Above you are the servants' quarters and a bit of storage, but your room is just off of the laboratory—a convenience you'll come to appreciate.

"The laboratory is"—he pushed open a heavy oak door at the end of the hallway and stood aside to let her go in ahead of him—"my pride and joy."

In a room that was clearly designed as a solarium, it was a decadent and breathtaking sight to behold. Rather than merely housing one or two windows, the entire back wall was fanciful wrought iron inset with clear-blown glass to give the sun a chance to illuminate every corner it could. And instead of plush chairs for some ladies' embroidering or tables for letter writing and china painting, the female sensibilities had given way to a true working laboratory with long waist-high tables and dark-stained stools.

"It can be drafty, but I've been keeping it so warm with the braziers you should be comfortable enough for the work."

"And to think most people have greenhouses!" she mused aloud, her fingertips tracing gently along the smooth worktable's surface. It was nothing like the grim rooms the village surgeon back home used. That had been a small brick building of poor means next to the blacksmith and not much of an example to go by.

But this! This was just as she'd hoped. Clean and open, it was a long rectangle of a room, the narrow worktable set in the room's center to run its length. Shelves of reference books, boxes, and various tools were set floor to ceiling along the inside walls, but the wall of fanciful flower-scrolled ironwork and glass had been left free of any obstructions, ensuring that the light could be used from every vantage.

In a tall cabinet in the corner, neatly labeled jars contained every hue of powder in black, ivory, and white alongside tins of compounds and chemicals she could only guess at. Also along the inside wall, on an ancient work surface with an untold number of burn marks and unique scars, was a configuration of burners and beakers with rubber tubing connecting various vessels and tying them all together for some unknown purpose.

Only unknown for a time. Soon, I'll understand what he's doing here and I will be a part of it! Perhaps even help him in some great discovery . . .

She turned about, admiring all of it, from the elegant shadows that the iron made on the wooden floor to the Latin motto carved into the door frame they'd just come through. *"Veritas vos liberabit."*

"The truth shall make you free," he translated softly, taking a seat at the table to give her room to explore. "Not very original, but my great-great-grandfather had a love for the classics."

"I think it would apply as well today."

"Of course, it does. I had a schoolmate that jested that it was a sad thing that truth didn't make you richer or happier, and now whenever I see the phrase I just remember his face and wonder."

"What exactly do you wonder? If he was right?"

Rowan shook his head. "Oh, I know he was right. It doesn't take too many years before you realize that the best philosophy is uttered by ten-year-olds and the rest is rubbish."

She had to struggle not to smile. "I hadn't realized that."

"Because you probably haven't wasted your time studying philosophy."

She nodded in agreement. "I don't think freethinking is ever encouraged if a young woman fails to master her music lessons."

He laughed. "I take it you won't be entertaining the staff with any private pianoforte performances?"

Her smile outpaced her determination to not be charmed

by her mentor. "And risk ending up on the doorstep for causing trouble? Mrs. Evans would insist on my removal if I sang a single note, Dr. West." She decided to redirect the conversation away from her shortcomings. "Whatever happened to your friend, the young philosopher?"

"He died of a fever that summer, along with his sisters and parents." It was a statement of fact, almost devoid of emotion, and Gayle was sure that there was more to the tale as an awkward silence held them in place.

"And here"—he walked over to another door at the end of the room and pushed it open for her inspection—"is your room. Not appointed with a lady in mind, I'm afraid, but you have your own water closet through there, and it should do well enough."

Gayle peered in and tried not to let her disappointment show. Unlike the pretty guest room below with its soft butter yellow walls and rosewood furniture, this was as stark and austere a tiny bedroom as she had ever encountered. A narrow wrought iron cot with a white cotton mattress was set against the wall, a single small dresser standing sentinel next to it. Two windows set high with white eyelet curtains kept the room from total gloom, but it was hard to see it in a cheery light. The floor was bare of rugs and the walls devoid of ornamentation beyond a framed mirror and a faded print advertising the Great Exhibition of 1851.

"It's . . . very nice."

"Mind yourself!" Mrs. Evans interrupted the exchange, her arms full of fresh bedding and towels. "I brought up a few things to make the room a little cozier for the miss."

Her relief was instantaneous. "How kind of you, Mrs. Evans!"

Mrs. Evans grunted in response, unceremoniously dropping her large bundle on the cot. "One of the footmen will carry up your things later. You can settle yourself in, I'm sure. You make your own bed and I'll collect dirty laundry once a week on Monday. See that you have it ready before breakfast. Florence will come in for a sweep and a dust that afternoon, but she's not a ladies' maid! You're to see to your own needs and keep your room in good order."

Gayle had to bite the inside of her mouth at the woman's tone, since she wasn't used to being addressed like a servant, much less used to making her own bed and "seeing to her own needs." But Rowan was right at her elbow, looking at her expectantly, as if he knew exactly what she was thinking and was happily anticipating some little temper tantrum on her part over Mrs. Evans's brisk treatment.

I'll sleep on the floor if I have to! And I'm not quibbling over a lack of wallpaper!

"Thank you, Mrs. Evans. Please assure Florence that I'll try not to overtax her."

Mrs. Evans's gruffness suffered a bit at the softness of Gayle's tone, and she wavered in the doorway before departing. "Will . . . will you be eating with the staff or . . ."

Rowan intervened. "Miss Renshaw will either dine with me on the first floor or, more often, in her room, I suspect. Her studies will keep her well tethered, I'm afraid, and as you know"—he rewarded his housekeeper with a smile that instantly turned the formidable creature into a blushing girl—"if she waits for me to have a meal, she'll die of starvation."

"You work too hard, doctor!"

"Not at all." He deflected her maternal concern, and Gayle marveled at the way he diplomatically turned his housekeeper into an ally. "I'm a tyrant of an employer and blessed to have you, Mrs. Evans."

Mrs. Evans retreated in a happy flurry, returning to her duties without another glance in Gayle's direction.

She sighed. "I don't think your housekeeper approves, Dr. West."

"She won't be the first not to do so, Miss Renshaw," he countered. "But on a somewhat related subject, I should point out that your door has a dead bolt."

"I see." Except she didn't see what in the world dead bolts had to do with Mrs. Evans.

"To protect your virtue," he added, instinctively providing another clue.

"I see," she repeated, with a little more confidence. "I shall be sure to use it, if only to reassure Mrs. Evans that my virtue is intact under your roof."

"See that you do," he said, a mysterious heat in his eyes making the command almost hypnotic. But before she could identify it, he'd turned away and returned to the workroom and the business of her apprenticeship. "I'll have a small desk brought up to your room as well. The laboratory is very good for studying, but you'll still need a private space of your own, I'm sure, for letters, journals, and any personal business you may have."

"Thank you."

Rowan began pulling down books, barely looking at the shelves as if he knew the volumes by touch alone. "How is your Latin?"

"Very good," she answered confidently.

"Have you studied Hippocrates?"

She shook her head. "Only vicariously, I'm afraid."

"We'll start with the classics. You'll read these, Miss Renshaw, and know them like you know your own history. I want you to absorb as much as you can, taking it all in, and when commanded, you should be able to quote it like the Bible."

She took the books reverently. *Hippocratic Writings*; *Hippocratic Aphorisms*; *Fasciculus Medicinae*; *Articella*; and *Pantegni*.

He placed his hand gently on the top of the page, breaking her connection to the words and drawing her back to the present. "Study them, Miss Renshaw, and while I may have asked you to be able to quote them like the Bible, I want you to be clear that this is no religion, although some of my colleagues use words like heresy and blasphemy for those who argue against this ancient wisdom. While there may be some elements of useful truth inside these texts, they are not infallible or inerrant."

"Oh!" she whispered in quiet shock. She had always understood that health was tied to the balance of the four bodily humors: black bile, yellow bile, phlegm, and blood.

Everything she'd overheard the physicians of her childhood saying had only reinforced that belief. "I thought that all doctors still believed in the four humors."

He smiled. "Belief is an action of faith. As I said, this isn't religion. We are in the service of science. If we have learned that we know anything for certain, it is that we know almost nothing for certain. The ancient Greeks and Arabs and their medieval followers have had a great influence on my profession and our approach to healing. But I am a heretic, Miss Renshaw."

"Why ask me to study them at all, if you don't hold to their teaching?" she asked.

"Heretic is from the root of a Greek word that means *one who can choose*, Miss Renshaw. You must understand a school of knowledge thoroughly before you can claim the wisdom to choose what to keep and what to disregard. And for you, it's a step that you cannot omit. If you truly want to keep pace with your masculine contemporaries, you must be fluent in the language of medicine—flawlessly fluent." He added another heavy leather book to the growing pile. "And remember, I said that there are useful elements of truth in these. Hidden, I grant you, but they're there for the keen and discerning mind."

The look she gave him was solemn and made his chest ache in its sweetness. She was so open and hungry for knowledge, eager for anything he imparted, and so trusting. It was a heady power to think that the imperious and unstoppable Miss Gayle Renshaw would look up at him like that, but Rowan knew the danger. And it was probably precisely the reason that it wasn't wise to have women at universities. She was so beautiful, a temptation to body and to soul, and a man would have to be blind and dumb to be unaware of the corrupting allure of such a student.

She'd make the crustiest old man forget himself. Lucky for me, she won't be here long and I can see this mess behind me before any true damage is done.

"We'll start here and then I can determine just how quick a study you are, Miss Renshaw." He eyed the daunting stack of books and calculated just how bruising a task they might present. "Start with the *Articella*. I'll check back with you when I return from my patient calls."

"Can't I go with you?" she asked impulsively.

He shook his head. "Not yet. For now, you read."

"But, surely, I could—"

"Read, Miss Renshaw. Read. And one of the first things you'll read is that 'life is short, the art long.'"

"Yes, Dr. West."

"Study, Miss Renshaw. Study as if your life depended on it, for I assure that in this instance, it will."

Chapter 4

Rowan adjusted the oil lamp on his desk and finished his final note on the day's calls. He'd begin having Gayle copy them out soon so that she could see the course of treatments for each patient and start to understand some of the practical work involved in diagnosing illnesses and providing care. It would be tedious work, but he doubted she'd mind it. Miss Renshaw's enthusiasm hadn't waned despite all his efforts to bury her in books and assignments.

In ascertaining the extent of her medical education, he'd learned just how tenacious Miss Renshaw really was. She said she'd learned all her herbal remedies by eavesdropping on a Scottish apothecary situated next to a milliner frequented by her mother. She'd augmented that wisdom with practical bits of advice from various housekeepers, cooks, and country women she'd come into contact with. When visiting family friends, she'd once gotten her hands on a book on anatomy, which was unfortunately in German, but the illustrations had been fascinating enough—until the book's owner discovered her in his library and removed the unseemly material from her wayward hands. Most recently, the surgeon in Standish Crossing had inadvertently provided a few more hints, but in the village, surgery was considered a rough trade, and since the man also pulled teeth, he was barely acknowledged socially, so he'd been an elusive source for her to use.

But of Gayle Renshaw, the woman, he knew almost nothing. Where exactly her family was from or how her parents had died were secrets she'd yet to reveal. His new apprentice was determined to keep her distance. From what he could deduct, she was born of country gentry and had been offered a life of some comfort and a middling education. But she'd blithely managed to pursue the most unfeminine interests of botany and science and acquire a better education than her parents thought suitable for their only daughter.

The next logical step in her education was anatomy, and he only hoped her Latin was up to the task. If she'd been allowed a formal education, it was groundwork that would have already been laid. But her boast of being a quick study was proving true. Even so, the books could only take her so far, and then it would be a challenge to get her access to a corpse and—

He caught himself with a frustrated groan, arresting the path of his thoughts. Miss Renshaw was to quit long before the grim work of a hands-on anatomy course, and he, of all people, needed to remember that.

The torture of his new apprentice was supposed to be a necessary inconvenience, not something he was beginning to genuinely enjoy. But as she'd demonstrated more and more of that keen intellect and tenacity, he'd started to look forward to every battle, test, and exchange with his unusual pupil. He'd pushed her harder than any apprentice had ever been pressed, and she'd simply borne it with a grace that often left him speechless.

"Sorry to interrupt, doctor," Carter broke in from the side panel door, hidden by one of the curio cabinets, his entire stance apologetic.

The fact that he hadn't used the main door from the hallway to Rowan's study spoke volumes. It meant he'd come straight up the servants' backstairs in his haste, which hinted that Mrs. Evans or the cook had put a fire under his feet. "It's fine, Carter. Yours is the face I am always happy to see."

"Nonsense! I'm the poor man constantly besetting you with the worst news of patients' calls at all hours, and don't think I'm not grateful that you don't snap at me for it."

Like my father used to. Carter had been a part of the family for as long as Rowan could remember, and before he'd graduated to long pants, he'd quietly sworn that no matter how tired or out of sorts he was feeling, he would never take it out on dear Carter. Every dent in the wooden molding around the private library room door told the tale of a brass bookend hurled at Carter's head for interrupting one of his father's happier moments mapping a future adventure or daydreaming of medical discoveries. His father's living had depended on his patients, but the man had never stopped resenting them for falling ill at the most inconvenient moments. "Never kill the messenger! Some wise Greek said it and we'll carve it over your bedroom door if it's any comfort."

Carter smiled. "Bless those Greeks, sir."

"What was it you wanted?" Rowan prompted diplomatically.

"Oh yes! I'm afraid it's to do with Miss Renshaw."

"Is Mrs. Evans unhappy? Is she proving to be a troublesome or demanding guest?"

Carter sighed. "Just the opposite, doctor. It seems Mrs. Evans is sure the girl is underfed. She's missing meals when you're not in the house, and the women have decided she's not ringing for trays—perhaps in an effort not to bother the staff."

"Ah! But now it's becoming a worry. . . . Has Mrs. Evans not offered to simply tell her that ringing for a tray or for tea is not a problem? We can't have her fainting from malnutrition, Carter."

"And there we are. It's all caution and care and not knowing how to address a woman who is neither truly an employee nor a guest under the roof. They're all pride and speculation downstairs, wanting to please but not wanting to overstep if she's not to be here long and not welcome."

"She's—" *Damn! I'm scheming to drive her out and my empathetic household isn't sure who to help. Mrs. Evans can't stand to starve her out but is wondering if I'd be perfectly happy to see it happen. What a world!* Rowan closed his notebook carefully. "Miss Renshaw is very welcome here, Carter. I would appreciate it if you would convey to Mrs. Evans that a tray be arranged for her meals, whether the lady remembers to ring for them or not. She is studying very hard, at my insistence, and has a tendency to lose track of the hours, so the fault is mine. But let's not punish the girl for it, agreed?"

"Agreed," Carter answered with relief. "I knew you'd see it just so."

Rowan smiled. *I'll never make a tyrant, and that's not a bad thing to boast at the end of the day.* "And would you please remind Mrs. Evans that since *I* am starving at the moment, if she could send up a tray of those wonderful little ginger cakes, I would be eternally grateful—and I will even promise not to track so much mud into the house."

Carter bowed before retreating back through the hidden doorway. "She'll send a mountain of them for *that* promise." And with that, he was gone.

And it's on to anatomy, Miss Renshaw. Brace yourself.

*　*　*

The sound of a bird striking one of the glass window panes awoke her instantly. Gayle lifted her head in a strange, breathless momentary panic at the stark transition from dreamless sleep to exhausted alertness.

She realized she must have fallen asleep while studying, her cheek sore from resting against the open pages of a book of anatomy plates. Unsure of the hour, she knew only that it was daylight and she could only pray that she hadn't

lost enough of the day for Dr. West to have noticed. A small
clock on one of the shelves read nine o'clock, and she stood
to brush out her skirts and smooth her hair as quickly as
she could. He was usually in the laboratory by then, and
her face flushed with shame at the idea of him catching her
like this, dazed and mussed over her reading.

*Had he come and gone already and just left me sleep-
ing?*

She wanted to betray no weakness of any kind, especially since it was clear he was sure she would beg off at
the first challenge or obstacle.

He's testing my resolve.

As a teacher, he was thorough, extremely knowledge-
able, and genuinely inspiring. He was also demanding and
ruthless when it came to her performance. At any moment,
he would require an oral recitation from her assigned studies, a defense of an assumption she might have uttered, or
an explanation of a medical technique or practice. Failure
to provide an adequate answer inevitably meant the reward
of more study, or the repetition of her lab work. No meal
was enjoyed in leisure without the inclusion of a lesson.
Even at the end of an exhausting day of patient calls, he
would make his way to find her and inquire on her progress.

For eight days and long into the nights, she'd done nothing but study—every waking thought given to the medical
arts and to not disappointing Rowan.

It was a strange slice of heaven sprinkled with a little bit
of hell. The freedom to learn the forbidden sciences and
arts of medicine, to have at her fingertips all the answers
she had craved to all the endless questions in her mind.
She'd sacrificed her future and her reputation to achieve
her hardscrabble hold on this chance—and it was more
than she'd hoped for so far.

Even so, she was surprised to be suffering from a touch
of homesickness. Not that she'd lived in Standish Crossing
for very long, but perhaps it was the care and security of
the life she'd abandoned that beckoned to her in the night.

She'd always chafed at the restrictions and confinement of her days before, but it was hard not to think with fond nostalgia on some of the leisure she'd forfeited. Even her room at Aunt Jane's had offered a garden view and every comfort. Here, the accommodations were drafty and Spartan. She'd never lived without a maid and had learned that she missed the companionship of one as much as having an extra pair of hands when it came to laces and buttons. Even so, it wasn't the lumpy, thin mattress or the bare room that threatened to spoil her paradise.

It was Dr. Rowan West.

His presence was unsettling. She hated the way her heart pounded whenever he came too close, a fluttering weakness that distracted and dismayed her. After all, he was her employer and nothing more. But already, her days and nights revolved around him—as a mentor and teacher, but also as her only link to the outside world.

A bell in the lab rang whenever he went out on call or returned—a signal to his apprentice to be at the ready to offer assistance—and it was a sound that still jarred her nerves.

It had rung just before dinner the night before, and she'd waited hopefully, indulging in a daydream where he burst into the lab, handsome and vibrant but anxiously seeking her out. Then he had commanded her to grab her coat and accompany him. *Come, Miss Renshaw! I need you!*

But naturally, he hadn't done any such thing and her plan to study until his return had ended up in the uncomfortable sleep on top of a pile of books.

He never came back. I'd have woken up immediately if the other bell had rung, but it didn't. The call must be serious for him to be out this long. Oh, well. At least I didn't have to endure another oral exam before retiring. . . .

Except she liked the way he pushed her. He expected perfection and credited her with the capability of it. When he corrected her, it never felt like an admonishment. And if she asked him to clarify anything, he would willingly provide examples or stories to ensure that she knew the content and the context of the lesson they were covering. Yesterday at breakfast, he'd even demonstrated a surgical technique on her kipper, much to Mrs. Evans's horror.

She moved to stretch her back and neck, massaging the base of her skull to dismiss the dull ache there. She knew better than to bother Mrs. Evans for a cup of tea, but Florence and the others were warming up to her, and Gayle wasn't too shy to head below stairs and ask if she could make up her own tray.

"Pardon." An unfamiliar male voice from the doorway interrupted her thoughts and startled her into a very unladylike yelp.

She did her best to recover quickly. "May I help you?"

"Didn't mean to frighten you, miss! Carter had his hands full with some business in the kitchens and I just let myself up as usual." His smile and friendly demeanor put her at ease as he moved comfortably into the room as if he'd been there a thousand times. Only an inch or two taller than she was and apparently of a similar age as herself, the slender young man was anything but intimidating, his cheerful blond good looks dismissing fear. "Are you assisting Dr. West?"

"Yes." She knew that Rowan wanted her to be discreet above all things, and she didn't want to jeopardize her position. She wished to be recognized as far more than an assistant, but Gayle was wise enough to choose her battles.

"I'm Peter James, Mr. Fitzroy's assistant."

When she failed to react, he went on. "Mr. Fitzroy is the chemist. I'm his apprentice and training to be an apothecary myself."

"Oh!" Gayle smiled, now dutifully doing her best to look impressed. *I wonder if he'd be as cordial if I told him that I was an apprentice as well.* "I'm Gayle Renshaw. Dr. West is out on a call at the moment."

"A pleasure, Miss Renshaw. His assistant, you say? Well, the doctor is out more often than he's in, and I'm used to it. I've come to check Dr. West's inventory there in the cupboard and make sure he's not in need of an order," Mr.

James explained. "I'm sorry if I startled you. The house knows me and I come every fortnight or so."

"I wasn't startled." The denial was foolish, but the impulse to lie was faster than her wits after only a few hours of sleep. "I simply . . . thought you were Florence bringing up a tray."

"Studying, are you?" His eyes rested on the stack of books and still opened texts spread across the table.

"Dr. West is . . . indulging me. I am very interested in medicine."

Peter eyed the Latin text and then looked back at her with a touch of awe. "That's quite an interest."

"I've always been fascinated with the practice of medicine. Ever since I was a little girl."

"Really? It seems an odd thing for a woman. Not to be abrupt, but my sisters never seem to lift their noses past their bonnet ribbons. However did it capture your attention, Miss Renshaw?"

His interest seemed so open and without judgment, and Gayle could detect no trace of sarcasm in his tone, so she found herself dropping her guard. "My father once said I was born asking questions, and I've always loved discovering how things work and what they're composed of—even to the sad end of several of my family clocks and our garden fountain."

"Oh, my!" Peter commented, offering a bit of jovial encouragement.

"When my older sister fell ill with scarlet fever, I was nine. She was seventeen and I idolized her. They banished me from her rooms, but I couldn't stay away. The doctor looked like a wizard with his white beard and all the magical items he pulled from his great leather bag. All those vials and strange instruments! And the way my parents seemed to shrink and defer to him whenever he entered the room . . ." She sighed, the memory taking on a life of its own. "I stole into Emily's room whenever I could to watch him tend to her. Everyone said in whispers when they thought I couldn't hear them that she was sure to die."

"But she didn't!" he guessed.

"She didn't." Gayle smiled. "I loved Emily more than anything in the world, and she didn't die that summer. And I knew right then that I wanted to be able to do that, to save someone's life and possess the knowledge of all the wonderful things that man had tucked away in that worn brown satchel."

"And what does your sister think of your surprising ambitions?" he asked.

"I can only imagine." Gayle returned to a more painful present by rote practice. "She died the following year in a tragic accident. She'd gone to stay with friends of the family and there was a house fire."

"I'm so sorry! How horrible for you!"

"Thank you for your kindness, but . . ." She did her best to set the dark turn in the conversation aside. "I'm sure it's the reason my parents were so protective and eager to keep me close—and never pressed me to marry." Gayle smiled at the thought. "So, there's the blessing! I became as independent and headstrong as a mule, and probably wretchedly spoiled. I never developed a talent for being told what to do, Mr. James, and now that I am on my own, I can pursue my interests as I have always wished."

"It's a rare and lovely soul that can find the bright side to these things, miss." Peter nodded his blond head, as if concurring with his own wisdom.

"Yes," Rowan interjected from the open doorway, his expression difficult to interpret. "Miss Renshaw is a determined optimist, if nothing else."

Gayle jumped a little, startled yet again by an unexpected presence, but this time, her heart only sped up when she saw him. She hated the guilt that poured through her, as if she'd been caught doing something illicit with the chemist and Rowan had walked in on them.

"How are we doing, Mr. James?" Rowan spoke directly to Peter as if she wasn't even in the room. "Did you get my request?"

"Yes, indeed! I brought more of the headache remedy

just for you, doctor. And your general inventory is adequate enough, but I notice that you're running low on the opiates. Shall I ask Mr. Fitzroy to compound more of your usual amounts?"

"Yes, and have them delivered as soon as possible. I cannot be out of them as some of my patients will have need soon."

"You use less than any physician I know, Dr. West, if you don't mind me saying." He smiled at Miss Renshaw. "Your doctor doesn't trust the new miracle drugs!"

"I don't believe in miracles. But when Mr. Fitzroy produces them, I am always grateful."

"And he meant for me to say as much to you, doctor! That new compound you suggested has our Mr. Fitzroy more cheerful than I've seen in years." Peter pulled a packet of papers from his jacket pocket. "I almost forgot to give you his letter on the matter. I was instructed to hand it only to you personally."

Gayle watched with some curiosity as the sealed bundle changed hands.

He read the papers in silence as she waited as patiently as she could for him to address her. Instead, he finished and turned back to Mr. James. "Well, thank you, Mr. James. I'll answer him by letter personally, but please convey my interest. You'll send the supplies we discussed right away, won't you? And otherwise, I'll see you in a few days."

It was a dismissal, and Peter James seemed to take it in stride. He gave Gayle a quick smile and nod before retreating to get back to his duties at Mr. Fitzroy's.

Alone in the room, a long, awkward silence spun out between them before Rowan finally looked at her.

Gayle forced herself not to fidget under his scrutiny. "Did you just return? Was it Mr. Fisher? You didn't say before you left, but yesterday you'd mentioned that he was apt to send for you."

"Did you have a nice visit with Mr. James?" he asked, completely disregarding her questions.

Gayle froze in place, then slowly stood away from the table to put herself squarely in front of him like a boxer preparing for the next round. "Say what you mean to say, Dr. West."

"I asked you why you wanted to become a physician and you refused to answer me. But the druggist . . . You confide in my *druggist's assistant*?"

It was indefensible and a small comfort to him that she did manage to look abashed and unhappy at the question. Her cheeks stained pink, but he knew better than to expect her to retract anything or make excuses.

"I'll speak to whom I wish about any subject I wish! Perhaps you've mistaken the bounds of your authority, Dr. West, if you think to command personal confidences and memories!"

Rowan wasn't about to crumble at the first display of her claws. She looked exhausted and he knew he was the sole cause. He'd barely been inside his own doorway before Mrs. Evans caught him to express once again how anxious she was about the presence of a female apprentice under his roof and set him in motion with a pronouncement that Miss Renshaw looked positively ill from the dreadful torture he was subjecting her to. He'd rushed upstairs with the intention of making sure that she was hale and hearty and apologizing for the ridiculous scholastic marathon he'd been putting her through out of spite.

But instead, he'd walked in on her practically sighing on Peter James's shoulder. Rowan couldn't remember when he'd been this angry.

"I see. You are right, of course. Why answer *my* questions when you can prattle away to Peter James?"

"It wasn't prattling." She looked at the floor, but the fleeting impression of a contrite child didn't hold. When she looked back up, she embodied defiance. "He was kind."

"And I am not?" He'd meant it as a question, a statement that she would instantly deny and assure him that he was all that was kind—but instead she just looked at him as if he'd spat on the floor.

"If I had told you some maudlin story about my dying sister, you'd have looked at me like some sentimental hysteric and that would have been the end of it. You'd have directed me to spend a bit of time in some ladylike charitable pursuit addressing orphans or embroidering slip covers! Or worse!"

"How is it that you know so much of what I 'would have' done? Are you that insightful, Miss Renshaw, or am I that transparent a cad?"

"It's not insight. It's caution! If I am cautious around you, doctor, I think it warranted, in light of what I've heard of your character. You are a very good teacher, but I am not cozening up to a villain."

"A wise strategy, Miss Renshaw." He crossed his arms. "Are you always so direct when speaking to a mastermind of evil? Wouldn't stealth serve you better?"

"I am respectful and compliant to all your instructions. I know that I've forced my way into your life and you'd like nothing better than to see me gone. I do not mistake you for a friend, Dr. West."

"Enough, Miss Renshaw. Whatever I may be, do you truly believe that I committed some crime in Standish Crossing?"

She shook her head slowly. "Whatever you are, Dr. West, it's not for me to say. Crime? Perhaps it wasn't a crime, what you did, but Aunt Jane was sure that if not for you, her daughter would be alive."

"And what *exactly* does Mrs. Hamilton believe? What scenario is she describing in her parlor over tea, Miss Renshaw? I ask only because, as a villain, I'm naturally curious, of course."

"She blames you for Charlotte's death."

"*How* am I to blame?" he pressed, the unrelenting icy ball in his stomach growing with each breath he took. "*Exactly* how, Miss Renshaw?"

"Sh-she didn't *exactly* say." The temporary chink in her armor at the confession didn't last. "She didn't have to! No one in Standish Crossing pipes up in your defense, and that in itself says a great deal, Dr. West. Charlotte was your fiancée. My aunt said that when you returned from India, you came to see her gravesite only once, and when Mrs. Hamilton confronted you in grief, she said you admitted your guilt and then left."

"I will say this only once. I did not have anything to do with Charlotte Hamilton's death."

"Did you not admit your guilt to Aunt Jane?"

And there's the rub. Rowan said nothing, loathing the taste of regret in his mouth.

"You're a liar." Gayle spoke softly, but with calm conviction.

His breath caught in his throat at the raw accusation. *Damn her!* "And how is it, Miss Renshaw, that you have ascertained that I am a liar?"

"Because until this moment when it served your purposes, you never argued directly against it. When I threatened blackmail, not even knowing the details, you never fought it. You never denied anything. And when I first told you my aunt's name, I swear your face became pale. If there is nothing to it and you are innocent, then why in the world did such a ridiculous threat work?" She crossed her arms. "If you were innocent, then why would you have confessed?"

It was the closest he'd ever come to striking a woman. He could explain nothing to her or offer a single defense without unraveling every promise he'd ever made to Charlotte's memory, but the injustice of having his choices thrown in his face was more of a slap than he'd anticipated. Everything in the world crystallized into a moment of pure frozen fury, and it was all he could do to simply turn his back on her and walk out.

Chapter
5

"I've taken on an assistant."

"Thank God!" Ashe's reaction was not ambivalent. "You need three!"

"One is enough." He raked a hand through his hair and settled without ceremony onto the nearest sofa. "Your recent insanity is contagious, Ashe. It seems I've decided to forgo convention and destroy my own peace of mind by actually hiring a woman."

"Really?" Ashe's astonishment was genuine, and he sat down next to his friend, staring at him as if he'd just spontaneously sprouted a unicorn horn. "You? How is that even *remotely* possible?"

"I'm not even sure. One minute I'm nursing a headache and so tired I can't feel my tongue anymore, and the next . . . I'm losing arguments with the devil's own daughter. Miss Gayle Renshaw is a force to be reckoned with."

"I like her already!"

"No, you don't. You aren't allowed to like her, Ashe."

"Why can't I like her? I love a good argument, and if

she's providing you with a nice debate or two, what's not to enjoy? So, you've hired a nurse to help with patients. Is that what you've done?"

"She wants to be a physician! Can you imagine such a thing? I have a *female* apprentice." Rowan relaxed his grip on a pillow and tried to sit back. "I'm in real trouble, Ashe."

"Ha! Where's the trouble? Every man in England would probably happily volunteer to see a doctor if he had the choice of a woman over one of the dour old men you tend to stand about with! Hell, that's probably why you've kept women out of the profession!" Ashe leaned in with a mischievous grin. "Can't stand a bit of pretty competition?"

"Who the hell said she was pretty?" Rowan snapped back.

"You certainly didn't, but there's no denying it now after the face you just made! Damn, Rowan! Did you hire her because she's beautiful? Has my saintly friend fallen prey to his desires?"

"You, sir, are an idiot—and should be extremely grateful to have friends who will tolerate you." Rowan abandoned his seat to pace in fury. "I happen to loathe Miss Renshaw."

"You don't have it in you, West. I've seen you spare a kind word to the worst sort of people. Hell, even in that dungeon I don't remember you ever say—"

"I *hate* this woman!"

"Careful." Ashe smiled. "That's a trap any man can lose his heart in." He poured himself a generous brandy from the small cabinet under his writing desk. "If you were indifferent, I wouldn't worry, but you sound like you're a bit too emotionally involved, Rowan."

"That's nonsense! You never hated Caroline!"

"Have you forgotten my fantasies of murdering her in her sleep?" Ashe jested, reminding Rowan of his own lost battle to guard his heart from the woman who was now his unconventional American bride. "I was besotted and didn't even know it."

"This is completely different!" Rowan had to keep his

hands clenched behind his back so that Ashe wouldn't see the fists that itched to punch his friend's handsome face for hinting at the impossible. "Trust me. This. She. Never."

"Well, if she's gotten you so spitting mad that you're making incoherent social calls, I'm not going to complain. Usually we're the ones invading your home and putting up our feet on your desk—and since I am now a devoted husband, my wife has informed me that the practice may have been quite rude. What a revelation!"

"It wasn't an invasion. Carter misses you dreadfully, though he'd hang himself before he said it. And you know the Jaded have never to ask. My home is open to all of you. You're family."

"You're growing maudlin these days, Rowan. Are you sure your lovely apprentice hasn't tied your tail in a knot?"

"She'll be gone in a week. Medicine can seem a romantic art until she's scorched her hands in the lab a few times and caught a glimpse of the pile of reference books I'm going to insist she memorize before next Sunday. She'll quit or she'll die of exhaustion. Either way, I'll have the harpy out of my hair in a matter of days."

"Hmm. That doesn't sound very Hippocratic of you. Didn't you swear to never do harm in that oath?"

"Surprisingly, no. Not specifically, although there is a bit about refraining from giving people poison."

"Well, that's something." Ashe gave him a wry smile. "I think I like you better surly and a bit menacing like this, Dr. West. Caroline will be astonished when I tell her you stopped by to growl over a woman."

"I did not—" Rowan caught himself before he took the bait completely. "Are you in Town for the winter?"

"No, we'll go to Bellewood and see my grandfather again just after Michaelmas. Caroline has insisted on it, and for once, I think I'm going to enjoy spending time in the country. If only to watch the old monster melt and fawn all over my darling girl. To this day, I don't think she realizes what pawns we were in that old man's game, but I have no complaints."

"He was quite the matchmaker."

Ashe nodded. "Too bad you don't need his services. I could have asked him to make arrangements for you, but since you're well on your way to bliss, we wouldn't want to interfere."

"Damn it, Ashe! You're worse than a housebound widow with this nonsense! I'll have Miss Renshaw off my hands in a week, and you, sir, will owe me an apology!" Rowan left the room, grabbing his coat out of Godwin's waiting hands in the foyer, anger making it a bit more energetic of a departure than he would have liked.

He'd wrenched open the front door only to surprise the lady of the house on the other side. Caroline stood on the doorstep with her ladies' maid, Daisy, both of them flushed and happy from their outing to the shops.

"Is everything all right with Ashe?" Caroline asked quickly.

"I was here for purely social reasons, Mrs. Blackwell."

"Then why do you look like a man with a porcupine in his pocket?" she asked, setting her boxes aside.

Rowan smiled. Ashe's American wife had a refreshing candor that made him glad for his friend. Life would never be boring for Ashe Blackwell with a woman like Caroline to contend with. "Madam, you do have a unique way with words. I just had . . . news to share with your husband."

"Good news, I hope."

"I've taken on an assistant." It came out clipped, and he almost winced at his confessionlike tone, but her cheerful reply made him groan aloud.

"Thank heavens! You need three!"

*   *   *

Misery.

She'd been an absolute harridan to the man, and after he'd stormed out, she'd wasted an hour facedown sobbing on her bed. What was it about him that made her want to spit and claw like a cat? He'd said nothing to counter her horrible accusations, and once again, she was left with the paradox of those sad, beautiful eyes looking back at her, his rugged countenance sober and furious at the sting of the charges she'd thrown in his face. He looked like a man offended and not like a man indifferent to his sins.

He's like that handsome Iago in Othello, *with all the appearance of a gentleman and trusted man, but if I forget what I know to be true, I'm lost.*

I'm tired and already, every time I see him, it's a struggle to remember any of it. Standish Crossing is a million miles away and none of it feels real.

What had Aunt Jane said? It was clearly spoken and I wasn't imagining it! She said that Charlotte would be alive today if she hadn't met Dr. Rowan West and fallen under his spell. She'd said that he was as responsible for the death of her daughter as if he'd been there to strangle her. And that he'd confessed as much and then turned his back on her and never returned to Standish Crossing.

And now I've called him a villain and a liar—in return for everything he's done for me. He opened his home and practice, and taught me, even if I have forced him to it; he's been gracious enough, hasn't he?

Peter James was barely an acquaintance, but she'd felt comfortable with him. He'd smiled and seemed encouraging when she'd hinted at her ambitions where Rowan had called them absurd and done everything he could in their first conversations to dissuade her. *I tell Rowan nothing of myself, not because I'm afraid of him, but because it's all too easy to like him.*

Perhaps I already do like him too much. Am I in danger, like Charlotte, of falling under his spell? But what danger could he represent? Haven't I already lost my reputation and perhaps my place in society? There's no going back! I have to amend things and convince him to continue my apprenticeship and take me forward.

I have to prove to him that I'm truly sorry.

Because she was.

Chapter
6

It was late in the afternoon when the bell finally rang, heralding his return. Gayle glanced quickly at the mirror, a
habit of vanity, smoothing one of the black braids of hair
back to tuck it up out of the way and into an elegant twist.
She'd deliberately selected one of her better work dresses,
the periwinkle print flattering her coloring and figure. It
was a feeble gesture, but she was afraid that she'd done so
much damage to the strange relationship they'd enjoyed
that perhaps even the smallest thing would help her cause.

She came down the stairs so quickly that she found him
still in the entryway with Carter.

"You look tired, doctor. And"—Carter was holding out
what remained of Rowan's mangled hat—"mishap, sir?"

"See what Mrs. Evans can do to restore the damn thing.
I must have accidentally sat on it in the carriage."

Carter gave it a dubious look—as the crown of it hung
by a single thread—before nodding: "We'll do our best."

Rowan gently caught his arm as he turned away. "Wait,
Carter. Don't bother Mrs. Evans with it. I don't think a

street urchin would want it in its current condition. Why don't you ask her to buy me a new one, instead? I have an account at that haberdashery off Drummond Street. Theo can drive her and she may even enjoy the outing."

Carter brightened considerably. "She'd like that a great deal, doctor. But don't be surprised if she isn't after you to get a new coat while you're at it."

"One thing at a time, Mr. Carter. One thing at a time."

"Dr. West," Gayle spoke to him as she descended the stairs, anxious to catch him before he announced that he was going to his room to rest.

Carter's look was disgruntled iron as he left with the doctor's hat to find Mrs. Evans. But Rowan's eyes were clear and his expression neutral. "Miss Renshaw."

"I'm . . . sorry." She'd intended to try small talk and remark on the unseasonably warm weather for his call, but the words of regret tumbled out.

Two steps from the bottom, she was standing nearly eye to eye with him, and for the first time, Gayle was aware that Rowan's eyes were the color of an English forest, dark green and brown in a potent blend.

At last, he spoke. "As am I." He picked up his leather bag. "If you don't mind, I'll drop this off in my private study on our way upstairs."

She walked with him up the staircase, surprised at the sudden forgiveness so easily given. "Thank you. I'd expected a bit more yelling and you've every right to do so. I was horrible this morning."

They reached the landing to the first floor and he opened the doors into his private study. "Yes, you were."

She opened her mouth to protest, but then realized he was smiling. "To what do I owe your good humor, doctor?"

"I made a social call on a good friend and his wife who both reminded me in their own ways that no matter what else may or may not be true—I did need an apprentice." He sighed and managed a cheerful shrug. "Theo took me on a ride around the park, and when I found myself reliving the morning and losing my perspective . . ."

She had to bite the inside of her cheek to keep from laughing. "You murdered your hat and felt better?"

"Amazingly refreshing and well worth it." He smiled, nodding as he placed his bag next to the large ornate desk at the room's center. Rowan sat on the edge of the desk to face her. "No more battles today, Miss Renshaw. Agreed?"

She hesitated. *He could have demanded that I behave from now on. He could have said,* Never again. *And I would have readily agreed. How can he be this kind after everything I said?* "Agreed. No more battles."

"Today."

"Why not require a more lasting truce?"

His gaze never wavered. "It's not in your nature, Miss Renshaw, and at least if you're openly fighting me on the battlefield, I don't have to worry about you cutting my throat in my sleep."

She gasped at the imagery but held her tongue.

"But I will request one more thing if you're in a giving mood."

"And what is that?"

"That you use that clever head of yours and make up your own mind. A scientist would hardly make a summary judgment based on the word of someone else and not trust his own experiences and observations."

"You want me to trust you."

"I want you to trust your own instincts. I want you to have proof before you start slinging libel in my direction, Miss Renshaw. Hearsay has its place, but not in this instance. Construct your own opinions and leave rumor out of it. If you decide that I am the worst of the worst, then so be it. But let a man demonstrate villainy before you call him one. Agreed?"

"Agreed," Gayle said, then she realized just how absorbed she'd been in their conversation and her quest for forgiveness as the library's ambience struck her for the first time. "Oh, my!"

Everything about the room was warm and inviting, with its floor-to-ceiling shelves of books and curios, every decoration placed almost at random until it was nearly impossible not to smile at the African masks leaning up against a statuette of the Roman goddess Ceres or the model of a Nordic ship that had decided to land next to an Arabian camel doll complete with bells.

The chairs were all overstuffed and upholstered in leather or brocades so worn that it was hard to discern the original patterns, but every one invited a guest to linger without any regard to their posture. Even the floor was a wonderful eclectic mix of various small rugs woven in one country or another until the sight of a bearskin peeking out from behind Rowan's desk came as no surprise.

Where the rest of his home was orderly and elegant, the character of his private sanctuary was completely unique— and she wondered if this were a better glimpse of the man. "Your study is . . ."

Rowan nodded. "Florence has finally forgiven me for her being the unlucky soul who has to dust in here. Mrs. Evans used to, but her arthritis isn't improved by this particular exercise. It's a jumble, but it's a good jumble."

"Where did all these wonderful things come from?" She circled to a curio cabinet filled with glass and ceramic figures blended in with strange pipes and antique devices.

"The men in my family for as long as anyone can remember have enjoyed traveling abroad for academic purposes. This little library was transformed into our odd trophy room and study. Other homes boast stags' heads and lions and, well, as you see . . . Wests hunt ancient scrolls and salt shakers."

"A hero's spoils!" She stood with a smile.

"If my grandfather's obsession with trying to discover the medicinal powers of rare water lily species can be qualified as heroic, or my father's fascination with the dark continent of Africa and ritual wood carving, then . . . yes. The West men are notoriously interested in all things most decidedly *foreign* and have historically succeeded only in the scholarly sense of the word."

"No fortunes made abroad?"

"My ancestors had a complete disinterest in anything remotely resembling a commercial interest in their travels. They sought the priceless rewards of knowledge."

"As did you on your travels to India, am I right?"

He nodded, a modest flush creeping across his face. "I did."

"And where are your trinkets and souvenirs? While your ancestors may not have had a talent for fortune hunting, they did seem to have a good eye for wonderful bits and pieces of the exotic world."

"My fortune is tucked away in the books in this room. Their contents should be enough for any man." He shrugged, as if embarrassed or uncomfortable with the topic. "But enough. Let's head to the laboratory and see if we can't make the most of the day."

Our battle-free day, he means. "Yes, that sounds wise."

They left the study to make their way up the stairs together, and Gayle reveled in the ease she felt around him again. "I'm a terrible person when I'm tired, Dr. West."

"Then your patients are in for the worst of it, Miss Renshaw. Women in confinement don't choose to wait until you're rested to bring you out on a wintry night for a long delivery, nor sick children with a cough, nor any patient for that matter. Fevers don't break simply because you're tired or you've been at one bedside nor another for three days straight." His tone held no reprimand but echoed with the sorrowful demands of their profession. "You'll have to learn to sleep whenever and wherever you can—and you'll have to practice your social graces when you're overtaxed."

"Another lesson learned," she said, unable to keep from smiling at the simple pleasure she felt when he looked at her with approval—but also recalling how she'd spent the night draped over textbooks.

They reached the laboratory door, and Rowan opened it for her as gallantly as a man bringing her to a grand ball. "Since you've shown an interest in chemistry, let's see if we can't get you to begin assisting me with my compounding, Miss Renshaw." He walked her over to the locked corner cabinet and the narrow worktable next to it. "Everything here must be clean and orderly. Everything taken must be returned to exactly the same place from where it came. One mistake with identical-looking powders and it's all too easy to dispense a deadly dosage to the wrong patient. So take care that you clean every beaker as you see, and put every jar with its contents just so. Do you understand?"

She nodded. It was daunting to think of the responsibility that came with the prescription of medicines. "Clean and orderly, yes, I understand."

He pulled down two black leather books with worn covers from atop the cabinet and set them down for her. "I keep all my combinations here, each annotated with ingredients and measurements as well as their sources."

"Their sources?" she asked.

"Not every chemist is as reliable as another, and I like to keep a good eye on where I've acquired an ingredient so that if potency is lost or there is a change in a patient's reaction, it may offer a clue."

"There's so much to remember."

He smiled. "Which is why we write everything down. In this book with the green ribbon, I make sure I record which patient a medicine is intended for and in what dosage. Naturally, the same information is reflected in my working journal, but this book stays with the supplies so that I can see at a glance the pharmaceutical record for a specific drug and sometimes see a trend in treatments."

"A trend?"

"Either to see that something is working or to catch myself in a tired routine if it isn't and ensure that I'm not doing more harm than good." He opened the book to a page so that she could see an example. "These formulas are extremely confidential and considered trade secrets, Miss Renshaw. I work closely with only one or two chemists to safeguard my efforts—and my patients' privacy."

"I understand."

"If there should be a fire in the laboratory, you must see to it that you get out safely, of course; but if there are seconds where you can take something with you to preserve it, you'll take these two books. Everything else, I can replace. But these . . ." He shook his head. "They're the legacy of three generations of physicians and my own research."

"What are you researching, Dr. West?"

"Heat."

"Pardon?"

"I'm trying to understand the correlation between heat and disease. The worst diseases spring out of the tropical heat, do they not? But why? What is it in the nature of heat that inspires death to move more quickly? Is it sweat that transmits these fevers? Then how? The very nature of fever is in debate by some of my colleagues. Some see it as an outside force imposed on a person's body that ravages and destroys, but others wonder if we are not built to create fevers as a ward and defense. Like a counterfire against the clutches of some unseen advocate. A dangerous defense, but one of last resort."

Defense against an unseen advocate. The words echoed in her head like some call to arms, and she found herself caught up in his passionate words. "But isn't the fever the disease?"

"Perhaps not, and wouldn't that be a revolutionary thing to uncover?" He led her over to another table and pulled down weather maps and charts as he spoke. "But we want to understand why would a particular disease strike one place but not another? And what if the seasons have more to do with it than we suspect?"

"It's fascinating!"

"I am studying the effect of temperature on the progress of various diseases. The Quakers swear to cold baths and chilled air to cool a person and slow disease's progress. Others claim such an approach is suicide. We close windows and pile on blankets and press in as much heat as we can. But if heat is the adversary . . . Well, you can see the endless dilemma that I am hoping my work will help to resolve."

"That's why you went to India!" Without realizing it,

Gayle had imbued her opinion of his journey to India with that of her aunt—and at the moment, she felt her cheeks start to warm with shame. *I have promised to form my own opinions and this seems a good place to start.*

"Yes, indeed. Cholera is said to have sprung from India, and there are other fevers inherent to other regions, that seem to spread without logic. Why are they deadlier abroad than their birthplaces? If the tropical heat is a source, wouldn't a disease like cholera or typhoid lose its bite in the cold and damp of England?" He pulled down a large atlas and opened it to a worn page covered with worn pencil marks and faint notes. "This shows the progress of the Black Plague, at least, what we know of it. And again and again, I keep thinking that there is a pattern here, influenced by more than ships. There are seasons at play, and social tides that I'm probably too slow to see. But if I could see the pattern and grasp its meaning, who knows what monstrous disease could be avoided?"

"And did you . . . learn a great deal in India, then? Were there answers there?"

He shook his head, his expression growing sad. "The answers may still be there, but I learned very little due to a bit of bad luck and poor timing." He waved his hand in the air, dismissing the pain of whatever memory she'd evoked with her questions. "Another man, another day will finish the journey, and I'd be a fool to complain. After all, I made it back in one piece. Now"—he walked over to the long table set directly against the glass wall—"I want to reset and clean all these containers so that we can begin a new batch of experiments. Some of the glass boxes we will heat and others will stay the temperature of the room and a third set, we'll do our best to keep cool. With equal samples of bacteria in each to begin with, we'll monitor the changes in each dish. As we compare the results, you must be extremely careful to record everything that you do so that we can write out our methods and brave the scrutiny and criticism of our colleagues."

It was all she could do to simply nod, almost speechless

in her euphoria at the inclusion she felt. She was doing the work of a man, and it was a giddy sensation to be trusted and treated like an equal.

He pulled forward a polished wooden box and opened it with a small key from his pocket. "Here is my microscope. See that you treat it with great care." He set it up, showing her how to assemble the instrument for use. "The light is best here, but you'll learn the nuances. I'll leave my key in this drawer so that you can use it whenever you wish."

"It's beautiful!" Gayle was almost breathless with awe at the small instrument.

"Not many women would say so, but thank you. It's a prized possession given to me by my father when I graduated from medical school. It's from the finest maker in Germany and is crafted in German silver." He unfolded a bit of felt with samples of feathers, leaves, and some shells. "It may seem silly, but practice looking at these objects with the different lenses. Give yourself the freedom to play and experiment and see what you can uncover. This is the immersion oil and you redirect the mirror below for the best light. See?"

She leaned over, sighing in admiration over its construction. "It's simply marvelous!"

"After each use, you'll oil these pieces to protect the brass and nickel fittings and wipe off the lenses and cases with this soft cloth to remove every fingerprint." He stepped aside to allow her to explore it at her will. "I want you to be as familiar and comfortable with it as you are with a pocket watch."

"I will!" And with that, she leaned over the contraption to look into the scope and lost herself in a new world of hidden sights and details and endless possibilities.

Gayle forgot everything and never even heard Rowan laugh as he left the room.

Chapter
7

"You have the handwriting of an angel." He spoke without thinking as he glanced over the copy she'd transcribed of his notes from the previous week's appointments and calls. He tried to be nonchalant as he set the leather-bound note-book aside. "Mrs. Evans swears she cannot read a word of my scrawl."

"Yours isn't completely illegible." She answered without moving, then finally glanced up from her work, and he immediately recognized the preoccupied expression that heralded a good question.

"Yes?" he prompted.

"According to this, women seem to be the origin of some diseases. Harboring them in our very anatomy as if we're malignant beings somehow . . . But it doesn't feel right. Or is it that I'm a woman and would instinctively be unhappy to learn such a thing?" She closed the book with an unhappy sigh. "I certainly don't feel like a dangerous creature."

"You don't see a correlation between the accusation of immorality in some women and disease?"

"I see it, but I don't see how it would only apply to women. Why would a woman's state of grace or lack of one fester disease to infect her 'pristine' partner where his immorality and indulgences are not a factor? The writers assume that his participation is irrelevant, or that his superiority is intact until he comes into contact with a woman of ill repute."

"I agree that the truth is probably more balanced."

"Is this . . . one of those areas of knowledge I am not supposed to be familiar with?"

He nodded. "Absolutely."

She did her best to look him squarely in the eye as she forged ahead. "So a man cannot spontaneously contract these diseases without being with . . . a woman of questionable virtue?"

"That's the general consensus." Rowan responded as neutrally as he could. Here was a subject rife with political and social dangers, and he wasn't sure which direction her mind was turning.

"Oh," she answered, a bit crestfallen as she absorbed the implications. "Dr. West, if that's the case, then . . . Before a woman falls, she is idealized as pure and desirable as such. It never says in the books how a woman is changed by . . . I meant, is there any medical evidence of a physiological change besides the obvious after a woman succumbs?" She took a deep steadying breath. "Is there anything that science has shown to prove this slant that women spontaneously harbor disease after . . . losing their virginity?"

"None." *Why do I feel like a man standing over hot coals?* As her teacher, Rowan was doing his best to track the scholarly points of the conversation, but as a man, it was hard not to be distracted by the delightful changes in her coloring.

"It's wretched." She pushed the book across the table, as if it offended her by proximity. "Women are viewed like separate creatures. As if we're not as human or that just by being female we require a science and medicine apart from the rest of it."

He put his hand on the book and set it aside. "The physical differences are undeniable, but I agree with you as I don't think women need to be shunted off into another category of study. You are very human."

"Then why is it that almost every condition women are said to suffer from is inherently tied to their reproductive organs or sexuality? Are we so singular in our natures? I don't see the medical texts pointing incessantly to the male reproductive organs every time *you* get the hiccups or discussing having them removed!"

He sighed. *Damn, there was that keen mind again, tracking like a falcon, a mesmerizing thing to behold in motion.* "It is a bit skewed, isn't it?

"Don't you think they'll have to decide? Either we're too innocent to be aware of our own physiology, or we're overly sexual and inherently dangerous creatures harboring the worst of diseases to prey on men? Don't they have to choose? Can both of those views exist side by side?"

"All good questions. I don't . . ." He'd never discussed sexuality so openly with a woman before. With his patients, even if a woman were pregnant with her sixth child, it was a careful dance of euphemisms and outright avoidance. "These books are written by men, Miss Renshaw. Remember the first time I told you that this wasn't a religion? It's science. But like anything else in the world, it's viewed through the filter of our beliefs. It's difficult to set aside social perceptions, and they can get in the way of theory and fact. A man sees what he wants to see sometimes."

"And what do you see? When you look at me?"

The question stirred his blood, ignoring the context of the conversation and causing a physical response that was unmistakable. Like hot, heavy sand, he could feel his flesh thickening, the taut tension building at the base of his spine all too pleasurable. But he did his best to ignore it. Rowan held his breath before carefully composing a civilized response. "You are definitely complicated and decidedly human, Miss Renshaw. And after this rattling discussion, I'm wondering if perhaps a female physician could break through all the wretched perceptions and work to protect her patients from all those misguided theories. Maybe you would help them to feel that they had an ally who understood . . . their plight."

She reached up to touch his upper arm, her fingers gripping the light wool of his morning coat. "Do you really think so?"

And there it was—that bright, fierce light in her eyes that made him want to kiss her senseless or just laugh and waltz her around the room. Her dreams were spinning out in her head, and he could almost see them, they were so vibrant and powerful.

And there he was—inspired by her intense hope and wishing he could shield her from the worst to come and give her whatever she needed to make her dreams come true.

I'm helping her move closer to a soul-crushing heartache when every medical school in the country slams its doors in her face. How's that for villainy?

It was time to retreat.

"I should be going." He stepped back, burying his hands into the deep pockets of his morning coat to hide his agitation. "I have more illegible patient notes to get caught up with, and I wanted to do some research and reading downstairs in my study. If you'll excuse me . . ." He bowed without waiting for her reply, and headed out the door with a single unhappy glance at the carving overhead.

Veritas vos liberabit.

Rowan's steps quickened. *The truth isn't setting anyone free, Grandfather. But as always, I appreciate the reminder.* By the time he reached the staircase landing on the second floor, he felt more in control and a new calm came over him. "I'm getting too comfortable with her," he confided quietly in a portrait of his great-aunt Mary. "And starting to talk to paintings."

He turned the corner and continued to the first floor and the unmatched sanctuary of his study. It was clear to Rowan that she was settling in, and flourishing. His plan to send her running had slowed to a crawl, and instead of frightening her away, he was aware that a new problem was developing.

He was enjoying her company too much.

He was looking forward to going over the laboratory experiments and hovering just to say stupid things like, "You have the handwriting of an angel."

Ashe was right. Passion begets passion, and not always in the direction a man desires. It was time to take charge.

My next call out—I'll take her. And if it's the call I suspect is coming, then the reality of life and death will supply the lesson I need, and she'll be gone.

Chapter
8

"Miss Renshaw, I've been sent for. Would you care to accompany me on this patient call?" Rowan made the offer from the doorway, his doctor's bag already in hand.

She looked up in astonishment. She hadn't seen him since yesterday's fiasco when she'd brazenly asked him about the unseemly topic of women's sexuality. Gayle had been so caught up in her reading, and so frustrated by the strange logic on the page, that she'd forgotten propriety altogether. For a few moments, it had just been an intimate conversation with a trusted friend—and he'd even offered her the first genuine encouragement she'd had on her quest. But then, it was as if she'd made a mistake or misspoken, and he was gone in an awkward rush.

Now, without warning, he appeared offering her a remarkable opportunity. For a moment, she was tempted to pinch herself since the scene was far too close to her daydream for comfort. "A patient call?"

"There's no time for conversation. You either wish to

come or you do not." He didn't wait for her response and simply turned to go.

"Yes! I wish to come!" She untied her apron as quickly as she could and tucked a scrap of cloth in the textbook she'd been studying before hurrying to catch up with him as he headed down the stairs. "Should I bring anything in particular for a call?"

He shook his head. "Just yourself. I have everything I need already present in my bag."

"Always? Or do you change what you carry depending on the call?" she asked.

"A good question, Miss Renshaw. And it's a bit of both. Give it time." He was all brisk business, and she felt herself responding in kind as a rush of adrenaline and excitement poured through her at the prospect of seeing him in action and being on hand to work with one of his patients.

When they reached the downstairs, Carter and Barnaby were waiting with their coats and scarves at the ready. "Shall I have Mrs. Evans hold dinner for you, doctor?" Carter asked as he helped Rowan into his coat. Gayle took her own coat and scarf from Barnaby and prepared for the crisp night air.

"No, not tonight. No need for anyone to stay up and wait for us this time."

"Very well, doctor."

Theo tipped his hat from his driver's perch atop the carriage as they came down the stairs. "Good evening, Dr. West. Miss Renshaw."

"Evening, Theo. We'll need to be fast as you can if you please," Rowan replied before he set in his bag and then helped Gayle to climb up into the cold confines of the carriage.

Theo pulled away immediately, and Gayle did her best to settle in and arrange her skirts to be warm, but also to give the decidedly taller and more substantial passenger the room he needed across from her.

"Who is the patient?"

"One of my younger patients, Miss Renshaw. His name is Jackson Blythe. He's sixteen, and I'm sad to say, this may well be his last night with us. His heart is failing him and there's not a remedy to be had." He leaned forward and gazed directly into her eyes. "It may be a long night, but I need you to stay close and do whatever you're told. No debates tonight, Miss Renshaw."

"No debates," she whispered.

The drive went quickly, and Gayle was left to her thoughts as Rowan made no conversation. The excitement of setting out was muted by the news that this would be a deathbed vigil, but she deliberately kept her chin level, determined to prove to him that she could hold her own.

When the carriage stopped at a rust-colored narrow row home, Gayle had to bite her lower lip to keep from asking a dozen questions, but they were up the steps and inside the door within a single breath or two, and all Gayle could do was watch as the scene unfolded.

"Thank God, you're here! I cannot face it! Not another minute of this, Dr. West! Please, don't think less of me, but I can't be in that room . . . I just can't . . ." Mrs. Blythe broke down in miserable tears. "I can't look at him like that anymore! I want my boy back! I want my son!"

"Of course you do," Rowan reassured her, nesting her hands inside his gloved ones. "We all want it."

"He's refused to eat or drink for days and I . . . God help me, I cannot . . ." She put a palm against her lips, biting her own flesh to stop the words. "He doesn't want to even try anymore!"

Rowan nodded. "Calm yourself if you can, dear Mrs. Blythe. I'll see to him now."

"He asked for you and I was . . . so relieved to think that you might come, but then—you'll think less of me! What mother would leave him . . . in that state? But I can't—" She pulled her hands away, her spine stiffening. "My sisters arrived two days ago, you see, to help, and they are convinced I should . . . *be in there!* And I'm the worst of mothers because I can't!"

"You are the very best of mothers, Mrs. Blythe," he interrupted her softly, signaling the women behind her for their assistance. "I never fail to see it and I never will, how good you are to Jackson and how much he loves you. Come, let your sisters be with you."

The older of the two reached Mrs. Blythe's elbow and addressed Rowan. "Shouldn't we all sit with him?"

Mrs. Blythe moaned, but Rowan answered quickly. "I would prefer to examine Jackson privately, and as he's asked to speak to me, it would be a courtesy if you'd allow it. For now, if you would take your sister to her own room to recover, and perhaps some tea? I can have my assistant make an infusion for you to help you calm yourself, Mrs. Blythe, if you wish."

"Y-yes. Thank you." Mrs. Blythe yielded to the hands that directed her, her hands covering her face as if she no longer wished to see where she was going or any of her surroundings. "Tea would be lovely."

Mrs. Blythe's sisters each took one of her elbows, the pair of them like gray geese in their plain gabardine dresses moving in unison to pull her away from the doctor.

Gayle watched them go, wobbling down the hall, when Mrs. Blythe began to wail. "He was going to be the man of the house! He was going to take care of me when I got old! He was . . ."

They quieted her, and a closed door muffled the rest of her litany on a lost future.

Rowan's steady voice anchored her back to the present, and Gayle was grateful for his instructions. "The kitchens are there. Mattie will show you the way, won't you?"

A young, pale-faced maid bobbed a curtsy from the end of the hall.

Rowan went on, "Make an infusion of valerian and chamomile for Mrs. Blythe, but not too strong." He opened his bag and handed her two packets of herbs before removing his coat and hat to hang them by the front door. "Wash your hands with soap while you're there and then come find me."

Gayle removed her own coat and scarf and then dutifully followed the maid to the kitchen and used the herbs,
boiling down an infusion to add to a cup of tea for the poor
lady. Mattie reassured her that a bit of honey would be welcomed, and Gayle was able to knock on the bedroom door
and pass along the tea to one of the waiting sisters without
too much of a stir.

Rowan wasn't too difficult to find; she followed the
sound of his voice as the bass of it carried down the stairs.
She found the open doorway and the young man they'd
come to see.

"Who . . . is . . . *that*?" Jackson asked, his eyes bright
with fever as they latched onto her face. "She's . . . beautiful."

"This is Miss Gayle Renshaw, my new assistant."
Rowan smiled and in a stage whisper continued, "I brought
her because I knew you'd feel better just looking at her."

"I . . . do." Jackson's innocent approval of the plan was
crowned by a playful wink in her direction. "Will she . . .
hold my . . . hand . . . and say . . . sweet things?"

"She has a talent for just that, my boy."

Her first instinct was to protest, but one look at Jackson
robbed his words of insult.

"At last." Jackson sighed, closing his eyes for a minute.
"I knew . . . dying . . . would have . . . its advantages."

Rowan didn't correct him, and instead checked his
pulse. "You're a natural flirt, Mr. Blythe." He glanced back
at Gayle. "You see? I've never been able to make her blush
and smile like that."

"You . . . are too . . . old. Clearly, she prefers . . . a
younger man."

Rowan reached under the covers to feel Jackson's feet,
frowning at the chill he felt there despite the pile of feath-
ered quilts on top of them. "You're probably right. Would
you like Miss Renshaw to come sit with you?"

Jackson shook his head. "Not yet. I want you . . . to tell
me . . . about the yogis."

"Again?"

"Again."

Rowan nodded, taking Jackson's cold hand into his. "They are so mystic and wonderful, Jackson. I couldn't believe my own eyes, but I saw a man control his own heartbeat, slowing it down until I was sure his soul would have left his body. But there he sat, for long hours, as peaceful as a still pool. Somehow, with his mind and will alone, his body became a simple, elegant instrument that he could manipulate at will."

"Control . . . his . . . own . . . heartbeat," Jackson repeated reverently in a whisper, his own breathing labored and uneven. "And it wasn't . . . a trick?"

"We were on a riverbank. There were no curtains or mirrors. They even allowed me to check his pulse. It wasn't a trick, Jackson. Some things are simply true, even if we don't understand them."

"I . . . like . . . that."

"My translator told me it was a form of prayer and that the holiest of men could achieve a state where they felt no pain. They could sleep on beds of nails and balance boulders on their heads that would crush an ordinary man."

"No . . . pain . . ."

"That's right. And without pain, do you see how they became invincible?"

"Yes."

"So, we'll try it, you and I."

Gayle was sure her heart would break at the sight of Rowan tenderly leaning over the boy, their eyes locked onto each other as they dismissed the world and there was nothing left but the care that Rowan had for him and the gentle courage of a dying child. Jackson's eyes shone with trust and love, and Rowan never flinched. Hours passed with the pair of them sustained with stories of India and mythical young princes interspersed with longer and longer silences.

Finally, Rowan examined his charge again, listening to his chest and then feeling his feet and hands as another wave of restless thrashing passed while Jackson fought to stay. Only when it had passed did Rowan push away for a minute, opening his leather bag to retrieve a small blue glass vial.

She recognized it as laudanum and put her fingers over her lips to stop a hundred questions from tumbling out. It wasn't the right time to ask him exactly what he hoped would happen as Jackson began writhing in agony trying to catch his breath. His color had worsened since their arrival, a bluish gray settling in under his eyes and around his lips.

He's dying and all I can do is watch!

Rowan put a palm on Jackson's chest and waited for the spasm to pass. "Here, drink this and we'll breathe together and banish this pain, Jackson."

The tonic was dutifully consumed, and then it was long minutes where Rowan seemed to almost breathe for him when Jackson couldn't.

"No pain," Rowan whispered.

Jackson nodded and smiled. "I . . . am . . . invincible."

Rowan enfolded his hands around the boys', trying to warm them one last time. "You are more than that, Jackson Blythe." Jackson's eyes closed with a smile lingering on his lips, one last rattling breath giving way to a terrible silence that swallowed hope. "You are so much more."

Rowan's voice cracked a bit and he closed his eyes before releasing the boys' hands and arranging him in a peaceful repose. He stood stiffly and composed himself. "Bring Mrs. Blythe in. Be quick about it, Miss Renshaw."

Gayle rushed to the door, opening it to an almost prostrate Mrs. Blythe, who at a single glance at Gayle's tear-stained cheeks burst into hysterical screams and pushed her way into the room to throw herself across her child's body.

It was the worst kind of scene, and long, chaotic moments before any order was restored. Only with the help of a draught of another tonic from Rowan's bag was Mrs. Blythe finally coherent, and with her sisters' assistance, led sobbing from the room to wail like a banshee in the privacy of her own chambers.

Rowan was like a quiet general, giving instructions to the housekeeper to send for the undertaker and where to inquire for services. He ignored Gayle entirely, and she was left to helplessly trail after him, weakly offering her tearful condolences and what little assistance she could before he'd packed up his bag and escorted her from the house to their waiting carriage and a patient Theo.

"I'm so sorry, Dr. West." She spoke as soon as the carriage was in motion, her cheeks still wet with tears. "It was . . ."

"It happens." His reply was terse. "What generally doesn't happen is the new experience of having an assistant standing around wringing her hands and crying like a child in the corner! How in the world can you comfort anyone if you're busy dabbing your own eyes like a sentimental fool?"

"I . . . I apologize for . . . crying, but he was . . . so young and so . . . sweet . . ."

"He was a patient and his death was inevitable. He was, truthfully, nothing and no one to you, Miss Renshaw. He was not your child! He wasn't your favorite patient! It's not as if you'd cared for him since he was small!" His voice was harsh, and Rowan's stomach clenched at the rough sound of it in his ears. *I'm angry at myself. I'm grieving and I'm lashing out at her for betraying her feelings when I wanted nothing more than to drop to my knees in there and out-scream that woman.* "You have to maintain an emotional distance if you're going to do your patients or yourself any good."

"I shall strive to pretend that I have ice running through my veins, Dr. West," she snapped back. "It's a trick you must be sure to teach me."

"I will! Don't think for a minute that anyone will be thrilled at the sight of a teary-eyed woman clutching a doctor's bag! Those tears will get in the way and cost someone his life, Gayle. You'll waste precious minutes mourning an unfair universe or wrestling with your feminine revulsion at loss, and you'll kill someone with that hesitation! If you cannot control yourself, Miss Renshaw, then you should pack your things and beg off!"

Silence invaded the small confines of the carriage and he waited, dreading the conflict and wishing he could take it all back and repair the conversation. True or not, he was sure he'd gone too far only because his heart was stinging from his own wounds.

The carriage stopped, and Rowan opened the door to climb out, reaching back to help her down. He dismissed a weary Theo with a single wave and escorted her up the steps into the unlit brownstone. He'd half expected Carter to defy him and still be up and at watch in the entryway, snoozing next to a candelabrum, but there was no one to greet them in the predawn darkness.

He lit a taper and turned to hold out his arm. "Here. I'll walk you up to your floor."

She took his arm, her fingertips barely resting on his arm, as if the physical contact was loathsome. Up the dark staircase, they walked without speaking, and he wasn't sure what to say after their hurtful exchange in the carriage. He should have been gloating at that glimpse of her tender heart and feminine weakness—instead his own pain had almost spoiled his ruthless plan. But he had no doubt he'd won the day and she would be gone on the morrow.

He stole a glance at her in the candlelight, moving gracefully next to him, the flickering light accenting the regal lines of her profile and the sensual turn of her neck and shoulders. *She is so impossibly proud. I feel like a ham-fisted idiot trying to break an Arabian without killing its spirit.*

They reached the landing on the third floor and he stopped, fighting the urge to beg forgiveness or explain himself.

Finally she spoke from the shadows, her voice soft and steady. "You're right, Dr. West. What good would I be to my patients weeping at every turn? Jackson needed you to be strong for him, and you were. It is a lesson I will never forget."

He held out the taper for her to take. "It is a lesson I should have found a better way to teach. But, here, take the light and try to sleep."

He started to go, but she stopped him.

"Rowan? Did those men in India really stop their own hearts?"

He turned back and she was so beautiful that his own heart seemed to arrest its rhythm in a bittersweet irony that made everything inside of him feel tangled and hot, restless and hungry.

"They did."

"It wasn't a trick?" A single tear rolled down her cheek, a wayward diamond in the candlelight that drew him closer and made him forget everything but the need to comfort her.

She was there and he was standing near enough to inhale the fragrance of her skin and absorb the heat of her body inches from his in the cool of the house.

She's leaving—she'll be gone—and I'm not sure I'm glad for it.

He was trapped in place, held by a desire to touch her and all too aware that he shouldn't. Ever so slowly, she tipped her head back as if inviting the kiss that seemed inevitable to him now.

Her breath fanned his chest and then his neck, and he looked down into her eyes, speaking aloud without realizing it. "Some things are simply true."

"Even if we don't understand them," she finished in a whisper.

He bent down, intending to take only a gentle, fleeting sample of the soft satin of her lips, but at the first brush of heated flesh to his, all his good intentions vanished.

* * *

It was the lightest touch at first, dreamlike contact that she could have credited to her imagination—the hot silk of his mouth passing over hers.

But then there was a fire that overtook denial.

This was no dream.

The pressure of his lips increased, and she matched it and yielded to it, all at once. Her mouth parted to taste him, drawing against the supple flesh of his lower lip and testing it gently to savor the sensation of her first kiss. It was not the chaste contact she'd envisioned. This was an act that evoked a fever in her blood and made her aware of every inch of her own skin, as if by tasting his lips she'd awakened her own senses.

His warm hand moved up her back to hold her close, and then he caressed her cheek with his other hand, his fingers gently trailing up her jaw line only to slide into her hair to cradle the back of her head, holding her a willing captive to the onslaught of passion she was greedily lapping up.

His tongue moved to explore her mouth and she welcomed it, the salty cinnamon of him pushing her hunger into a spiral of need that she didn't fully recognize and couldn't control. Arcs of electric heat began to connect the hardening peaks of her breasts to a languid pool of restless wanting between her thighs.

Her breath mingled with his and she marveled that she wanted nothing but this. More of this. More of him. More of whatever could come from the sustenance that he alone provided—for this felt like a feast of taste and touch and she took all that was offered only to beg for more.

More. Yes, please!

His strong arms encircled her, pulled her even closer against the hard, firm plane, and she moaned at the delicious feel of her feet leaving the ground by the merest inch. *Just one kiss and I am already lost.*

The jarring sound of the candle holder striking the hard wooden floor and the sudden plunge into darkness as the candle was extinguished pulled her back to an awareness of the world beyond his arms.

Gayle pushed against him, shame and confusion tumbling in as cruel substitutes for the warm security of his embrace as he instantly released her. She was grateful for the darkness as tears threatened, and she fled to the laboratory and firmly closed the door behind her.

Heart pounding, she waited—unsure of what she could say if he followed, or if she would have the strength not to open the door and beg him to kiss her again. Her breath came in a ragged, uneven rhythm that had nothing to do with fear, and she leaned back against the door to wait.

The faint sound of his footsteps retreating down the dark stairs gave her the answer.

Gayle closed her eyes to fight the urge to step out and call him back. But she knew better.

Enough. Enough lessons for one day.

* * *

The laboratory and her room were directly above his personal apartments, a fact he'd omitted in that first tour of the house. He could hear her pacing, a frenetic energy that was unsettling to track. He was always aware of her movements, thanks to the aging floorboards, and every late night of study had been telegraphed beneath her feet without her knowledge.

But this was a little different. Rowan was trying to imagine if she were pondering an escape from his unwanted advances, or more directly, how to take her revenge against her teacher for overstepping his bounds.

He undressed quickly, experience dictating that even an hour or two of precious sleep was worth pursuing. But he doubted that even exhausted, he'd enjoy much success in the chase tonight. His body was throbbing with unsatisfied lust, and he winced as he freed his hardened cock from the confines of his pants. He eyed the washstand with a sigh, dreading the cold-water remedy that awaited him.

That kiss. Has it been that long since I've touched a woman? Have I lost every aspect of my mind to do such a thing? I preach respectability and get all riled when she accuses me of being any flavor of lecherous villain . . . and then I kiss her.

Hell! I might have done more than kiss her if that madness had gone on for another few seconds.

It had been a difficult day, and even with the inevitability of Jackson's passing, it had hit him harder than he'd expected. Then to know that he'd hurt her. That he'd deliberately taken her on that call to try to shake her resolve and shove the reality of life and death under her nose.

So much for my claim to villainy!

She'd reacted as he'd hoped, with all the tearful sweetness of a woman confronted with the death of a child. His own pain had made him rough with her because he'd been so disgusted with himself. Grieving for Jackson, all he'd felt was envy that she could cry so openly and then fury at his underhanded ploy to break such a heart.

And then . . . he'd kissed her.

Impossible.

Unthinkable.

Undeniable.

Here was a desire that had edged past lust and caught him completely off guard.

One taste and he was a man walking out of the desert.

And all I want to do is drown.

Chapter
9

Gayle retied her apron for the third time, and then caught sight of herself in the small polished metal mirror on the wall.

I look so nervous; anyone seeing me is going to think I'm up to something.

She'd hardly slept and had had disturbing heated dreams about kisses in darkened stairwells when she did manage a fitful slumber, so she knew there was a difficult day ahead of her. She dreaded seeing him again, but also longed for him to come quickly and put an end to this anticipation.

She closed her eyes and put her hands over her face. "As if yesterday wasn't hard enough." She made a quick vow not to think about what had happened on that staircase and simply move forward.

She dropped her hands, taking comfort as a new idea came to her. *I wasn't myself. Jackson's death hit me harder than I'd expected and so I was . . . not myself.*

Gayle paused, waiting for the delicate logic to fail, but it seemed to hold. She'd been so disappointed in herself, crying like that in front of Mrs. Blythe. It would have been an unthinkable mistake to throw herself at Rowan like that—but in her weakened emotional state, she'd done the unthinkable. She'd wanted so much to feel comforted, to be held and to connect with another person.

But even that might not explain why it had felt like more than just a kiss.

Because the overwhelming hunger she'd experienced had shattered her understanding of her own nature. She'd never been stirred to so much as flutter an eyelash at a man before and had just assumed that she was too serious in her ambitions to leave allowances for flirtation. Gayle had coolly ignored any man who showed an interest, seeing all of their gender as a barrier between herself and her freedom.

Her regret and shame at the incident would have made it easier to paint Rowan as the aggressor, taking advantage of her confusion, but he'd kissed her only when she'd invited it, and he'd released her the instant she'd protested.

All the more reason that she was more determined than ever to regain control over her runaway imagination and not give him any excuse to sever their contract.

What if he means to send me away because of what happened? What if he accuses me of seducing him? Or of a lack in moral character?

She shuddered at the thought. She knew it was difficult to defend her behavior. *Not one word of refusal or outrage! Instead I was moaning like a wanton and begging him for more.*

Their conversation about the duality of a man's expectations came back to haunt her. A single kiss had alerted her to its power to derail her rational self. *All the rules of society and decorum's restraint evaporated like so much smoke in a rainstorm, and now I just feel like an idiot for ever wondering why anyone would even bother with it. From the outside, it all looked so ridiculous. The notion of people mashing themselves together—it was distasteful to even think of it.*

But now . . . Now that I've tasted his kisses, it's all I can think of!

And it wasn't revolting at all. It was . . . Her mind failed to provide a single appropriate word for the molten sweet intoxication of being in Rowan's arms.

Well, I won't be bothering with—

"There you are, Miss Renshaw! I brought you up some lavender water to refresh you after such a long night." Florence's interruption was a welcome breeze of distraction, her petite frame moving about the room with the busy energy of a bee in a garden. "I'll set it here, and then I'm to ask if you'd like more pillows."

"Thank you, Florence. I'm sure I have enough."

Florence shook her head, undaunted. "Bed pillows, perhaps, but there's not a frill of lace or embroidery to be seen. Cook said ladies suffer without a bit of embellishment, and while Mrs. Evans was sputtering a bit about dust covers—I just thought I'd come up and ask."

Gayle laughed. "You're a champion of embellishment, are you?"

"Even my room has a touch of tatting, Miss Renshaw, and I'm no lady!"

"You're very much a lady, dear Florence, and I'll leave all the embellishments to you." She finished pinning up her hair and pushed a carved tortoiseshell comb into place in her curls. "Truthfully, I never noticed since I never seem to be in this room, unless I'm stumbling to bed. Please don't trouble Mrs. Evans."

"You have to trouble her a little, or she'll fret herself and make Mrs. Wilson nervous, and there goes the menu!" Florence explained patiently as she moved to remake Gayle's already made bedding. "Dr. West won't thank you for all this 'lack of trouble,' and that is a bit of good advice, miss."

At the mention of the doctor, Gayle lost some of her carefree humor but tried not to show it. "Very well. I'd love another pillow. This chair for the desk could benefit, don't you think?"

"Yes!" Florence turned back to survey the room, tapping her foot. "You've even swept! You have to leave me a few things to do, miss. Mrs. Evans will think I've skipped off the way I come back downstairs so quickly after being sent to look after you."

"You've enough to do without tidying up my room. Besides, I know all the extra trouble I cause for dinner trays and such. I have to show my gratitude somehow."

"You are sweet! I like to bring you trays, and we worry downstairs—you being up here all the time by yourself."

"I'm in heaven learning as I am, Florence. Please reassure them all that I am very happy in my work. And Mrs. Evans most of all! I know she doesn't approve of me."

Florence smiled. "She likes you in her fashion. She's just slower to show it and feels terribly responsible for the house. Barnaby says, when she isn't too near to catch him, that she's all hiss and no scratch!"

"Yes, but does she ever purr?" Gayle spoke without thinking, and then they were both laughing at the idea of a contented Mrs. Evans with nothing to do but rearrange her own fur.

Rowan cleared his throat and marveled at the way the beautiful girl laughing and talking to the house maid instantly transformed into the haughty and enigmatic Miss Renshaw. The ice had returned to her eyes and he was almost grateful for it.

Almost.

Florence scurried past him with a shy smile, and Rowan stepped inside the room to see what lay ahead for him and his apprentice. He noted that her bags were definitely not sitting by the doorway, so his first guess was that the only tangible result of all his Machiavellian wrangling was to forfeit her trust. *I kissed her and now she's looking at me as if she isn't convinced that I'm not going to lock the door and force myself on her. Damn. What a mess!*

"Florence is a good girl. It seems you have an ally in the house."

"I like her." Gayle crossed her arms, a habit he was beginning to enjoy since it betrayed more of her thoughts than she realized. "It's good to have at least one ally."

"Only one?" He sat at the end of the table. "This isn't exactly enemy territory, is it?"

"I'm using my personal experience and observations, Dr. West, and would like to wait awhile before answering that question."

"Ah! Reserving judgment are we?" he asked, casually leaning over on his elbows. "Fair enough."

"Did you want any—" She stopped midsentence and then rephrased her question. "I was going to study the texts you left on surgical techniques, but if you have something else you wanted me to do . . ."

"I've given you enough books to keep you buried for a month, haven't I?"

"I wasn't complaining."

"Would you? Complain? Ever?" he asked, each question coming out a little more seriously than he'd intended. "You're quick to argue, Miss Renshaw, but I haven't heard a whisper of complaint about the work you've been assigned."

She pursed her lips together. "Was that your goal? To bury me in books until I cried *enough*?"

"You are a puzzle, Miss Renshaw. To everyone else, you seem a bit more tenderhearted, but to me . . . I am gifted apparently with drawing out your worst traits."

"No. It isn't you. I am deliberately my worst self in your presence."

"Why?"

"Any feminine weakness, any vulnerability or display of tenderheartedness will only earn me your scorn. I wanted to make sure that I proved to you that I could be as focused and frank as any man. I would never want you to think less of me."

"And I only reinforced that, didn't I?" He stood up to prepare to go.

"I don't wish to invite your . . . sympathy or comfort, Dr. West. I'm sure you . . . only meant to be kind with your attention last night, but I'll ask you to maintain your professional distance from now on. I cannot allow you to think of me in that way."

He could only nod, unwilling to apologize since even at that moment, a part of him wished to kiss her until the brittle cold in her violet eyes gave way. *My own little touch of insanity, to want you, Miss Renshaw, but I'll do my best to keep my thoughts to myself.*

"When Jackson Blythe died last night, I was cruel." He put his hands on the table and dropped his head. "Well, at least I know the cause, and now if I argue on the side of praising all those delightful feminine traits of compassion you possess, I would go against my own previous wise teaching, wouldn't I?"

"You were right to reproach me after Jackson's death. I was an idiot to lose my composure like that, and it didn't help Mrs. Blythe in the slightest—or Jackson."

"I'm right. I'm wrong. It's an amazing tangle, Miss Renshaw." He straightened his frame and took a deep breath. "Like a Gordian knot."

"I don't understand."

"It doesn't matter. Go on as you wish, Miss Renshaw. I won't touch you again."

"Th-thank you."

"Tonight, if I'm not out on call, I'll expect you to be able to tell me how to successfully amputate a man's leg."

And he left wondering if she were the only woman on earth who could be happily diverted by the prospect of learning how to carve up a man's flesh.

So long as it's not mine.

* * *

Lady Pringley was his most difficult patient, but also his most wealthy and influential. She was an infamous gossip whose acid-edged comments had contributed to the destruction of more than one unlucky soul, but somehow she had a soft spot for Rowan. The woman's patronage was both a blessing and a curse. The blessing came in the prestige it gave to his practice and the increasing number of regular patients from her elevated circles that paid handsomely for his services. The curse was that the woman vacillated between treating him like a pampered pet and a personal servant—and neither one was a role he enjoyed.

"What kind of physician can't cure a headache, for God's sake?" Lady Pringley snapped at him as she readjusted one of the pillows at her elbows. She was reclining on a fainting couch in the sitting room off her bedroom, and from what her maid had told him on his way up, she'd been in a temper all morning.

"Rendering you unconscious with opiates is not a cure, Lady Pringley."

"Well, it feels like one!"

"To your detriment, your ladyship, but let's see if we cannot find a better solution to your discomfort this morning that will keep you from drooling into your tea later this afternoon, shall we?"

"Dr. West!" She gasped in shock, only to smile the next instant like a schoolgirl. "You are too abrupt!"

Rowan knew his patient all too well. For a woman complaining of a terrible headache, she was rather prim and pert, and at the prospect of torturing her "personal physician," she appeared very bright-eyed and alert. Lady Pringley enjoyed a variety of mild complaints to employ him regularly, and he was too wise a man to point out that only a woman as healthy as she was could find the energy to complain and cajole him as she did and frighten every debutante to the point of hysterics from London to Bristol.

Lady Pringley leaned forward like a bird of prey eyeing a pigeon. "So now I can be abrupt. Why are you not married, Dr. West?"

"That *is* abrupt." He took out his stethoscope in a blatant ploy to ignore the question. "I'll have to ask you to cease speaking for a moment while I listen, your ladyship."

She complied, but not without giving him a blistering look that would have frightened a lesser man. He took his time, moving the drum about and pretending to evaluate her heartbeat and breathing, silently praying for patience. At last, he had to lean back and pronounce her healthy. "You have a strong and elegant constitution, Lady Pringley."

"I have a headache, nonetheless, Dr. West," she insisted archly. "Well?"

"Are we still talking about your headache?" he asked innocently.

"Don't be daft. You are too handsome not to be married, Dr. West. How is it that you are not?" Lady Pringley gave him an openly evaluating look. "Have you some secret vice or terrible flaw that would prevent you from marriage?"

What I want to know is what I've done to deserve this line of questioning. . . .

"Come, your ladyship! You know better than to ask a bachelor such a thing! A man cannot admit to regret, and if I aspire to a wife, I would have to neglect my patients and my practice. There are not enough hours in the day for a proper courtship or social pursuits, not for a doctor. She would have to drop into my lap, and I never sit still long enough, Lady Pringley."

"Shall I find a wife for you, then?" Lady Pringley reclined back, anticipating her favorite treatment. "I have an excellent eye and I know exactly the sort of woman that would suit."

"Do you?"

"I do, indeed." She closed her eyes. "A vicar's daughter, perhaps or the offspring of one of your own professional peers. You'll need an obedient and devoted little thing, completely content to occupy herself with embroidery or a hobby of economy while you are out on calls. I imagine her as bright enough to anticipate your needs but not too chatty! You are a personable man, Dr. West, but I know what's best, and a man should never look to his wife to provide too much conversation!"

He took out the peppermint liniment and rubbed it onto his fingertips and began gently massaging her temples and scalp. She practically purred as his hands worked small circles against her skin to relax her and banish her "headache." "You're very astute, but I must decline the offer, your ladyship. Truthfully, Lady Pringley, I am a wretched thing and not very lively or entertaining. I think a wife deserves some levity and cheerful company, does she not?"

He was overplaying it, and he knew it, but it had the result he'd hoped for. Lady Pringley was amused by her melancholy physician and distracted by the debate itself and not its subject.

"True! A man can be too serious and be punished with too serious a wife, in my opinion. It is a dreary profession you have, sir." She sighed with sympathy for his plight. "Not as depressing as an undertaker, but close enough!"

"This is exactly the moment when I'm supposed to argue about the nobility of medicine and protest a bit so that you can trick me into admitting that I'm not so dreary after all."

"You're such a clever man. Be dreary if you must, but young girls these days are often drawn to men with somber dispositions. They'll see you as a delightful challenge, thanks to all the poetry they consume!"

"I'll be on my guard, your ladyship."

"I do wish you'd let an older woman enjoy the innocent pastime of matchmaking." She pouted, opening her eyes to give him a piercing look.

"I don't need a wife, Lady Pringley, I need a—" His breath caught in his throat in surprise at what he'd almost blurted out. *Here's a twist. . . .*

"What do you need, Dr. West?" Lady Pringley pressed, her interest piqued.

"I need a good assistant." *I almost said partner, didn't I? And I thought of Gayle, working and practicing medicine with me. What would that be like—to have the spheres of your working life and your family life blended to coexist?*

"Oh, pish! I wish to invite you to one of my holiday gatherings, Dr. West. Nothing too fancy to make you ill at ease, but you know you are a dear personal favorite of mine, and even if you refuse to do more than grouse about in a corner, I want to see you present!"

He rolled his eyes, knowing she couldn't see him as he continued to rub the ointment into her neck and shoulders. *Like a trained monkey that will entertain her guests . . .* "I'll make no promises, your ladyship, for I wouldn't want to disappoint you."

She was drawn back to his private study on the first floor, as if being there would give her something that she needed. She'd spent the morning studying surgical techniques for amputation, trying to memorize every anatomical detail she could, while also finishing a few tonics he'd asked her to have ready for delivery on the morrow. But the words on the pages had blurred, and she'd finally accepted that her mind was already wandering and she could use a change in scenery.

I won't touch you again.

But standing in the delightful clutter of his family's collections was like being with Rowan—without the tension and awkward fire between them. Here she could let her fingers trace the spine of his books and play over the silhouettes of his knickknacks and omit worrying about inconsequential matters like permission or propriety. She knew Rowan was out on a call, and was sure that if the bell rang for his return, she would hear it in time to make a quick and timely withdrawal before he caught her.

"Quite a collection, isn't it?"

Startled, she yanked her fingers back as if she'd blistered them and then took in the sight of the tallest bear of a man she had ever seen completely filling the open doorway. Although her first instinct was to run, Gayle did her best to look nonchalant. "Yes, it's marvelous."

"I wish *I* could see Rowan's marvelous collection!" a muffled voice came from behind the first man, and another gentleman dressed in the height of fashion pushed his way past to come into the room and occupy one of the leather chairs without ceremony. "My God, Michael! While you may be notoriously quiet on your feet, you still make a hell of a wall!"

"Language, Ashe! There is a lady present!" Michael corrected him, and Gayle smiled as the giant suddenly seemed far less frightening as he awkwardly colored at his friend's gaffe. "She doesn't know either of us from burglars, so mind yourself."

The gentleman he'd called Ashe stood instantly, a graceful blond lion of a man with ice blue eyes, and gave her a courtly bow. "I beg your pardon. I am Ashe Blackwell, a harmless friend of Dr. West's, and I apologize for my wretched language. I am a man still in the process of reformation, but bound to improve, so my wife says." He waved a hand toward his companion. "And this moving mountain is Michael Rutherford, also a relatively harmless friend of Dr. West who is likely to lose his powers of speech in the presence of a beautiful woman. Well, any woman, for that matter. Mr. Rutherford is shy."

"I am not . . . shy." His reddening face told another tale, and Gayle found herself completely charmed by the unlikely pair.

"I'm afraid Dr. West is out on a patient call," she began, wondering how Carter could have forgotten it and let in visitors. "I'm not sure when he's expected to return."

"Please don't worry on our account," Mr. Rutherford said. "We've a terrible habit of making ourselves at home and didn't mean to surprise you."

"I'd come to apologize to Rowan, but I think I've changed my mind." Ashe's smile was enigmatic as he held out his hand to take hers. "You must be Miss Renshaw."

"H-he spoke of me?"

"At great length," he answered, politely releasing her hand. "You are the promising new assistant."

"He said promising?" she asked, openly skeptical.

"My memory is impeccable. I'm certain he said something very similar." Ashe's wicked sense of humor twinkled in his eyes, and Gayle enjoyed the jest.

He said nothing of the kind! But who can fault Rowan for complaining when I've been such a terror? "Yes, that sounds like exactly what he would have said. And you've come to apologize, have you? Should I ring Carter to bring you some refreshments?"

Michael finally ventured a step into the room. "We should go."

"No!" Gayle interrupted him, horrified to think she'd driven off Rowan's guests. She did her best to go on more calmly. "I'm the one who's—I'm the one who should be going. I have a great deal of work to do upstairs in the laboratory and several pages of notes to finish before Dr. West returns."

"You should stay! How else will we find out more about you?" Ashe said, openly disappointed.

Michael cleared his throat and tried again to take control. "Ashe, she has work to do and an endless debate about who should stay and who should go seems a bit silly, don't you think?"

Ashe nodded. "He's right. Running away just because we've bumped into Rowan's new assistant would be the height of rudeness. Please, Miss Renshaw, ignore our presence. All his friends find their way to his study from time to time. We've made it our unofficial gentleman's club— and Rowan is far too kindhearted to protest when the Jaded hide from the world amidst his things."

"The Jaded?" Gayle was sure she'd missed something.

"Damn it, Ashe! He's not likely to want to mention that to her!" Michael snapped impatiently.

"Language, Michael! There is a lady present!" Ashe's admonishment was accompanied by a mischievous smile. "Now she's going to think it's a bawdy club, the way you're over there puffing away!" He turned to her directly. "A silly nickname for our small circle after a misinterpreted comment or two when we'd returned from India."

"You were both in India with Rowan?" she asked, rapt in attention.

Mr. Rutherford intervened once again. "And on that note, we'll bid you good day. Come, Ashe. You can return and apologize to Rowan another time, especially since it now seems you'll be apologizing for today as well. It was our pleasure to meet you, Miss Renshaw." Michael bowed awkwardly, his expression pained at the attempt at social niceties. "Come, Blackwell, before I drag you off to prevent Rowan from killing you."

Ashe was nonplussed. "Rowan is a doctor. I've never seen the man kill so much as a mouse." But he also began to retreat. "I am sincerely sorry if I've offended you. I meant to be playful, but my wife has told me more than once that I am an impossible man. Michael is right. We should be going. I'll let Carter know that we—"

"Mr. Blackwell! Mr. Rutherford!" Mrs. Evans greeted them from the doorway. "I didn't realize you were here! It's been ages and I'd have sent up a tray for—" She spotted Gayle and her delight withered to stern disapproval. "I'd come in search of you, but didn't expect to find you here, Miss Renshaw."

Gayle did her best not to look the part of an errant schoolgirl caught by her headmistress out of bounds. "You were looking for me?"

"Florence has just come from upstairs and informs me that something is bubbling away, quite unattended, in Dr. West's laboratory!"

"Oh!" She ran past Mrs. Evans without a backward glance at either man. "Oh, God!" She took the stairs two at a time, numb with disbelief. *The tonic! I couldn't have left*

it on the burner—could I? A morning's work, and worse, I
could have burnt the house down in my carelessness!

Just as Mrs. Evans had described, there was the container bubbling away, its contents overflowing in an unhappy brown waterfall that smelled more like burnt shoe leather than soothing lemon balm. Her next impression was that the small disaster would take the rest of her afternoon to clean up, but the smell would linger for days. Gayle felt close to tears. She grabbed a leather cloth to pull the beaker off the gas brazier only to spill more brown sludge onto the table and floor.

Ruined.

The bell alerting her to Rowan's return rang merrily and she could only sigh. Since his friends were downstairs, she didn't think to hurry. It was the first social call she was aware of him receiving, and Mr. Blackwell and Mr. Rutherford would certainly warrant a bit of his time before he made his way up to the laboratory to check on her progress.

Rowan, however, must have had other ideas.

She was on her hands and knees under the table scrubbing the hot tarlike substance from the floorboards when he came in, and Gayle had to bite off a groan. The embarrassment of being caught on the floor was overwhelming, and for a split second she almost hoped he wouldn't spot her there.

"Miss Renshaw?" His feet stopped in front of her.

She closed her eyes as if to wish him away. "I . . . I didn't expect you so soon."

Oh, God. Please don't let me cry. He's going to say something about ignorant distraction or how women who can't concentrate shouldn't be trusted with his marvelous laboratory . . . and how will I argue against it?

He bent over to peek under the table. "Are you all right?"

She managed to nod, not trusting her voice.

"Can you tell me the main arteries of the forearm and hand?"

She blinked twice before replying. "The brachial artery,

the ulnar artery, the radial artery, and . . . the digital, meta-carpal, and the deep and superficial palmar arches."

"Very good." He slapped the tabletop lightly with his palm in approval. "Well, I'll be downstairs in the study if you need anything."

As if he always talks to women under tables . . . as if I hadn't ruined anything . . .

"Yes . . ." she answered, shock giving way to gratitude. "Thank you, Dr. West."

After he'd gone, Gayle remained under the table and just sat back on her heels, almost afraid to move for fear of spoiling the moment.

I think I may have turned a corner with him.
I just wish I knew where I was going.

Chapter

11

On Wednesdays, he took calls in his ground floor office. Amidst his usual working-class patients, it had become quietly known that Dr. West did not turn anyone seeking aid away and did not demand payment for his services of those without the means. His small household staff was familiar with the day's demands, and everyone was at the ready to help as needed. Carter collected cards and orchestrated the lists so that everyone was seen either at a previously appointed time or in the order that they'd arrived to wait. Barnaby, the footman, provided an element of security, along with Theo, and downstairs, Mrs. Wilson baked extra bread to give to anyone whose prime complaint might be hunger.

On this particular Wednesday, Rowan had determined that he would include Miss Renshaw in the day's proceedings. It was a bold move, considering the potential for gossip, but he was hoping she'd be perceived as a nurse, and he couldn't keep her locked in the third-floor laboratory forever.

At least, not with a clear conscience.

He'd instructed her to wear her plainest dress and white laboratory apron to try to mute her presence, but it was hardly successful. Her plainest print was a flattering jade green that set off her dark hair and remarkable eyes, and even with an oversized white apron, she was simply stunning to behold.

You look like an aristocratic beauty in a poor disguise, Miss Renshaw. Oh, well—into the front lines you go.

"He's crying, doctor."

The mother's voice barely carried over the infant's unhappy screams, and Rowan smiled. "He is, indeed, Mrs. Dorsett. Why don't you just sit there and I'll take a look at this loud, young fellow and see if he'll tell us what the bother is. Come here, handsome man." He lifted the small baby out of her arms and signaled Gayle to come with him to the exam table. He deliberately kept his voice low and even, instead of trying to compete with his charge. "My stethoscope is there, in the first drawer under this table. Pull it out and let's have a listen to his lungs."

Gayle found the instrument easily. "Here you are."

"I can tell you already without using it that he seems to have ample strength and a clear cry, so that's a good sign." He laid the boy down carefully to unwrap him a bit for the examination. "See? His color is good, though admittedly a bit red in the face from his efforts. Then we listen, like so . . . in between the cries . . . for any wet drawing sounds . . . but he's a beauty." He took the earpieces out to allow Gayle to try to listen. "Can you hear it? The air moving freely? Like a high-pitched sound, and there should be a little muffled wind on the intake and just before he breathes out. Yes?"

"Yes!"

"So, we know it's not pneumonia or an ailment of the lungs. His mother said nothing of coughing or fever, so that's a clue. What next?"

"It could simply be colic. I would feel his stomach. Is it distended or hard?"

Rowan pulled up the boy's little shirt and a gentle exam confirmed all. He put her hand under his to demonstrate the pressure and pattern of his search.

She gasped. "It's hard as a little drum!"

"Poor fellow! See how he pulls his legs upward? He's miserable, but this will quite literally pass." He rolled the infant over, keeping his own warm hand pressed against the baby's stomach to offer some temporary relief. "It's colic, Mrs. Dor—"

Rowan stopped himself as they both realized that Mrs. Dorsett, who was all of seventeen, had fallen fast asleep in the chair behind them.

Gayle surveyed her with sympathy. "She's a child herself. Has she no help?"

He shook his head. "Not that she's spoken of." He turned back to the table. "All right. Ring for Barnaby and Florence, and then while we're waiting for them, let me show you a few simple techniques to help our patient. You see? I can use the slight heat and pressure of my hand. Sometimes it helps to rub his back or belly in a wide circular motion, and if we sit him up and do so, just make sure he's reclined and comfortable. None of this is a cure. We'll make sure she gives him fennel water before his feedings and look into her own diet for the cause. Often, he'll just outgrow the trouble in just a month or two and her burden will ease."

She rang for the servants, and Gayle and Rowan worked quietly side by side with the fussy baby until his cries slowed and he dropped off to slumber. Barnaby arrived and surveyed the scene. "Who am I to take?"

"Can you carry Mrs. Dorsett into the library without waking her? It's dark and quiet in there, and the reading couch will be perfect for her to rest for a while. Let everyone know not to disturb her, all right, Barnaby? And then keep an eye out so that when she does awaken, there's no panic. Florence will have her boy, and tell Carter to slip several shillings into her basket before she goes."

"Easy enough!" he answered softly, then stepped aside into the room as Florence pushed past him.

"Oh! A dear baby!" she exclaimed quietly, happy to be called to take him from Gayle's arms. "I'll see to him, doctor, no worries there! The kitchen is warm and quiet this time of day, and he'll be a little prince for me, won't you, sweet?"

Both mother and baby were sorted away for rest and care, and Rowan wrote down the instructions for the fennel water for Gayle to give her later.

And so the day went. Any hope he'd held of his apprentice being put off by the press of his less noble patients and their complaints died quickly. Instead, he found himself enjoying a Wednesday as he hadn't in a long while. Gayle set many of them at ease, and her interest and questions were never misdirected. She was quick with her hands and never in the way. The morning seemed to fly, even as his entryway filled with patients.

"Ah, Miss Featherstone!" Rowan looked up from the pile of cards with a smile. This would be one visitor that would try the patience of any apprentice, so he was curious to see what Gayle would think of Ada Featherstone—for the young woman was never well, no matter what anyone said or did, and could not be convinced that she would survive the month. A spinster in her midthirties whose brother had left her money enough for a little bit of pretense but not enough to secure a husband or fend off pity, Ada had made her health, or lack of it, her singular pursuit. He wasn't oblivious to the quirky element of romantic fantasy that dear Ada attributed to their weekly appointments, but he hoped that it was better to harmlessly indulge her than offend her. "What brings you to my office today?"

"I am . . ." Ada hesitated as she spied Gayle, her expression a bit wary. "I am suffering. But who is this?"

"This is Miss Gayle Renshaw. She is assisting me today."

Miss Featherstone eyed Gayle as if she were a rival on the battlefield. The drooping feathers in her bonnet quivered with the emotion of their owner, and she sniffed her dismissal—but withheld her disapproval, to Rowan's relief—as she finished her study of his new "nurse." Then she proceeded to devote her attention to Rowan as if Gayle were invisible. "I am dying, Dr. West. I am sure of it!"

"Come, Miss Featherstone." He led her to one of the chairs across from his desk and took its companion to sit near her. "How can you be so sure? You look better today. Did you not find any relief using the remedy I prescribed last week?"

She sighed dramatically. "I did, at first! You are a genius, Dr. West, and you know I rely entirely on your care. But now . . . I'm dizzy. Nearly all the time! Before it was just headaches, but with this new terrible symptom, I'm in a terror! I could fall! I could break my neck! Or faint in the street!"

"Oh, dear." He nodded, trying to give every appearance of a man deep in thought and temporarily stumped by the news. "We cannot have you at risk, Miss Featherstone!"

He looked back at Gayle, standing in the corner patiently. "I need my stethoscope, Miss Renshaw."

He listened to Ada's heartbeat, pressing the small drum just to the edge of her collar and averting his gaze to protect Miss Featherstone's keen sense of modesty. Then, setting the instrument aside, he gently felt her throat and glands, looked into her ears and eyes, and shook his head. "You must take better care of yourself, Miss Featherstone, and see that you relax in the afternoons. You should take a nap each day before teatime."

"I try! But it is so difficult when one is suffering to think of rest! I'm terrified that if I recline too much, I'll expire right there."

"Then we must remove this terror so that you can recover." He held out his stethoscope to Gayle. "I'm afraid it seems that you"—he paused dramatically—"have overexcited blood." Gayle was behind Miss Featherstone and gave him a puzzled look, but he pointedly ignored her and continued. "It's a common condition for women with artistic and delicate constitutions, such as yourself."

"Oh, my! Overexcited blood!" Ada repeated enraptured.

"It is *not* life threatening, but it would certainly feel

worrisome and cause all of the symptoms that we've been battling."

"What can I do?"

"I'll have to send for a special compounding mixture from a colleague of mine who has been researching this very thing. Please allow me to send over a tonic with instructions by noon tomorrow. But you must swear that you will take only the careful doses that I prescribe and not take too much! It is extremely potent, but very efficacious for your condition if managed properly."

"I swear, I will follow your instructions to the letter, as always." She fanned herself with her gloved fingers. "Is it . . . terribly expensive?"

"Dreadfully so!" Rowan proclaimed. "But I refuse to let you give me a penny until we see you better! I've taken an oath, Miss Featherstone!"

"Oh, my! How wonderful!" Miss Featherstone rose from her chair, energized by the prospect of a new diagnosis and exotic tonic. "I knew you would resolve it! Thank you, Dr. West!"

She sailed out, her bonnet feathers happily waving at them as she left, and Rowan turned back to face his suspicious apprentice.

"Overexcited blood?"

Rowan shrugged. "I know there's no such thing, and thank you for not spoiling it. Miss Featherstone is . . . I do what I can to keep her happy."

"Is she ill at all?"

He shook his head. "Not in all the years I've known her."

"And these special tonics and mixtures?" she asked.

"Variations of sugar water, ginger syrup, and lemon or sweetened flour paste pills when her symptoms are acute." He went back to his desk to make himself a reminder note to send Miss Featherstone's latest "remedy" by morning. "I may assign you to designing her next tonic if you'd like the practice."

"Wouldn't she be happier if she knew she was fine?"

"No! And I'm not sure that she wouldn't really lose her

health if another, less scrupulous, doctor was in the picture."

Gayle crossed her arms. "Does she pay you for your services?"

"Not yet and I never expect her to. I've told her that I will send her a bill as soon as I've successfully treated her and she is better. But I can hardly bill a woman when I've 'failed' to relieve her suffering, so the agreement works out beautifully. She gets to come every Wednesday and show off her best bonnets, and I make sure she's not on some quack's doorstep taking opiates."

"She's insane."

"She's lonely. Where is your compassion?" he chided her gently, unsure of where the violet storm in her eyes had originated or why. "Ada is difficult, but not any more than most."

"She's a bit . . . too familiar with you, Dr. West."

It was close enough to jealousy to make a strange, joyful fire uncurl around his chest. *Hell, I'm wrong, but I think I'll enjoy the misconception and that delightful little pout for now.* "Many patients feel a bit of ownership and entitlement to their doctor's time and attention, but don't blame poor Ada for it."

A knock on the door ended the debate, and he was sorry for the interruption.

A middle-aged man came into the room, the scent of gin immediately permeating the small room. He crushed his hat in his fists as he bobbed a mumbled greeting at Rowan before he caught sight of Gayle. "I ain't droppin' my pants in front of the likes of her!"

Rowan bit the inside of his cheek to keep from laughing. "Miss Renshaw, it seems I'm in need of a few things from Mr. Fitzroy's." He pulled a short list off his desk and handed it to her. "Theo will drive you."

For a moment, he thought she was going to refuse him, but then the man went on even more loudly to say, "A man's gotta right to keep himself to himself without some woman lookin' on! Bad enough my tackle's gone red and itchy, but *she's* not gettin' a peek!"

"Yes, Dr. West. I'll see to it right away." She took the folded paper from him so swiftly he could hear it leave his hands, and she left the men to themselves.

Rowan turned to his unhappy patient, praying that Gayle would come to appreciate the courtesy of respecting a man's privacy and being spared the sight of what promised to be an embarrassing rash.

Chapter
12

It was mortifying to be sent away, but Gayle was not so proud that she couldn't see the sensibilities that had driven her out of the room. For all her stubborn determination to prove herself, she'd taken one look at that man and decided that for once, retreat truly was the better part of valor.

Rowan's anatomy books had provided her first frank look at the male form, and while she'd grown accustomed to the drawings, the reality of a sputtering, unshaven, ruddy drunk dropping his pants with Rowan at her elbow was unthinkable.

So much for all my bravado! And so much for the villainous Dr. West!

She'd spent a great deal of time with Rowan, but today had been the best day she could remember. Yesterday's fiasco had been rewarded with an opportunity to work side by side with him on over a dozen patients. Today, it had been impossible not to admire how polite and respectful he was to each patient, no matter how mean their dress or the state of their arrival. Each one was made to feel important and cared for, and it was clear that the entire household enjoyed participating in the doctor's Wednesday practice.

She'd listened to heartbeats, set a broken wrist, and even incised an infected heel.

Paradise!

And at every turn, there was Rowan. She'd forgotten her vows after they'd kissed not to smile at him and to keep a reserved distance from him at all times.

It was difficult not to warm to a man who peered at you under tables and let you spend a day learning how all those mysterious Latin phrases could come to life with a patient standing before you.

"Here we are, Miss Renshaw!" Theo gave her a bemused look as he opened the carriage door. She'd been so deep in her thoughts of Rowan and the day that she'd missed the ride altogether and was now shocked to realize that they'd stopped in front of the apothecary's.

"Ah! So we are!" She stepped down lightly. "Thank you, Theo. This shouldn't take very long."

Theo nodded. "Mr. Fitzroy prides himself on being quick with orders, so no worries there! I'll wait with the carriage for you."

"You're very kind." She smoothed the line of her coat over her skirts and headed into the shop. It was a long, narrow space with a counter along one side and behind it were hundreds of small wooden drawers of every cunning size and shape imaginable.

A portly man with spectacles came over to her, addressing her from his side of counter. "Can I help you, miss?"

"Yes, I—"

"Miss Renshaw!" Peter James hailed her from a doorway in the back, his arms full of a large wooden crate. "I apologize for interrupting, but it's such a surprise to see you here!"

"You know this young lady?" the older man asked archly.

"Yes, Mr. Fitzroy. This is Miss Gayle Renshaw. She is working with Dr. West."

"I am his assistant." It was pride that made her blurt it out, but she'd said as much to Peter James when they'd met, and Gayle didn't see the harm in underscoring her position—especially with a dour man like Fitzroy. "I am very interested in the medical arts."

Mr. Fitzroy adjusted his spectacles. "I'd thought Mr. James was spewing nonsense when he told me that Dr. West had a woman helping him in his laboratory. I've known Dr. West for too long to think he would even consider such a thing."

Gayle held out the list, as if Mr. Fitzroy hadn't spoken. "Dr. West asked me to give you this list and bring back the items on it. Naturally, if there's anything you can't provide, please let me know."

Mr. Fitzroy took the paper from her as cautiously as a man reaching for an asp. He glanced at the list, then back up at her. "I'll send along the order later this afternoon."

"I'll wait. Dr. West expressed some need for the items as soon as possible and I have the carriage outside."

Mr. James put down the crate he was holding to set it aside. "I can pull the order, Mr. Fitzroy. I don't—"

"No! Don't be a fool!" Mr. Fitzroy huffed. "*You* can see to it that Miss Renshaw, who has expressed an *interest in medical arts*, doesn't go poking about my inventory in my absence! I shall pull this order personally!" And with that, he set about pulling powders and striding around his shop before stomping into the back of the store out of sight.

She was embarrassed for Peter at being spoken to so rudely in her presence. But also for herself for being treated like a wayward child who needed a minder. "Mr. Fitzroy is . . ."

Peter leaned forward, keeping his voice low. "He's all bluster. Don't worry." He led her over to a display of small brown glass bottles toward the front of the shop as far away from the doorway Mr. Fitzroy had gone through as possible. "Here, we'll pretend to look at smelling salts and enjoy our wait, despite him. What say you?"

She nodded, picking up a tiny jar labeled "Licorice-spiced Ammonia," and played along. "I never knew there were so many varieties."

"As many as the ladies who practice swooning, I like to think!"

She laughed. Peter had such a relaxed air about him.

Peter picked up a different bottle. "Not to pry, but I'm sure you have an easier time with your employer. Not once have I heard of West barking at anyone. He's got quite a good reputation—though his staff never talk much—so maybe secretly he's even meaner than Fitzroy."

She shook her head. "He's very kind. And his staff never talk because he treats them like family."

"A world traveler, though! How envious I am of a man who can set out and see the exotic wonders of the world! My uncle once went to Scotland, and my family fussed over him as if he'd been to the ends of the earth, can you imagine? But none of them have ever left London, so who's to say what impresses one man and not another!" He opened up a small jar as if to sample it. "Dr. West went to India, didn't he?"

"Yes." She crinkled her nose as a scent like wet dog wafted over. "For medical research."

"Has he told you about it? India, I meant." He capped the offending vial. "He was ill there, terribly ill from what Mr. Fitzroy said. Dr. West was all skeleton thin and looked a bit haunted when he returned—not at all like the man who left London."

"Ill? Was he?"

Peter nodded. "He'd never say, so it's a bit of a mystery. But he went off with a bounce in his step. We heard he'd stopped to visit friends in the Lake District and picked himself up a wife on his way out of the country. Lost her though before he reached Bombay. Maybe it was grief that took the starch out of him." Peter shrugged. "He was gone for almost two years, but you wouldn't have recognized him."

"Travel and experience can change a man. But you—you think he was ill?"

"Who can say? It wasn't just his appearance that was different. He had all these new friends that no one seemed to know. Have you met his gentleman friends?"

Something in her tightened defensively as their friendly chatter strayed into what felt like Rowan's very personal business. But before she could express her dismay, Mr. James went on as cheerfully as a lark. "I have! Mr. Blackwell is my favorite. Recently married, much to everyone's surprise, to some American girl. An actress in Piccadilly attempted suicide when she heard, they say—he was so popular with the ladies! If ever a man was destined to die a bachelor . . ."

Relief flooded through her. *I'd forgotten how well he knew the house! Naturally he would know of Rowan's circle—better than I would.* "His wife is an American?"

Mr. James put back a bottle he'd been taking, his expression sobering. "I was being rude, wasn't I? I feel so comfortable with you, Miss Renshaw, that you have me rambling on like an old woman. Forgive me, I am tied so often to my workbench that I spend most of my time in the social company of delivery boys, cart vendors, and servants. It makes for wonderful stories, but I get carried away."

"There's no need to apologize." She waved off the trespass. "I've done the same, telling you more of myself than I should have at our last meeting! And with Dr. West's fascinating friends like the Jaded, who could blame you for wishing to share a good story?"

Peter's eyes flashed at her mention of the Jaded, but before he could let her in on the cause—

"Mr. James!" Mr. Fitzroy's clipped call brought both of them instantly around. "Carry this package out to Miss Renshaw's carriage and then see that you're downstairs finishing sorting away those deliveries. It's my time and money you're wasting, sir!" He set the bag down on the counter. "Please thank Dr. West for his patronage, Miss Renshaw, and let him know that I can have anything he needs run over—*without* troubling you."

"I will, Mr. Fitzroy and it's no trouble. No trouble, at all." She walked out nearly blinded with fury at the apothecary's tone with Peter behind her.

"All bluster, remember?" Peter whispered behind her, then hailed Theo. "Here's the box, sir. Shall I put it inside the carriage?"

"I'll take it." Theo took the good-size box from him, tucking it safely under one of the carriage seats. "We'd best be back. Thanks for the hand, Mr. James."

"Anytime!" He tipped his hat to Gayle. "It really was a pleasure to see you again, miss. A real pleasure!"

She climbed back inside, and the carriage pulled away smoothly into the traffic on the street. Gayle was grateful to have her errand behind her and cheered to have seen a familiar face. *Poor Peter! The next time I am tempted to kick Rowan in the shins, I'll have to remember how fortunate I am that he is nothing like Fitzroy.*

She looked at the brown paper-wrapped box underneath the seat across from her and a new thought robbed her of some of her mirth.

I wonder if Rowan feels as fortunate in the association with me for an apprentice. He's made it all too easy to forget how I came to be here and why we cannot be friends. I feel like a snake he's allowed in his garden. Peter was rattling on about Rowan being changed, and here I am, benefitting from whatever secrets he's keeping.

And what was that about him being ill in India? Was it from grief over Charlotte's death? He said he'd suffered from poor timing and bad luck. Did he almost lose his life?

Gayle sat up straighter and leaned back against the cushioned seat. "I'm just going to ask him," she spoke aloud. "I told him I'd do my best to reach my own informed opinions, and I'm going to stop letting my imagination run riot about jungle fevers and ask the man."

And then I'm going to see about mixing up a tonic for Miss Ada Featherstone so that she keeps her eyes and hands to herself!

* * *

By the time she'd returned, it was late in the afternoon, the last of his patients had apparently been seen, and the house was quiet. Carter pointed her to Rowan's ground-floor office, and Gayle pushed the door open only to discover the man asleep behind his desk. Rowan's long legs were stretched out to rest unceremoniously on his leather doctor's bag, using it as a footrest, and he leaned back against the wooden back of his desk chair, his head tilted over to one side in precarious balance.

Gayle smiled at the sight. He hardly looked comfortable, but he was slumbering so soundly, she couldn't imagine disturbing him. Instead, she realized it was a rare opportunity to look at him unabated and without any repercussions.

He was a handsome man by any assessment, but Gayle marveled that it was the sum of his parts that gave him such charm and not even one thing in particular. There was a rugged quality to his chiseled features, so that the clean lines and classic beauty to his face were unmistakably masculine without being coarse. He was unfashionably clean-shaven, but Gayle liked it on him since it made him seem younger and more accessible to her.

Asleep he looked almost boyish, with the soft curls of his dark auburn hair with its mahogany streaks set back from his face. His lashes were as thick and lush as the prettiest maiden's, and she smiled remembering how her mother had once lamented that men never paid a single thought their entire lives to the bounty of grand eyelashes they'd been blessed with but admired them on ladies and spurred women to unknown torture to achieve the same effect.

Rowan would never be mistaken for a man of leisure. His frame was muscular and athletic, with his broad shoulders and narrow hips. His hands were clasped lightly to rest on the flat of his stomach, and the wool cloth of his trousers clung to his thighs and outlined the shape of his legs.

She'd studied more of the male form than she'd ever anticipated, and a hundred scientific terms jangled through her head as she surveyed him. But still, the potency of Dr. Rowan West was impossible to dismiss in terms of sinew, muscle, or bone.

The wicked ability to stare at him unchecked was heady, and the longer she acted the voyeur, the more a strange heat in her blood began to grow. She took two steps closer, near enough to lean over and drink in the details of the beauty of his hands and wrists, the pulse at his neck, and the faint smell of cedar and spices from the soap that he used.

Here is a man.

She tried to conjure an image of Rowan without the layers of respectable clothes and was almost breathless by the mental exercise. The top buttons of his shirt had come loose and there was the smallest hint of a shadow of hair peeking out. *Is he covered in hair like that? Is it soft or coarse to the touch? What would it be like to lie up against the flesh of a man—so alien but so alike at the same time?*

"Excuse me, Miss Renshaw." Carter came up behind her and Gayle nearly jumped out of her shoes. "Sorry to disturb you, doctor."

Gayle put her fingertips over her mouth to keep from screaming when she was equally startled by Rowan's prompt and level reply. The sable brown eyelashes she'd admired barely flickered to betray his alertness. Rowan didn't bother moving a muscle, except to smile. "Not at all, I was just resting my eyes."

The panic that seized her made her wish the floor would open up and swallow her whole. *Had the man been awake the entire time? Was he just pretending to sleep while I stood there sighing and cataloging him like a trollop?*

"I . . . I was just . . . Here are the items from Fitzroy's." She backed up, nearly tripping over Carter, and put the package on the table by the door, her hands trembling terribly. "I'll be upstairs if—"

It was simply too much. She turned and fled the room, the sound of her heels pounding out a drumbeat of retreat that Gayle was convinced would echo her humiliation through every room of the brownstone.

Chapter
13

Cleaning up the laboratory was a simple task that kept her hands busy, but unfortunately still left enough energy to think too much. She'd refused a dinner tray and decided to work into the night until she'd exhausted herself and regained the intelligent self-control she was so proud of. Gayle swept the floors, wiped down the windows and wrought iron framework, and then began washing and drying all of the empty glass vials and jars.

Anything to avoid being still.

If I focus on the work of the day, being in the exam room and the patients I saw and even my introduction to Mr. Fitzroy, I may survive this embarrassment and forget the worst of it.

Not that Carter could have known—or Rowan for that matter—what I was thinking when I was . . . standing there. Looking at him. Ogling him. After all, Dr. West had even made a jest about having his throat cut in his sleep, so he probably thought I was plotting murder.

Not picturing him naked.

Gayle bit her lip and set the last wet jar out of the sink and onto the wooden tray. Her plan was to carry the tray over to the table by the window so that the light and air in the morning would finish drying them.

She grabbed the handles and lifted the tray, then gasped at the weight of it. Anyone less stubborn would have emptied a few of the contents to lighten the load, but Gayle was too distracted by the jumble of her thoughts to consider it.

If only it were just physical, this odd pull he has with me. But the more I know of him, the more I wish to be near him. The way he respects his household staff and the way he spoke to his patients today—my father always said it was how a gentleman treats the common man that betrays the most about his character.

And why am I so obsessed with Rowan's character? Why does it matter so much what he thinks of me or of anything beyond medicine?

It matters because I'm falling in love with him.

The shock of the revelation made her fingers go numb and breathless, the heavy tray of vials and delicate glass containers sliding out of her hands and striking the hard floor with a soul-jarring crash. The expensive crystal shattered in an explosion of sound, and she cried out in horror at the clumsy mistake.

Gayle quickly began to kneel to try to salvage something from the shards to ward off her useless tears. *He'll be furious when he sees . . . and what am I doing? Acting like a mindless ninny because I've lost my heart to a man who barely tolerates me.*

"Don't move." His voice was gentle but firm from the doorway into the lab.

"I'm sorry for the dreadful mess. I can clean it—"

"Don't! Move!" It was a firmer command, arresting her movement this time as she registered the unexpected urgency in his words. Gayle straightened, her cheeks burning with embarrassment, unsure if he meant to lecture her where she stood or if the mishap were somehow worse than she'd estimated.

He lit several lamps to ensure that he'd have the light he needed to see and came toward her.

Before she could ask what he intended, he'd bent over to use his handkerchief to brush aside the largest sharp pieces from a small area in front of her. And then he knelt on one knee and gingerly began plucking the glass slivers and tiny shards from the hem of her skirt. In the glow of the lamplight at her feet, she now realized that the last few inches of her skirt had transformed into a glittering display of nearly invisible bits of broken glass.

"I could just shake them out, Dr. West." She had to swallow, for a lump had formed in her throat at the sight of him at her feet—so intimately close, so tenderly focused on his compassionate task.

"Just stand still, Gayle."

And there she was—trapped in an impossible moment of chivalry.

He worked efficiently and quietly, cleaning up a small section of the hem of her skirts and petticoats to brush it with his handkerchief-wrapped fingers, pulling out the glass that remained, then clearing the floor to allow himself to shift over a few inches and repeat the process.

"You don't have to do all this." She was breathless at the sensation of his hands moving against her skirts, never making contact with her ankles or slippers, but still *there*, his head bent and level with her thighs, his forehead a scant inch from the pleated fabric, and the temptation to reach down and touch his hair was making her dizzy.

"I'd rather this than finding my kit to teach you how to pull glass splinters out of your ankles. I imagine they're too pretty to be scratched up needlessly, Miss Renshaw."

"I don't think you're supposed to imagine what your apprentice's ankles look like, Dr. West."

He laughed but didn't cease his efforts. "I'll do my best to refrain from doing so, Miss Renshaw."

"I'm . . . This is awkward, Dr. West. You wouldn't do this if I were a man."

"You're absolutely right. I would have gotten the scissors and just offered to let you cut off your pant legs and then I'd have left the matter of your stockings to you."

"Oh." She tried to ignore the shocking image of Rowan cutting her out of her clothes. "I see."

He mercifully changed the subject. "It was a long day."

She shook her head. "It was a wonderful day."

He smiled. "Wednesdays in this house are not every-one's idea of wonderful, but I'm glad you thought so. The hours fly for me on these days, and there is a selfish plea-sure to having everyone about to lend a hand. Even if Mrs. Evans does fuss a bit at the state of her floors after-ward."

"So many different patients on a single day—I loved it!"

He moved again, now kneeling almost directly behind her. "Good. I was afraid I'd exhausted you and caused this—"

"I am *not* prone to accidents."

"Of course you're not."

"Please don't mock me. How is it that every time I wish to convey how reliable I am, something happens and one of us is kneeling on the floor over some mess I've made?"

"Fate," he replied gently.

Why isn't he yelling? There's a month's wages for most physicians on this floor—but the man is speaking to me as calmly as if we were talking about the weather.

"Why are you so . . . kind to me? You needn't be. I mean, I don't expect you to be kind, Dr. West."

"Perhaps that's why."

She closed her eyes, wishing she knew how to fight off the sentimental tears that threatened and ward off the maelstrom of emotions inside of her. *I am not falling in love with this man—I won't! I've come too far to surrender my dreams and transform myself into a joke.* "I'll pay for the glass. I'll replace all of it, Dr. West."

He shook his head. "There's no need for that. I'd needed an excuse to visit the glass shop and—"

"I'm not Ada Featherstone! I'm not some addle-headed woman that you need to coddle! You have every right to be angry, Dr. West, and I insist on being allowed to restore what I've broken."

"Gayle," he spoke softly, the use of her first name capturing her attention. "Trust me when I say this. There may well be an extensive list of things that invoke an angry reaction from me, and God knows, I'm not always very good at keeping myself in check, but broken glass—hasn't been on the list for a very, very long time."

Rowan sat back on his heels and shifted again, this time returning to his starting position in front of her to survey his progress. "I'm almost done, Gayle. Just hold still for another few seconds, and allow a small liberty."

"A s-small liberty?" she asked, but the answer was swift and left her speechless as his hands lightly trailed up her ankles and calves, circling the muscles there to gently caress her up to the back of her knees.

"Just one last check for any glass slivers that may have strayed onto your stockings."

"Oh!" His touch was efficient and feather soft, but the miasma of fire and delight that spread up her limbs to form a molten pool between her hips was intoxicating. Her knees turned to rubber, and she bit the inside of her cheek to stare at the ceiling as a thousand wicked thoughts nearly overcame her. The splay of his warm fingers were telegraphing electric sweet storms all over her body, and she wasn't sure she could survive another pass of his hands without betraying herself with a moan or a sigh.

"Ah, there's one." He sat back on his heels and sucked a small piece of glass from an index finger to discard it with the rest. "Not life threatening, Miss Renshaw, but you don't deserve a miserable end to a wonderful day."

She nodded in stunned silence, one hand gripping the worktable's edge to keep her steady on her feet and the other pressed against her chest to keep her heart from pumping out of her ribcage.

"Well, I've pushed it under the table far enough for now, and Florence can bring up a dustpan in the morning to clear it. As for this, I'll just throw this handkerchief into the bin." He stood like a graceful panther rising from the floor. "You should get some rest, Miss Renshaw."

All she could do was nod, like a mute child, miserably blushing but hypnotized by him.

"Good night, then."

Rowan left her there, returning to the second floor, and Gayle began to cry.

Some things are simply true. Even if you don't understand them.

Chapter
14

Mrs. Evans finished dishing out the lamb stew, and then deliberately put another large spoon of meat onto Rowan's plate. "You're getting thin in the face, doctor."

"I'm not, but I'll eat my delicious, hearty lunch all the same and send my compliments to Cook, please, for another Thursday meal that has me completely recovered and in good spirits." He took a bite or two before Mrs. Evans finally withdrew a satisfied woman. "She hovers but she has a good heart, and I know for a fact that she's one of your staunchest defenders below stairs."

"Is she? I think she's still convinced that I'm going to burn the house down."

Rowan laughed. "That may also be true."

"And who is she defending me against?" Gayle tasted some of the stew from her own plate and savored the dish. Mrs. Wilson's skills were incomparable and a welcome amenity. "Do I have enemies in the house?"

"Evil doctors who might forget to see that you have tea

in the afternoons during grueling sessions about diseases of the bones."

"I don't like tea."

"How startling and unladylike of you!" he teased. "Well, that warrants a recitation or two. Let's see. Shall we discuss the symptoms and signs of cholera?"

"I had rather discuss a cure." She pushed her plate aside. "Is there no treatment known for it?"

"Every physician I know claims to have the answer to that question, but I haven't heard proof of one. Snow recommends an intravenous injection of saline fluid, but it's somewhat hit and miss by all reports. The best cure is to prevent its spread."

"From contaminated water."

"You are a good student, Miss Renshaw. Can you name the— "

Carter cleared his throat in the doorway, in his usual fashion, and reluctantly interrupted the lesson. "A note was just delivered, doctor."

"Well, let's have it then." Rowan held out his hand.

"It's for Miss Renshaw, doctor." Carter walked over with the small silver tray.

"For *me*?" The thought was extremely distressing since no one she knew was aware of her whereabouts, but Gayle took the folded note with a trembling hand. "Thank you, Carter."

Carter retreated, and almost instantly, the mystery was solved. "It's from . . . Mr. James."

"Peter James?" Rowan asked, openly displeased. "Peter James is sending you notes?"

Gayle stared at the signature, disregarding the note's contents as she absorbed the implications. "I'm sure it's . . ." She looked back up at Rowan, her face growing hot in embarrassment. "It's nothing." She tucked the object into her skirt pocket, intending to send a terse reply back to the young man advising him that she was not open to receiving invitations to step out.

"Fitzroy tells me that Mr. James has nearly completed his training and will be looking to open his own venture soon."

"Really?"

"A good apothecary and surgeon can always make a good living, though it can be tough to find the savings to get started. But Mr. Peter James strikes me as an ambitious young man, and Fitzroy said the young man seems extremely optimistic and has even spoken of taking on a wife."

"Has he?" She put her hands in her lap so that he wouldn't see her fingers curling into her own palms in frustration. She was as romantically interested in Peter James as she was in rocks, but openly arguing the matter didn't seem wise.

"I overheard Florence saying he was quite the catch."

Then again, wisdom is not always my strong suit when I lose my temper. "Are you jealous, Dr. West?"

"I have no right to be, Miss Renshaw. You are not my property, and if you wish to step out with the apothecary's boy, then who am I to protest?"

Without warning, she found herself smiling at him. By any measure, practically beaming, and the look of raw confusion on his face only added to the strange mirth she was feeling. *He called him a boy. He's so jealous he could spit. It's . . . a bit wonderful, isn't it?* "You're absolutely right, Dr. West. I'm not anyone's property." She broke off a small piece of bread to soak in her stew. "Can we not speak of something else, then?"

"Joyfully," he groused and refilled his glass with ginger water.

"Were you ill in India?"

"What? Why? Who said I was . . . ill?"

"It was meant to be a question to provide a neutral diversion," Gayle supplied. "You said yourself that you'd suffered some bad luck and poor timing when you were there, and I was just curious. You said not to listen to rumors, so I thought I would simply ask."

"Ask me something else."

Her curiosity was entirely piqued at his reluctance to touch the subject. "Have you ever broken a bone?"

He shook his head. "No, much to the surprise of my parents, I'm sure, since I had a propensity for sliding down banisters and climbing trees."

"Have you ever suffered a contagious fever?"

"I survived scarlet fever as a child, and I'm not oblivious to the way you're trying to get around me, Miss Renshaw."

She ignored his last comment and pressed on. "When did you lose your parents?"

"My mother died when I was fourteen from stomach cancer and my father passed away when I was twenty-three of a heart attack." He took a sip from his drink. "You realize that by asking all these questions I could demand quid pro quo."

Again, she quietly ignored his suggestion. "Are you an only child?"

"I am."

"Were you in India during the Troubles?"

She could hear his breath pull in through his teeth as he winced. "It's not a good story, Miss Renshaw, or I would tell it."

"Then tell me something else. If I promise not to bring up India again, or ask about what happened there to change you so completely, will you promise to tell me the truth about something else in exchange?"

"Perhaps."

"Please tell me the truth about Charlotte."

"Veritas vos liberabit?" He pushed his chair back and stood from the table. "I don't long for my freedom anymore, Miss Renshaw. And the price you would have me pay is too high."

"Dr. West, please!"

"No. No, Miss Renshaw. The truth doesn't set anyone free in this instance. It doesn't heal the scars from the past or make your decisions any easier. If I'm a liar, then what difference would anything I say ever make?"

"You aren't a liar. I should never have said such a thing."

"You have decided to keep much of yourself shielded from me, and as you said, we are not friends. So I believe I will invoke the same right, Miss Renshaw. You have no right to pry into matters that do not concern you. And I am at liberty to keep the ghosts of the past in my own cupboards."

Once again, it was Carter who was forced to intervene from the doorway. "Another note just arrived, doctor."

"Oh, for God's sake!" Rowan crossed the room impatiently. "If the butcher is corresponding with you, Miss Renshaw, we may be forced to have a review of the rules of the house!"

"It's for you, Dr. West."

Rowan tore open the page there and read it instantly, and Gayle had to fight to hold her tongue as the butler looked on.

"Carter, tell Theo I need the carriage." He looked up at her, the storm in his eyes unabated. "We'll discuss Snow's *On the Mode of the Communication of Cholera* in depth when I return."

And with that, he was gone.

* * *

"Still hate her?"

"Shut up, Ashe." Rowan surveyed a healthy-looking Ashe Blackwell with growing suspicion. "She's my professional apprentice in my strictest employ. Just tell me what you needed. I find it hard to believe you wouldn't just come to the house if you needed a headache powder."

"Blame me." Michael appeared behind them, a stealthy trick that still amazed Rowan. Michael Rutherford was a giant of a man, and his talent for materializing out of thin air was nothing short of unsettling. "I'm glad you came. We needed to gather quickly, and I knew the pretext of a medical call would bring you by the fastest means."

"A dirty trick." Rowan dropped his doctor's bag on the floor with relief. "But I suppose it worked. Are the others coming as well?"

Michael walked over to the fireplace to warm his hands. "Josiah, at least, but let's hope. Galen has taken his wife to see her family for the holidays before visiting the Earl of Stamford for Christmas."

Ashe stood from his writing desk. "Can I get anyone a drink?" He began to pour out three brandies without even waiting for a reply. "Did I tell you Caroline received a letter from her aunt that said there's talk of a civil war in the States?"

"It's inevitable if they don't change course," Michael pronounced grimly.

Ashe shook his head. "It won't come to war. From what I can tell, Americans enjoy squabbling more than anything in the world. They'll spit invectives and jig up to the cliff's edge, and then someone will come up with a compromise."

"It's slavery, Ashe. Where's the compromise there?" Rowan asked.

"We gave it up without losing our way of life. The Americans in the South will see the moral sense of it and adjust, you'll see." Ashe held out the drinks to his friends.

"Was this the reason for the summons? Not that I don't enjoy a good political debate. . . ." Rowan pulled his hands from his coat pockets to accept the glass. "I need to get back to my laboratory."

Ashe grinned. "Such dedication to your research! Nothing to do with that goddesslike apprentice awaiting your skilled and experienced guidance, of course. I am impressed."

"I'm here!" Josiah Hastings came through the door, still wearing his coat and hat. "Michael's note made it sound like your house was on fire, Ashe. I left so quickly I think I forgot to close my front door!"

Josiah almost fell onto the long couch against the wall, settling in with his legs akimbo and arms outstretched. He looked tired and distracted, with his shirt buttons mismatched and his face unshaven. "Why aren't we at West's brownstone?"

Michael sighed. "We can't always meet in Rowan's library. I thought it would be wiser to change our patterns for now."

Before Rowan could ask Josiah how he was feeling these days, Rutherford lifted one hand as if to call their impromptu meeting to order.

"Gentlemen, there has been an interesting development and it affects all of us." Michael gestured to Blackwell, as if to beckon him forward. "Show them, Ashe."

"I received an anonymous letter this afternoon. It was literally pushed under my door, and Godwin just added it to the regular post and brought it up with the usual cards and letters. But it caught my eye immediately, and . . . well . . ."

"It's addressed to the Jaded."

"I take it that it isn't a social invitation to a Christmas gathering?"

Ashe shook his head firmly. "Absolutely not. I sent for Michael, thinking he'd want to see it, and then Rutherford immediately sent off for the rest of you—and here we are. It's definitely a threat."

"Let's hear it, then." Josiah sat up, shedding the laissez-faire aura he'd been projecting, transformed by concern for his friends. Ever since their escape from a dungeon in India and their arrival in England, they'd realized that their lives were still in danger. Beginning with a direct attack against Galen, someone was doing their best to draw out the Jaded and to try to hurt them.

Ashe read it aloud, his voice clear and even. "Our patience is running out. It's clear that you have it in your possession. And while we may not yet know which of you has it, it is only a matter of time. Surrender the sacred treasure, and you can keep the rest of the riches you have stolen. Fail to yield her before the full moon, and your numbers will be diminished. Watch for the sign and be ready."

"I swear I'm tempted just to throw it all out into the streets and let another man lose sleep over the whole business." Rowan finished his brandy as if to underline his sincerity. "To hell with stolen riches!"

"Speak for yourself!" Ashe was quick to protest. "You don't have a women's college to fund!"

Rowan smiled. "Ah, how could I forget?" Then he sobered and looked to Michael. "My house has already been overturned twice by the police in the last year, no doubt on this anonymous entity's behalf. I'd say they've eliminated the brownstone as a possibility for holding whatever this *sacred treasure* is."

"But none of us have experienced any burglaries, or visits from the police. Why not?" Josiah wondered out loud.

"Not any burglaries that we know of," Ashe corrected him. "I've seen your painting studio, and I think a battalion of thieves could have waltzed through there without you realizing it."

"Very funny." Josiah crossed his arms defensively. "All right. They claim to know who we are and now just want this sacred treasure. What next?"

"What is it, do you think? Or who? Did it say *her*?" Rowan asked.

Michael's expression was grim. "There were no statuettes or figurines in our pockets, unless someone failed to put it on that blanket when we divided the treasure aboard ship—and I don't believe that's possible. And we sure as hell didn't haul a woman out of there . . . so it could be a miscue. Honestly, I think they may have it wrong and we simply don't have what they're after. But how do you communicate that without putting all of our lives at risk?"

"I'll write to Darius. I need to make sure he's aware of the letter and that he takes extra precautions," Ashe offered. Darius Thorne had been his cellmate during their confinement, and the men were as close as brothers despite their different temperaments.

"Is he still in Edinburgh?"

Ashe nodded. "Happily buried up to his neck in medieval scrolls when I heard from him last."

"What about Galen?" Josiah asked, then took a small sip of his brandy. "Can you get word to him at Moreland's?"

Michael nodded. "I'll write to him and make sure that

nothing is left to chance. Hawke may even have a few ideas of his own on what this all means."

For a few moments, silence fell as they each absorbed the implications of this new threat and the changes it might bring. Ashe tossed back his drink in a single motion, then set his glass down forcefully on a side table. "So much for letting our guard down."

"What sign? Should we be looking for another note instructing us on where and how we're supposed to hand back sacred treasures?" Rowan threw up his hands in frustration. "What if we've already missed it?"

"The next full moon is a week from this Saturday, gentlemen," Michael said. "One way or another, we'll know soon enough what the writer of this letter intends—sacred treasure or no."

Chapter
15

The next day, Friday, while Rowan was out on a call to the curate's house for his wife's lying-in, Gayle was doing her best not to pout. After Wednesday's incredible success, she couldn't believe the setback in her progress. But he'd quietly refused to take her on calls and given no explanation as to why.

She could only guess that it had everything to do with the inconvenient note from Peter James and the foolish fight that had followed.

If only we could find some middle ground, he and I.

She turned back to her letter to Aunt Jane. It was a fanciful construction of blatant lies about her travels, and Gayle hated every insipid word of it as she read over her description of an imaginary Italian piazza. She'd never been especially skilled at lying and was sure that wishing for such a talent would invoke myriad divine punishments. But the letters were a necessary evil, she told herself, putting the pen back to paper. Better that Aunt Jane be satisfied with these weekly travelogues until Gayle could come up with a better plan to keep peace with her only living relative. *I love the architecture of the cathedrals here and the wonderful paintings.*

She frowned as she paused to chew on the tip of her pen. *Should I accept that I am a horrible person and get a book on Italian paintings or swear off this nonsense and just—*

"Miss Renshaw! Miss Renshaw!" Mrs. Evans's voice was a screech of panic as she came up the stairs, and Gayle instantly pushed away from her little desk and ran out into the hallway to intercept her on the staircase landing.

"What is it?"

"Please! Dr. West is out, but—" Mrs. Evans put a hand to her throat in alarm. "Florence has cut herself terribly in the kitchens and—"

"I'm coming!" She outpaced Mrs. Evans easily on her race to get below stairs to the basement floor where the kitchens were located. Her heart was pounding at the exercise but also with fear for the dear maid who had done so much to make her feel welcome in the house. Just as she reached the door to the kitchen, she stopped and took one slow breath to steady herself.

A physician doesn't run into a room like a wild animal. Rowan radiates calm and then takes control.

She pushed through the door and surveyed the scene. Florence was on the floor in a pool of blood with her arm wrapped in a blood-soaked towel, cradling it in her lap, and looking whiter than her own apron. Mrs. Wilson was kneeling next to her, openly weeping.

"Ye've got to put it up over yer head! Put it back over yer head!" the cook urged her tearfully, but Florence was too dazed to obey.

Gayle immediately moved to kneel on the other side of her and assess the damage.

"We were cuttin' onions and she were helpin', dear thing! We were chattin' away, and then . . . I don't know! Blood's everywhere and I thought a bit of flour and holdin' it up—but then there was so much blood!" Mrs. Wilson was beside herself with distress.

"Raising the arm is a good first step, Mrs. Wilson. Calm yourself, and let's find some clean cloths and see about clearing this large wooden table to get her up off the floor, all right?"

Carter and Mrs. Evans burst through the door, and Gayle barely looked up. "Mr. Carter, if you'll help me lift her, I want to get her up onto this table so that we can see the damage."

"Yes, miss!" Carter moved instantly, and even Mrs. Evans shifted over to help Cook clear a space so that Florence could be comfortable.

"I need ice if you have it and the coldest water you can find." She held up Florence's arm and steeled herself to take a closer look. "Mrs. Evans, can you see about getting more cloths? If there's nothing handy, perhaps something from Dr. West's office on the first floor? And his suture kit from underneath the examination table, if you would!"

"Yes, miss! I'll see to it right away!" Mrs. Evans disappeared faster than a rabbit down a hole.

The cut was deep and dramatic into the palm of her hand and had cleanly sliced into the meat of three of her fingers to reveal bone. Ice was provided and Gayle washed the wound briefly with the water to try to clean it and get a better view. Florence moaned, and Gayle ruthlessly applied pressure with a new cloth as she held up the hand and tried to think.

Blood is dramatic but Rowan said to always stop and think first. The cold will slow the bleeding and raising the hand above her heart should help as well.

Florence moaned again.

"There now, dearest. You've scared poor Mrs. Wilson and Mrs. Evans, but you'll be just fine. I am here and we'll get this hand tended to and set you to rights." Gayle spoke as confidently as she could, concerned that Florence appeared to be drifting in and out of consciousness.

She turned back to Mrs. Wilson without letting go of her grip on Florence's wounded hand. "When did it happen? How long ago?"

"Ten minutes or more, I'd say."

Ten minutes. Unlikely that she'd ever bleed to death from such a thing, but with her fainting, I can see how it would have put the idea in their minds. "It's all fine, then. I know it looks dreadful, all this blood, but you mustn't worry." She took another fresh dry cloth from Mr. Carter and changed out the soaked one in a single smooth movement that immediately kept a viselike pressure on Florence's hand. "The bleeding's already slowed, see?"

Mrs. Evans returned in a breathless flurry with a basket of clean white squares and a wooden box with sewing supplies from the cabinet in Rowan's office. "He uses these!"

"Thank you, Mrs. Evans. If you'll set the bandages there, that will keep them handy as we change them out when they get soaked." She looked around the table at their faces, all earnestly looking to her for instruction as Florence lay so still. "Our greatest concern is infection. Mrs. Wilson, do you have any vinegar or alcohol in the kitchen? It will be painful, so I'd prefer to use it while Florence won't mind as much."

"I have some apple vinegar!"

"That will do very well."

Carter brought more ice and Gayle applied it as generously as she could to slow the bleeding even more while she organized her thoughts and prepared for the next steps. With the three of them looking on, she flushed out the wound with vinegar and then carefully but quickly sutured the cut palm and fingers as best she could. She was fairly certain that only the fleshy muscle of the fingers had been damaged, but with the palm, Gayle had to pray that none of the tendons were severed to affect poor Florence's dexterity.

Logic dictated that the fewer stitches she used meant fewer invasive punctures of the maid's hands, and Gayle hoped her instincts were right to trust that the body's unseen abilities to recover and rebuild would increase the less she interfered with them.

She finished her sutures, cut the thread, applied another

liberal dose of vinegar and then ice just as Florence started to come around.

"Did I . . . Why am I on the kitchen table?"

Everyone smiled in relief. "No onions in the soup to-night, thanks to yer clumsiness!" Mrs. Wilson chided gently with a warm squeeze of Florence's shoulder.

Gayle gently dried off the hand and began to wrap it up. "Here, I'll finish with this and Mr. Carter can help you down whenever you're ready."

Mrs. Evans folded her shawl and put it under Florence's head. "No rush! Rest here for a while and Barnaby will carry you up to your room. Shouldn't she rest tonight, Miss Renshaw? Wouldn't that be best?"

Gayle nodded, momentarily speechless at being deferred to by the intimidating housekeeper. But they were all looking at her with a new respect, and Gayle wasn't sure what to say. "Certainly."

Rowan's voice broke in from the doorway. "Is everyone hiding? Is everything all right?"

It was a cheerful chaos as everyone in the room except Gayle began to relate the terrifying excitement they'd endured, praising his assistant's miraculous intervention and swearing that she'd saved poor Florence's life. Even Florence tried to contribute, holding out her bandaged hand and tearfully confessing that she was sorry to have missed most of it.

Rowan nodded, calmly agreeing with their praise and quietly taking in all the details in the room. The blood on the floor and the table. The soaked bandages and his suture kit on the sideboard. The vinegar bottle and the melting ice in the ceramic bowl next to it. The beautiful wrap on Florence's hand.

And Gayle.

Calm and still.

Flawless.

"I am glad that Miss Renshaw was here. Florence, take your time and I'll just leave you in Mrs. Evans's and Mrs. Wilson's capable hands for now. Carter, we'll give everyone the night off after all this excitement, and I'll fend for myself this evening. Miss Renshaw, why don't I walk you back upstairs?"

He held out his arm for her to take and was surprised at how meekly she moved to allow him to escort her out. Her fingers were warm through the cloth of his coat sleeve, but he could feel them trembling.

He slowed as they reached the first-floor landing, unable to stop the questions from coming. "You're never this quiet, Miss Renshaw. Are you all right?"

She lifted her head, the black silk curls of her hair falling back from her cheeks framing violet eyes that shimmered with unshed tears. "It was . . ."

"Terrifying?" he ventured cautiously.

"Exhilarating."

Exhilarating. Intoxicating. Indefinable.

His brain echoed with her confession, adding sentiments all his own for the woman standing in front of him. "Yes," he whispered, his fingers moving up to cradle her face, tenderly drawing her closer for a kiss. "What a marvel you are. . . ."

"Kiss me, Rowan."

He didn't need the command, but the permission pushed open the floodgates of his desire for this mercurial creature, so vibrant and lovely. Weeks of trouble and torture, and she was warm in his arms and soft, her head tipped back and her red lips parted eagerly, and Rowan was sure that no man living could have resisted temptation.

He kissed her as if she were truly his, as if there was nothing in the world to prevent him from touching her as he wished—all the while sure that at any moment she would remind him otherwise.

Gayle felt alive with an urgency, so forbidden and naughty, it made her almost giddy. The turn of the stairs would hide them from any casual looks from the floors below, but at the moment, she wasn't sure if she trusted her senses to hear anyone coming—she was so trapped in a whirlwind of excitement. The possibility of being caught in the open didn't dampen her feelings, but only made the seconds seem sweeter and more precious as they ticked away.

He kissed her and it was her first kiss revisited, but instead of fairy-light brushes of silk at the start, this was the bone-melting feast that she'd left off in a panic. Only this time, all her fears were forgotten. Even the fear of discovery should have made her consider hurrying up the stairs, but the languid heat building in her blood bid her to savor every step.

These were the kisses she'd been unable to escape in her dreams and now she only wanted to press closer, opening her mouth to taste more of him and to allow him to taste her. His hands cradled the back of her head and his fingers fisted in her hair to send the first shivers down her spine at the power of being held thus—captive to her own lust and his.

Again, she was surprised at how much of her body awakened when he was near—through layers of clothes, her skin shimmered with warmth, and she became aware of even her toes and the backs of her knees and the small of her back.

She'd forfeited her reputation to come to London, and suddenly, it was as if there were no barriers to be seen between what she could have and what she wanted. A small part of her started to protest, but Gayle wasn't in the mood for internal debates. This was about freedom and power, and she seized on both when she kissed Rowan.

She loved the way he smelled of cedar, smoke, and cinnamon. She loved the way he held her so firmly, but also the way they fit together—as if by grand design. The adrenaline from the crisis made every inch of her tingle with heightened awareness. His kisses seared her lips, branding her with possession; the texture of his mouth was intoxicating.

But she was also aware that she could have blamed only the very first kiss on her nerves and Florence.

If that were the only thing behind all of this . . . I'd have already pushed him away.

But she didn't want to push him away.

She wanted to experience all that there was between a man and a woman. A lifetime of constraints and requirements that had always appeared like a steel cage around her, now yielded like cobwebs at the first brush of her hand.

She did more than give in to his advances. She matched every move that he made, hungry for the thrill of Rowan's touch. He gently pulled her lower lip into his mouth to suckle the sensitive flesh, tasting her and inviting her to taste him.

One kiss flowed into another, and Gayle threw herself wholeheartedly into the lesson.

He lifted her up to place her on the next riser up, equalizing their height and fitting her more closely against him. His mouth shifted over to capture an earlobe, and she gasped in surprise at the unorthodox shimmer of sensation that snaked down her spine, but held completely still to savor the unexpected pleasure of his teeth latching onto her earlobe. He pulled back only to encircle the outer shell of her ear with the tip of his tongue, and her fingers clutched at his shoulders as each exhale he made demonstrated a new application for fire and ice.

Buttons on her blouse, the ivory ribbon at her throat, he stopped to undo them, his eyes never leaving hers, and she wondered how the absence of a man's kisses could be as potent as their presence. The dark forest green and browns of his eyes glittered with excitement as he unwrapped her like a gift, but he wasn't rushing. The unspoken question was very clear.

If I wish to protest or cry foul, this is my chance.

She waited for an inner voice that might have conveyed a twinge of reluctance or dismay at what was unfolding, but there was only the drumming of her heart in her ears and the slow, delicious heat building between her thighs, dampening her curls there and fueling her growing anticipation.

He lowered his head again, this time to taste the ivory column of her throat. Gayle closed her eyes and prayed that her heart wouldn't stop from the sweet agony of this torment. Her blood was already on fire, and she suspected that it didn't bode well since he'd hardly bared more than a few inches of her body—and there was nothing she didn't want him to touch with his mouth or view with his eyes. There was nothing she wanted to hold back from Rowan's touch.

Her collarbone and the pulse there must have drawn his attention, and they took another step up toward the second floor, her desire refusing to wait as several more buttons on her shirt gave way to allow him to explore as he wished the hollows and rises of her neck and shoulder. One of his hands reached up to touch her breast, and even through the layers of her clothes, the heat of his palm and the warm pressure of his fingers threatened to make her knees give way. Her nipples hardened against the friction, and she arched her back, moving against his hand and wishing that there was nothing between them.

Rowan's head lowered to kiss the initial swell of her breasts, nibbling up against the edge of her corset in a courteous exploration that nearly undid her. They moved up another step, and Gayle was forced to cling to him to stay upright.

Wicked. I am a wicked woman. All I can think of is that I'm wearing too many clothes and I want his mouth— there! Everywhere!

His hands both pressed up to cup her breasts, his thumbs passing over their peaks, sending sparks of pure lust through her and hinting at what was to come. His mouth returned to hers, and suddenly she was molded to him, drinking in his heady kisses that bruised and healed her at the same time. She no longer wanted to draw out their play on the stairs. She just wanted to be alone, where anything that was encumbering him from taking her virginity could be removed.

Rowan did everything he could to keep himself in check, but she was magic in his arms. Her hands roamed across his chest, encircling his back, and the play of her fingernails through his shirt was beyond tantalizing. All he could do was picture her fingernails raking across his bare back and his flesh thickened even more.

A faint crash from the kitchens made them both lift their heads and freeze into position, but the sound faded and there was no other indication that their tryst was about to be discovered. Still, for Rowan, it was a reminder that making love to Gayle Renshaw on the stairs probably wasn't the stealthiest of choices.

"Gayle," he whispered, hating the raw need that made his voice so rough. "I won't be able to stop. . . ." He intended to slow things down so that she could comprehend where they were going, but words failed him. Rowan caught her hand where she was clutching at the lapel of his coat and guided it down to his hardened cock, pressing her fingers over its length through his pants with the intention of shocking her into reason. But instead, her palm naturally smoothed down the ridge of his flesh, her lips parting at the discovery of his arousal, and Rowan was a man lost to the power of her touch.

She was a fearless thing and looked up at him with eyes wide and hungry. "Please, Rowan."

It was all he needed to hear. He lifted her up easily, one arm behind her knees and the other at her back, and carried her up the last three steps, down the hall, and into his bedroom to kick the door shut behind him.

He set her down near the bed, and they both eagerly began to address the matter of her being overdressed for the occasion. Her shirt was already unbuttoned and off her shoulders, so it was easy to dispense with it altogether. As he kissed the white column of her exposed neck, he unhooked the waist of her voluminous skirt and pulled it up over her head, both of them laughing as they were enveloped momentarily by a makeshift tent of heavy silk flounces.

"Wait." Rowan threw her skirt across a chair by the bed.

"I don't want to wait, Rowan."

"We have to use our heads for just a few seconds, here."

"I don't want to think. If I stop to think, it might end somehow, and I don't want it to stop."

He groaned at the wicked effect of her words on his body, a whiplash of lust cascading down his spine to tighten his body to the point where he feared he'd spill himself at the first touch of her flesh to his. "Damn it, let a man . . . manage this, Gayle."

She kissed his chin, her pearl white teeth nipping at his jaw, and Rowan conceded slightly, tossing her onto the bed. He wasted no time in locating the tin of French letters in the bottom drawer of his nightstand, and Gayle watched him with open curiosity.

"Condoms. We can't be too reckless. . . . I won't see you hurt from this, Gayle."

"Then don't hurt me, but please, Rowan, don't stop."

Rowan put them within reach on the table by the bed and decided there'd been enough conversation for one evening. "Let us see about getting you out of that remarkable construction, Gayle."

He had to help her unfasten the tabs on her modestly hooped petticoat, the flannel hem weighted for winter, and then remove all her additional petticoats for volume and warmth, her corset with its whalebone stays, and at last a nearly sheer muslin chemise and pantalets, taking care not to tear the last in his zeal to reveal all of her. Unlike an ordinary abigail, Rowan found himself kissing her throughout, reveling in the process that revealed a little more of her with each pass of their hands.

Finally, there were no more layers and even her stockings had joined the mound of her clothing next to the bed. She was as naked as the day of her birth, and he stepped back to survey the bounty before him, savoring the sight of her. "You are perfection."

When he'd first seen her, he'd likened her to a cameo, a beautiful thing but hard and heartless. But this was no carving. The beauty in his bed was as fiery and elemental as a nymph, and the more of her he'd revealed, the more he felt like she was his own Galatea brought to life before him. She made no effort to hide herself but knelt on the bed to face him holding on to the bed curtains for balance. She was ivory and smooth, but the pink flush of her cheeks and the movement of her breathing made sure there was no mistaking her for a marble carving.

With her black hair tumbling down behind her in a lustrous cascade of silk curls and her arching black eyebrows like raven's wings, she was a presentation of delicious contrasts—even the dark triangle on her mons drew the eye and made her thighs look even more sumptuous.

She bit her lower lip, unknowingly plumping it and adding to its raspberry color. "Rowan, you're staring."

"Shhh. I'm worshipping you with my eyes. There's a difference." Rowan pulled off his boots as he spoke, grateful to keep his balance. He put one knee on the bed and slipped one of his arms around her waist to pull her against his chest. "And now I'm going to pay homage with my body."

He climbed up onto the feather mattress, deliberately leaving one side of the bed curtains open so that the firelight wouldn't be shut out. He didn't want to be denied the sight of her. Her breasts were just the way he liked them, firm and heavy, naturally fitting into the palms of his hands. Her nipples jutting out defiantly in dusky rose pink that invited a man's mouth, and at the first touch of his hands, she shivered and purred in response and he knew he'd met his match.

She was pure innocence and pure passion—the duality of perception and reality collided and a new lesson was initiated, but Rowan knew that he was likely the student.

Gayle leaned into his hands; the strength of his touch left scalding trails of pleasure wherever he moved them, fanning his fingers up her ribcage to hold her breasts, squeezing them just to the point of eliciting a gasp only to pinch and smooth their peaks and make her knees melt away in response. It seemed sinful to accept the pleasure he gave her without return, but for the first few minutes, it was all she could do just to stay upright.

He kissed her, and she feasted on his kisses while her soul discovered the remarkable power of a man's hands caressing the bare skin of her back and shoulders, her arms, and her stomach. He nestled her even more tightly against him, and then there was little he couldn't reach. Her breasts grew heavier and her nipples even tighter at the warm friction of his shirt front against them.

"Rowan . . . am I to be the only one undressed . . . in this . . . process?"

He smiled and it was the grin of a gentle rogue who was in no hurry to explain the rules. "Wait."

He pulled back the coverlet to nestle her down into the bed but kept the bedding from interfering with his line of sight. "I would have you warm and naked, Miss Renshaw, and spread across this bed just for me."

"How is this, then?" She stretched out her arms and legs, playfully obliging him, unaware of the incredible havoc she was wreaking on Rowan's plans to take things slowly and gently.

Gayle expected him to make a jest, but instead his eyes darkened, and then he was hovering over her, his mouth replacing his hands, stoking her desires in a hundred ways she'd never expected. Here was a gentle assault that she didn't want to defend against. She clung to him, spurring him on and writhing up from the mattress to offer him more of her body for his wicked tongue and silken lips. Her fingers entangled in his hair, and she closed her eyes at the bliss of Rowan's kisses between her breasts or in the indent of her belly button.

He tormented her by deliberately avoiding the obvious points of her need, nibbling around the ivory globes and running his tongue at the crease underneath her breasts, but never even grazing the nipples that now burned and ached with neglect.

"Rowan . . ."

His lips latched onto one tip, and he drew her into his mouth to lave and suckle her puckered flesh until she was mindless from the sensation. Her fingers tightened their grip but then slid down to his shoulders to ride the rippling build of need that began to grow inside of her. A river of subtle electricity began to flow between her breasts and down her belly to pool between her legs.

There. I want his mouth there, too.

It was an impossible thought, formed before she could think of a thousand reasons why such things weren't done. But Rowan's hand slid over the soft curve of her belly, through her wet curls, and touched the source of her quandary.

His fingers were hard and warm against her tender skin, dipping into the folds of her body and finding the wetness there. For a fleeting second, she felt ashamed of it—unsure of what he would think of her or her body—but the shame didn't last.

"Ambrosia." He sighed. "Your body is ambrosia."

His finger was slick with her even before he penetrated her with it, and she bucked at the sensation of this intrusion, her muscles clenching to hold him in place—but whether to forbid it or to beg him to stay, she wasn't sure. And then there was a friction against the swollen bud of her clit that made her shudder and try to hold as still as she could—for this was nothing but heaven on earth.

Back and forth, his fingers swirled around and over it until she completely surrendered to the flood of fire beginning to rage through her body. The pressure of his touch never changed, but the speed of the circling dance grew tighter and tighter until there was nothing in the world but her core and his hand against her. Gayle clung to him, unable to voice her feelings as she began to lose control of her body, unable to do anything to stop it.

She opened her eyes and accepted it all.

Chapter
16

Her world exploded in an inner fire that transformed into crystalline ecstasy that shattered inside of her. She cried out but wasn't sure if it was her own voice calling his name as wave after wave rocked through her to finally ebb to a warm, delectable glow.

It was several long seconds before she returned to her senses and realized that Rowan was just holding her now, kissing her cheek and stroking her hair.

"Well?" he asked softly.

"You're still dressed, Dr. West."

He laughed and kissed her before he sat up. "I can amend that, if you have the strength. But if you'd rather wait—"

Gayle sat up as quick as a cat and ignored the trembling in her thighs as a new excitement seized her. She began to unbutton his white linen shirt but lost a little momentum when the heat of his body through the thin material distracted her. It was like touching a firm, hot wall through muslin, and at the first hint of crisp dark auburn hair on his chest, she felt like swooning in anticipation.

His hands took over, making quick work of his shirt and demonstrating no regard for slowing to preserve buttons. She pushed back to watch, breathlessly taking in the sight of Rowan stripping himself out of his clothes.

Shy. I should be shy. But I can't seem to take my eyes off him. Whatever maidenly instincts I should have to cover my face or blush and look away . . . I cannot find them now. Oh, God, he's so beautiful. . . .

Skin, muscles, and the delightful answer to her question . . . an even darker auburn swirl of chest hair across his chest only to narrow to a tantalizing line that disappeared into the linen of his breeches.

Skin, muscles, nerves, sinew, and bone made a man, but as Rowan was revealed to her, Gayle wasn't sure how anything prepared a woman for the realities of it. He was pulsing with power, rippling muscles and lean lines that were directly opposed to her soft curves, and she couldn't help but stare at the proud tower of his arousal. It jutted out from his hips from a thatch of dark curls, far thicker and longer than she'd guessed, with a swollen head the size and shape of a plum. She hesitated to consider the question of capacity. *I was insane at the use of a single finger inside of me. What will I be once I am well used with his cock?*

There's not a statue or painting at an art museum that comes close.

It looked like a weapon, but also to her excited eyes, like a thing of beauty.

"I've never had a woman watch me undress before."

"Does it . . . displease you?"

"No. I like it very much."

"You put all the drawings in my books to shame, Rowan. I . . . It's as though I've never seen a man before. Not that I have—but Hunter's *Examination of the Physiology of Man* made me confident I had."

He smiled. "What do you want to do, Gayle? I could sit here for a while, but I'm risking a cold."

"I want to touch you."

She reached out to touch his chest, enjoying the thick hair that teased her fingertips, but even more, the firm muscles and skin behind them. She wasted no time, spreading out her fingers to gain as much coverage as she could, moving her hands at will in great arcs to smooth over his body and claim every inch of him for her own pleasure.

His nipples were far smaller than hers and almost brown, but she smiled when they tightened after a pass of her palms, and she bit her lower lip in concentration as a hundred new ideas flowed into her brain. *Like me. Different enough, but his body responds just as mine did. So whatever he does to me, I should mirror it and invoke a reaction.*

She explored and played, and he allowed it, as much as he could, kissing her when she gave him the chance, but she wriggled from him, unwilling to give up her quest to learn every point and junction of his physical being. His cock jerked and jumped as she leaned over his thighs and accidentally trailed her hair across his erection.

You're a minx, Gayle Renshaw. God help me, I think I'm going to have a heart attack if you keep this up for long.

She'd straddled his thighs and was close enough to his penis so that every exhale made him grit his teeth. She dipped her finger down to touch the clear bead of silken moisture coming from its tip. "Is this your essence?" she asked with innocent curiosity, and then before he could reply her tongue darted out to sample the taste of him. "Hmm . . ."

The gesture made him forget everything. Lust swamped him at the sight of her pink tongue licking him off her finger, as if she were licking honey off after sampling a dessert.

He'd never seen anything like her natural sensuality.

He pulled her over, gently tossing her down against the mattress to spread her legs, unable to indulge in any more delays. He opened the small metal tin by the bedside and ignored the cold sensation of the French letter encasing his cock. *Warm, soon enough, boy. Warm and buried and blind, thank God!*

He reached between her thighs to assure himself that she was still wet, the silken folds swollen and sensitive, and then positioned himself above her. There was one second to absorb the moment, teetering on the brink of ruin as surely as the sun would rise—and he felt no fear. The sight of her beneath him, her arms thrown back and her violet eyes glowing with desire, black curls nesting above the ripe pink of her flesh already slick with her release—here was a moment he would never forget. He fisted the length of his erection and dipped just the tip of his penis into her entrance, teasing it against the hot little bud of her clit until she was writhing beneath him, breathlessly begging him for more.

He wanted it to be as pleasurable for her, but he accepted that it was going to be all too easy to forget himself—it had been far too long since he'd had any woman in his bed and he didn't know if he could hold back.

"This . . . might . . . hurt . . . for just . . . a bit. . . ."

"I trust you." She lifted her hips to urge him forward, her legs parting even wider, and Rowan gave in to a primal need to take what she offered.

He slid into her in one slow, unrelenting stroke that tore through her maidenhead and left them both gasping for air. It took every ounce of willpower he possessed to lie still for a few seconds and allow her body to adjust, her muscles clenching and unclenching, her passage protesting as it stretched and burned to give him room to move.

She kissed his shoulder, a single tear falling down her cheek. "Rowan? I think I liked the kissing better."

He smiled but groaned into the mattress at the delicious humor of her predicament. He lifted his head to cradle her face in his hands, to comfort her. "Wait. The worst is over and now it improves." Even as he spoke, he slowly began to move, demonstrating what lay beyond.

He kissed her to ease her, and as she relaxed beneath him, Rowan felt a surge of relief. He was buried deep inside of her, but as her channel grew wetter and wetter, it allowed him to withdraw and return, teaching her the rhythm of it. Her legs wrapped around his hips, and the zeal of her kisses returned to push them both into a spiral of desire. Within seconds, they were both moving against each other, pleasure replacing all pain as she arched against his chest. His cock thickened at the sensation, and he savored each thrust, amazed at the strength of her hold on him and how quickly passion had recaptured her.

Gayle took in the paradox of conquest and submission. Her body betrayed her mind, refusing to wait for her to compose descriptions or try to understand what was happening—a new kernel of red-hot tension began to grow inside of her, and this time she knew what the culmination could be and she welcomed the fire.

There was not an inch of her that wasn't his, that wasn't in contact with him or basking in the glow of his body to hers. Gayle marveled that a woman could yield so much without thought, but the reward of passion and pleasure tipped the scales.

There was nothing elegant in the raw tangle of their limbs or the pounding of his flesh into hers, and she loved it. It wasn't refined or measured. It wasn't science or art. It was sex, and Gayle heard a woman moaning and realized that it was her own voice.

She turned her head into the pillow to scream, muffling her cries as he lifted her hips up, parting her thighs even farther, and drove himself into her again and again in a merciless onslaught of sensation. And it was heaven.

This was a transformation no book could ever have described. This was a completion that defied words, and she came again in a free fall that tore apart every illusion she'd held about what this would be—and what woman she would become.

Rowan watched her climax, felt it as her channel seized his cock in a mind-bending hold, and his own scalding orgasm spun out from his hips, shaking his frame and forcing him to bite the inside of his cheek to keep from yelling the house down.

It stretched out for endless seconds, and Rowan was grateful that she appeared to be unaware of him after her own climax—it gave him a few breaths to try to collect himself and recall how to use the English language.

Damn! Too long . . . Ashe always used to say that a man could go too long and end up a gibbering idiot, but until this moment, I never believed him. . . .

He slid away, only long enough to remove the wreck of the condom and find a flannel for them both. As his breathing became normal again, he tended to her as best he could, drying off her thighs and clearing away the small amount of blood from the injury to her maidenhead. "There. All better."

A foolish enough thing to say, but he pulled the covers over them both and held her close so that he could trace the last shimmering waves of pleasure as they faded from her skin.

Who knew a kitchen crisis would land her in my arms?

Florence hadn't been in real danger. After all, men could lose a hand and still not bleed out so long as pressure was possible and the flow allowed to coagulate. It was the infection that killed them, but even that threat had been diminished by her level-headed approach to the crisis.

She'd proven herself under pressure and without guidance.

But Rowan waited for the inevitable, when that beautiful head of hers assessed the facts. He braced himself for the worst and wondered how long it would take and if he could distract her with—

"I just fell into bed with you over a few cut fingers."

He propped himself up on one elbow to gauge her mood. "Yes."

She bit her lower lip and then smiled. "Well, that seems a bit off, doesn't it?"

He kissed her cheek, the platonic gesture altered to suit him as his lips lingered to trace the delectable line of her cheekbone up to her temple. "I'm in no position to argue, unless you're about to accuse me of bedding you over a few cut fingers."

She giggled, and then stopped abruptly, evidently shocked at the uncharacteristic laughter slipping past her lips. "I'm sure I should be feeling a twinge of regret. . . ."

"Are you?"

She shook her head. "No."

"What are you feeling?"

"I'm embarrassed to say it."

"Close your eyes then and let's hear it, Miss Renshaw."

She dutifully closed her eyes, and he waited patiently, using the back of his fingers to stroke her bare shoulder and arms.

"I'm changed by the experience."

"Yes?"

"I'm a wanton thing, Rowan. All I feel is a desire to try it again. Perhaps the books had it right, and once a woman is—"

He kissed her to stop her from finishing her thought, and her eyes fluttered open, a new warmth blazing in their depths and confirming that he had her complete attention. "All of our natures are the same, Miss Renshaw. We are physical beings and drawn to each other with a power that men have wrestled with for as long as we've been out of caves. But you—you are perfection and just as you should be. But this—this is extraordinary, Gayle, this connection between us, this fire. Science doesn't apply."

She nestled against him, her hand splayed against his heart, innocently stoking his desire by toying with the hair on his chest. "I'm hardly perfect, Rowan."

"No one is." He held her close, wishing he could freeze

the moment in time where she was content in his arms. "About Charlotte's death—"

"I'm not sure I want to hear about that at this very moment." She pushed against him, sitting up and covering her breasts with the coverlet. "Rowan, I . . . I'm naked and I don't think I want to even hear her name on your lips. I realize that's not very logical, but I promise I'll listen attentively when I have at least three layers of clothing on and a better idea of where my shoes are."

"Well, there's a new medical theory! You could prove that people's ability to listen may be tied to their clothes."

She hit him with a pillow, playfully trumping the debate. "Talk, then!"

"Well, since one topic is unwelcome, let's try another. Every instinct I have is urging me to do the honorable thing, Gayle, and ask you to marry m—"

"Wait!" She put her fingertips up against his lips, her eyes darkening with distress. "I need time to get used to all of this! I planned—I plan so much of my life, or at least, I try to, but this? This is nothing I'd planned. Please, Rowan. Just give me time."

"Time." He lifted up one of her hands and kissed the soft well at the center of her palm. "Yes. I shall do my best to give you all that you need."

"Thank you." She leaned over to reward him with a kiss.

"Can you tell me more about yourself and your family—while you're naked?" he teased gently. "Or does that subject also require shoes?"

She looked away, diverted by her hands, and this time his patience wasn't rewarded. She didn't offer to share anything about her mother, or herself, and Rowan sensed it was better to retreat and give her more time. Even after she'd literally bared herself to him, Miss Gayle Renshaw was still a creature apart and practically unknown to him. With a sigh, he turned to a more immediate matter.

"Very well." He held out the package of condoms. "I know it's an unromantic topic but a necessary one. If you

would . . . here is a tin of them. I don't want you to think
that I'm assuming anything or taking for granted your con-
sent to any future encounters, but—better that you have
them, Gayle. Please, put them in your bedside drawer or
anywhere you can discreetly access them without Florence
or Mrs. Evans coming across them."

"I will." She took the tin, shyly at first, but then lifted
her chin, a woman determined to be practical. "You're
clever to think of it, and I'm grateful. You're just being
considerate of my . . . of our position."

"I meant what I said. I won't see you hurt from this,
Gayle."

"Can you . . . help me dress?"

Without covering himself, he shifted to the edge of the
bed and began retrieving her clothes for her, kneeling to
gather her stockings and taking a few extra seconds to locate her missing shoes. As she watched him, Gayle was
surprised to realize that she felt more awkward about him
helping to put her together than she did about him taking
her clothes off.

He stood, surveying the pile on the bed, and shook his
head. "I'm no ladies' maid, but let's just see if we can't
think in reverse and accomplish this thing."

"I'm . . . Perhaps I just need help with the hooks to—"

"Nonsense! A gentleman is always on hand to help, and
I'm not going to forgo this chance to assist you." He held up
a stocking, and then knelt by the bed to put it on, his hands
sliding up her legs and lingering at her thigh to retie the
satin ribbon that held it up.

"Rowan! I . . . I need to dress. Can you at least put your
own shirt on first?"

He nodded and slipped his own white shirt on to partially shield his body from her appreciative looks. "And so
you shall. I promise to behave."

She had to bite her lip to keep from protesting when that
was exactly what he did. No matter how distracted she became or how delicious the light teasing touches of the
backs of his fingers proved against her ribcage, legs, and

breasts, Dr. Rowan West was a man of his word. Her drawers and chemise were restored, her corset rehooked, and then came the layers of petticoats and her hooped farthingale.

The fire in his eyes smoldered as he performed an abigail's duties. Rowan brushed out her skirt and lifted it up over her head, sliding it down, caressing her arms as he did and encircling her waist with his hands as he fastened the hooks at the back.

"Almost done," he said, dipping his mouth down to nuzzle her neck and kiss her there, finding the most sensitive spot above her shoulder blades at the base of her neck. His tongue laved her skin and she shivered, her skin pebbling wherever his fingers trailed.

"Rowan . . ."

He retrieved her shirt where he'd thrown it over a chair, helping her into the lacy white thing, its sleeves marred a bit with Florence's blood, and reworked the carved buttons, starting at her waist.

Finally, he placed the lace shawl over her shoulders and used it to playfully hold her captive for one more kiss.

She pushed away from him breathlessly, the color in her cheeks betraying her passion. "This is . . . ridiculous, Rowan. I'm ridiculous."

"Hardly." He smiled but stepped back to try to respectfully give her the freedom to compose herself. "But consider yourself officially in charge of the health of the house, Miss Renshaw, for I swear, the next time Theo accidentally shuts his hand in the carriage door or someone twists an ankle, I'm going to have trouble controlling myself."

She playfully punched him in the shoulder. "You're a wicked thing, Dr. West!"

The clock in the downstairs hall chimed five times and Rowan winced. "The house will be up soon. Carter comes early with coffee and a tray, Gayle."

"I'll leave now. I'd rather not wait and meet him on the stairs."

It was time to let her go.

I'm already in love and she won't hear of it.

Damn! I don't think I'm going to survive the heartache she's capable of handing me—but there's no chance in hell I'm walking away now.

I'll just have to teach Miss Gayle Renshaw that science and love can exist side by side.

Chapter
17

He'd left her to her work for most of the day, but finally by midafternoon, Rowan had demonstrated all the self-control and patience a man could muster under the circumstances. He grumbled to himself as he climbed the stairs, convinced that in a more sane world he'd have gotten to spend the day in bed with the irresistible Miss Renshaw after she'd breathlessly agreed to marry him, and he wouldn't be reduced to feeling like a man forced to nibble at the edges of happiness.

Although, if I liken the woman to cake in this conversation, I think I'll end up starving to death if she interprets it the wrong way.

He opened the door to the familiar sight of Gayle perched on one of the stools sitting up to the long worktable closest to the windows. She had several texts fanned out around her as she balanced on her elbows, chewing on the tip of her pen. She was deep in thought, and Rowan's breath caught in his throat at how lovely she was with her dark hair pulled back in a simple chignon, a few tendrils escaping to trail down her long white neck to draw the eye toward her ample cleavage. She was wearing her blue day dress in her usual effort to look professional and plain, but the effect was ruined by the dress's fashionable tailoring, expensive jet buttons, and the unmistakable elegance of the model.

She'd look beautiful in sack cloth and ashes.

"I see that you are dressed, Miss Renshaw."

She looked up with a smile that almost made him drop the offering he'd brought. "I told you that I have trouble concentrating without at least three layers!"

"I still say it's theory until you test it properly."

"Are you suggesting I attempt to study . . . *without clothes*?"

The distracting turn of their conversation almost derailed him from his mission as the delightful prospect of Miss Gayle Renshaw wearing nothing but a copy of *The Lancet* sent his heart racing. "I'm going to keep my suggestions to myself, for the moment. But before I forget why I came up here, or change my mind—I wanted to give you something."

"Oh." She pushed away from the table to stand and face him, her expression suddenly more wary and less playful. "Unless it is an assignment, Dr. West, I'm not sure it's appropriate to—"

"Damn it, Gayle! Let a man finish one thing without debate! Agreed?" Rowan snapped.

"Agreed." She crossed her arms and waited. "Well?"

The sight of her tapping her foot was comical, and Rowan's flash of temper evaporated. *God, I'm enjoying every minute of her company—even when she's trying to drive me to bedlam. But now let's hope the truce holds.* "Do you know how Charlotte Hamilton died?"

Gayle nodded. "A fever, I thought. But after moving to Standish Crossing and listening to Aunt Jane, I wasn't as sure."

"Here, Miss Renshaw. It's my case study of Charlotte's death, for you. I wanted to understand what had happened, so I created this. It's just a few notes I made about the fever that took her life—from the facts I'd pieced together once I'd returned from India. You might see something that others have missed or just confirm the worst." He held out the slim packet of paper. "I trust your judgment, Gayle."

She took it from him, slowly, her eyes never leaving his face. Rowan wasn't sure how to feel as he walked the fragile line between personal honor and promises to the dead. It was a gamble to give her his notes. They were incomplete, because he'd broken off the work after going to Standish Crossing and learning the truth. But he hoped there was enough that she might see the inconsistencies and choose to give him the benefit of the doubt. *Use that keen mind, Gayle, and figure it out—and then perhaps you can see your way clear to loving me.*

"Thank you, Rowan." She set it aside, her cheeks turning pink. "I'll be sure to look at it when . . . I can concentrate."

"But you have on at least four layers, from what I can see. Would you like me to leave you alone so that you can read it in private?" The offer was sincere, even if he longed to stay. "Unless you'd like me to stay and interpret some of the harder-to-read scribbles."

She took a step closer, her fingers outstretched to trace the outline of his lapel. "This is a terrible problem, Dr. West."

"What? My coat?" He held as still as he could, anticipation unfurling inside of him at the flirtatious movement of her hand.

"You're . . . proving to be a terrible distraction. I don't think I could read a children's primer with you in the vicinity."

He captured her hand with his and pressed her fingers inside his coat and up against the measured pace of his heart. "That *is* a problem, Miss Renshaw. But I think I have the solution."

"Yes?" She tipped her head back to look up at him, her lips parting slightly.

"We must dispense with this passion so that you may concentrate." He reached up to begin lazily working the knot of his silk tie.

"Here?" she asked in alarm. "W-we can't . . . here!"

"How can you be so playful and direct spread across my bed and here, so shy?"

"I am not shy! But you—" She lost her train of thought as he pulled his shirt open and took a step closer. "Rowan, I don't want you to treat me differently. I'm worried that you'll see me as a woman to *spread naked on your bed* and not as a serious student. I'm not abandoning my apprenticeship to . . . play about!"

"I don't want you to abandon your studies."

"Good."

"But neither am I going to let you ignore what's happening between us, Gayle." He took one of her hands to draw it over his skin, pushing her hand down over the hard muscles of his stomach, his breath whistling through his teeth as his flesh thickened and tightened in response. "I'm drawn like a moth to flame. How is it that I cannot seem to stop myself from wanting to touch you? And taste you?"

"We should stop. Someone might come up. . . . Mrs. Evans is forever sending up trays."

"You're right. We should stop." He eliminated the space between them, pulling her into his arms. Her head tipped back and he could see the mischievous light in her eyes as she enjoyed the forbidden nature of the game. He made quick work of the buttons of her dress to expose her neck and worked his way lower with the professional speed necessary to outpace her objections. "Perhaps an anatomy lesson is in order, Miss Renshaw."

"I love . . . anatomy."

"Very well." His tongue flicked out to send a lightning storm across her skin. "And what muscle is this?" He teased the triangle between her collarbone and the firm rise of her breast.

"P-pectoralis minor . . ." She arched against him, and he had to hide his smile.

So much for her inability to concentrate.

"And what muscle am I using to do this?" Rowan licked the curve of her body, his tongue trying to pleasure her into undoing a few more buttons and participating in the game.

"Oh . . . the tongue . . . is several . . . lingualis inferior, superior . . . oh, Rowan!" She groaned, surrendering to the electric fire his touch evoked and read his mind by undoing the next two critical buttons so that he could access her breasts. Her nipples pushed up from the top of her corset, puckered and tipped as if begging for attention.

"And what is this?" Rowan deliberately ignored the pert peaks for a few seconds to torment her and settled his mouth against the outside of her throat. "Miss Renshaw?"

"I can't . . . remember."

"A penalty, then. My apprentice must pay a penalty." He shifted to put his mouth just over her breast, caressing her only with his breath, blowing against the taut skin until he could see her trembling with need.

"Rowan!"

He pulled her nipple into his mouth, encircling the sensitive tip and suckling her until she was bucking and writhing against him. He released her only when he suspected she was on the brink of crying out. "Come, Miss Renshaw. Let's on with this lesson. What is this?"

And this? And this?

He chose every tender place on her body that he could reasonably reach within the confines of their embrace, but the persistent torment was taking her far past reason. "Proper Latin, Miss Renshaw."

"Yes, oh, yes . . . please!"

"Not a proper answer, Miss Renshaw." He sighed against her skin, his hot breath fanning over her and sending another ripple of lust through her body. "Another penalty, I'm afraid." He lifted her up by the waist and set her on the table, both of her breasts exposed for his hands and mouth; he wasted no time in demonstrating that just her nipples alone could send her over the edge.

"Oh, God! Rowan! Please!"

"Shh! You should be concentrating, Miss Renshaw. Here comes the final exam question."

He gently pushed her back so that she was lying on the table with her bottom just to the edge, her legs wrapped around him for balance. With a textbook under her head for a pillow, she was quite a sight looking back at him with her breasts pushed upward and her skirts and petticoats bunching up around her thighs.

"R-Rowan? I'm—"

He bit back a jest about this being an oral exam but smiled all the same as he wickedly initiated the "penalty" she'd earned. He bared her sex, parting the seamless slit in her drawers to reveal the satin folds of skin topped with black curls that made the world fade. The sight of her, dripping with her arousal, was enough to make him abandon all attempts at clever banter.

There would be no more talking.

He ran his fingers over her flesh, parting her lips and uncovering every sensitive fold and contour for his mouth to sample. He bent over to kiss her, his mouth, his teeth, his tongue all part of the dance as he teased his way up until the engorged pearl of her clitoris could no longer be ignored. His tongue found it, a flicker of wet friction that he kept featherlight, working over the tiny core of her sex, until he knew she was completely in his power.

For the writhing stopped and his siren was as still as glass to let this magic work and find the release she craved. Rowan slid his hands up from the ripe curves of her bottom and captured her breasts, throwing new fuel on the fire to ensure that she was his. He waited until he could feel the first spasm between her hips, and then he pinched the beautiful rosy tips of her nipples just as she pushed off from the brink, sending her into a mindless climax. Her thighs tightened around him, but he deliberately moved even faster against her clit, driving her on and on until she began to sob with it.

Only then did he relinquish in speed and lower his mouth to press his tongue inside her entrance, drinking her crème and savoring the taste and smell of her pleasure on his skin. It was heaven, the salty-sweet flavor of her climax on his tongue, and Rowan ached to drown in it—to bury himself to the hilt inside her and lose himself there.

He leaned back and found the wrapped French letter he'd optimistically tucked into his coat pocket. He stood, and moving quickly, he freed his erection and encased it in the protective membrane. He wasted no time in sliding her closer to the table's edge, so that her legs were wrapped around him. The worktable was the perfect height, and he lifted her firm bottom to rake her hot pink slit against him and ensure that he had all the lubricant he needed to take her.

Her skirts were still pushed up around her waist, and Rowan took a long, slow breath to try to steady himself and revel in the sight of Miss Gayle Renshaw's perfect sex exposed to him, honey dripping from her body from her release—all at his bidding. He notched the swollen head of his penis just at her entrance, instantly coating it in her juices.

Her eyes fluttered open in shock. "You're so warm!"

"As are you, Gayle. Come see, see how I'm going to come inside of you."

He lifted her up so that she could see his wrapped cock pressing up inside of her, the plum-size head of him stretching her and drawing her labia apart to push up against the taut little button of her clit. Slowly, he moved his hips forward, thrusting up into her inch by delicious inch, burning his way inside of her—a slow torture that made her shudder and claw at his shoulders.

"Yes . . . oh, Rowan, all of it! Please just . . . I want to feel all of you there. . . ." She gasped, shivering as he withdrew almost all the way to tease her channel, her inner muscles clenching and unclenching at the unexpected loss of him. "Rowan!"

He plunged forward, smothering her cry with his mouth, drinking in her moans of pleasure as he buried his entire length in one smooth thrust, nearly lifting her up off the table. She gripped his cock with her wet channel and tilted her hips to give him even better access—and it was Rowan's turn to moan at the sheer power of the act.

Standing, he found himself thrusting into her with all his might, lost to the sensation of his cock working up against the very entrance of her womb. Gayle fell back onto the table's surface, overwhelmed by the experience of so graphic a sight.

The sound of the wet friction of their bodies was undeniable, and it fed her lust, a fuel of the mind that made her even wetter, spasms of pleasure beginning to unfold in her mind.

Even then, Gayle's hands fisted into her petticoats as a world of want and pleasure enfolded a universe of desire and pain. He was so thick and large, a velvet sheathed battering ram that she was sure held the power to tear her apart—but it was a raw power that every fiber of her welcomed. Every thrust of his body into hers pushed her that much closer to the edge of an internal precipice.

More! There must be more!

Any thought of restraint or control vanished. She tried to meet his thrusts, instinctively matching his efforts with her own to add to his pleasure—and her own. "Rowan, more . . . please, more!"

He roughly dragged her off the table, his own breathing labored and fast as he withdrew his rock-hard penis from her to successfully get her down. Gayle started to tear up, bereft at the aching void between her legs and the denial of the release she'd been so close to attaining, but there was hardly time to ask what he intended when she found herself bent over the stool and her skirts and petticoats tossed unceremoniously over her head. The draft on her bare bottom was strangely stimulating, but then there was the searing wet heat of his body nudging her legs apart and she sighed in relief.

Again, he penetrated her in one firm stroke, but this time, there was no question of begging him to go deeper, harder, or faster. It was all she could do to grip the crossbars of the stool, balanced as she was with her breasts hanging over the edge of the seat, her feet leaving the floor as he caressed the limits of her body with the unyielding length of his cock, pounding into the hungry confines of her until she was sure she'd faint from it all.

Lightning arced down her spine, and when she heard him cry out and felt the molten tide of his release, even through the membrane of the condom, she came once more, an explosion of the senses that left no room for thought.

It took long moments for them to recover, no sound in the room but their ragged breathing from the exertion of their coupling and the all too real sounds of the sodden withdrawal of his body from hers. Rowan held out a white cloth that he retrieved from one of the drawers so that she could clean herself as he turned to do the same and put his clothing to rights.

She did what she could to recover a modicum of modesty, straightening her skirts, adjusting her corset top to cover her breasts and rebuttoning her dress. Gayle bit her bottom lip, amazed at how quickly her plans on firmly lecturing the man on the boundaries of their professional relationship had evaporated. He was simply too charming and she'd overestimated her willpower.

"Rowan. I meant what I said." She faced him, squaring her shoulders. "Nothing has changed."

"I never thought I'd enjoy teaching so much." Rowan was all smiles, apparently missing the shift in her mood.

"Please, don't! Don't denigrate what I've accomplished and make it sound so . . . cheap!"

"I never intended to. It was meant to be a jest at my own expense, not yours! Even you have to admit that this . . . development . . . between us is a wonderful gift we didn't expect." He walked back to her, his face full of a sincerity that made her feel worse, as if she were being callous.

She tried again. "Last night was glorious, and this—I'm not going to deny how much I'm enjoying this but—"

"We can't go back and undo what's been done, Gayle.

It's as if you would make less of it or you'd rather we blithely ignored what's happened."

"I'm not your mistress! I'm your apprentice. This changes nothing!"

"It could change everything, if you'd allow it."

She was afraid. She was afraid and the words caught in her throat. She was afraid that now she would be nothing more than this—that giving in to passion meant she'd forfeited everything else. "Please . . . I need time to consider . . . all of it.".

"You have it! I've not forgotten my promise, Gayle. I'm not trying to press you. I can respect your need for discretion, and you have to trust me to keep this a secret. The last thing I want in this world is to see you sacrifice your reputation or your integrity. But"—he took a deep breath to steady his temper—"I'm not apologizing, Gayle. Not for wanting you or for . . . feeling about you as I do. I'm not going to let you pretend that I jump at every skirt that brushes my legs. This is—"

A faint bell downstairs echoed up faintly through the house, and they both looked at each other, aware that their quarrel had just been interrupted.

Rowan walked to the door to listen for a few seconds. "It seems I have a visitor."

"You should go."

He hesitated, but at the sight of her standing stiffly on the other side of the table, so prim and untouchable— unwilling to look at him—he marveled that he'd lost so much ground. Minutes ago, she'd been as warm and passionate a woman as he'd ever imagined, but now, her violet eyes were frosty and aloof.

She'd retreated in fear and transformed into the woman he could never have.

"We're not finished, Gayle."

He left her there, and crossed his fingers that it would be a quick social call.

* * *

"Dr. Jessop, this is an unexpected pleasure."

"You've not been to the Society for some time, and frankly, I'd heard a rumor that I simply had to see settled."

Damn! Already? How is that even possible for them to know about Gayle and—

Jessop continued, "Why will you not support the creation of the Clarecourt workhouse?"

The flood of relief at the news that it was an old political topic and not related to his new difficulty made Rowan take a deep breath before he could compose his thoughts to answer. "Because I don't believe that you can warehouse the poor just to ease your own consciences."

"You'd see them sleeping on the streets, begging and falling to crime? Her Majesty was most impressed with the idea of the least of her subjects being cared and provided for! The workhouses offer them a life of productivity and the sustenance and structure they need to reform themselves."

"Reform? Poverty isn't the fruit of wanton choice or a condition of the wicked. The workhouses are charity of the worst kind. You imprison them, and whatever Christian kindness you profess, Robert, they'll see little of it once those gates are locked."

"It's not a prison!"

Rowan tried to take a steadying breath. "I will not support the confinement of the poor. I cannot." Memories of the dark and cold of the raja's dungeons loomed, and his revulsion was too powerful to hide. "I will continue to tend to anyone who comes to my door and do my duty until my strength gives out. It's the only charity I comprehend, Dr. Jessop."

"Every time your name comes up for some accolade or advancement in the Society, do you not wonder why you are then dismissed or overlooked, Dr. West?"

"I can only imagine."

"Why must you stand apart? Why can you not support the resolutions and efforts of your fellow physicians in the

Royal Society? Why, Dr. West, must you always be so re-
bellious against the obvious wisdom of your betters?"

Rowan walked over to the shelves next to the fireplace,
reaching up to adjust one of the small wooden African
figurines that had been moved during Florence's efforts to
keep the family curios dusted. "I'm a West. I don't think
we've ever managed to find the path to acclaim or success."
He shrugged and turned back to face Jessop. "I'm not a
political man. I'm just a physician."

Robert sighed, his shoulders relaxing as some of the
stern lines in his face disappeared. "And a damned good
one despite your youthful tendencies. I speak out of care
for you, as a friend of your grandfather. You waste your
time and efforts with your emotional approach to our profession, Dr. West."

"And how is that?"

"Besides the dangerous precedence of your Wednesday
clinic, you are known for your liberal sentimentality. A
good bedside manner is overrated, and all these nonsensical questions about how one is feeling have little weight on
treatment and cure. The patients will muddle your diagno-
ses with all their blather and sighs! After all, they are hardly
educated enough to understand the complex workings of
their own bodies—why inquire after their opinions?"

Rowan shook his head, this argument all too familiar.
Every month or so, Dr. Jessop would stop by for the same
philosophical debate and insist on Rowan's participation.
"You go too far, sir! They may not understand the science,
but there is insight to be had, and a calm and involved patient can't hurt in our efforts to heal."

"Your clients are wealthy and used to offering far more
than mere opinions. You put them in charge when you pla-
cate them with these games."

"Careful, Dr. Jessop. I strive for balance in my profession. And while some may see the populace as fodder for
their laboratories, I refuse to ignore a person's humanity so
that I can feel more secure or important."

"I don't ignore a person's humanity. But it hardly matters if I set aside science and progress to waste my time listening to patients prattle rather than seeing to their diseases." Dr. Jessop stroked his mustache and then sighed, rising from his chair and effectively signaling an end to his visit. "I've lost another evening in your stubborn company."

"For which I am grateful." Rowan followed him to the doorway. "I will see you at the lecture series next month."

"Yes, yes. Come and meet some of the new students. Perhaps one of them will suit for an assistant and you can devote yourself more readily to that experimental approach to infections you presented in the spring. You need help, you know!"

"I know." Rowan shook the other man's hand. "Thank you again, Dr. Jessop."

Dr. Jessop finally retreated, mumbling down the stairs in his usual fashion. "Visiting foolish young doctors! That's *my* charity! A statue. A man should have a statue raised for visiting foolish young doctors. . . ."

* * *

"Everyone is always accusing you of being too softhearted." Gayle sighed, stepping into the room.

He turned back, realizing that she must have been on the other side of the library door listening. "Except you."

"You're practically a saint, Rowan."

"Saints don't burn with desire. A saint wouldn't be considering at this very moment how to separate you from that dress and pull you down onto this bearskin rug."

She blushed. "You have a good heart. And he's wrong to ask you to change."

"Eavesdropping is a terrible habit, Miss Renshaw. Haven't you learned that by now?"

"I didn't intend to listen at the door. I followed you down because I didn't want you to leave without . . ." She shook her head. "All the most important things I've ever discovered, I think I've overheard by eavesdropping, Dr.

West. It's a hard thing to give up. Besides, how else would I know what the Royal Society thinks of my mentor?" She smiled at him and playfully plucked at his sleeve. "No offense, but it's hard to look at you and see a revolutionary in danger of toppling the medical industry simply because you don't mind holding your patients' hands or asking them how they feel."

"None taken, but don't say that I didn't try to warn you. If I'm a heretic for these blasphemies, and if Jessop and the others have their hackles up over my objection to the latest social reforms, what do you think they're going to say when I introduce you as my pupil?"

"I don't care. Someone has to be first."

"Easy to say, Gayle. You have less to lose."

The mischievous light dimmed in her eyes, and he watched the familiar retreat of her emotions as she withdrew from the topic. "You're right, of course. I'll try not to—"

A knock at the door cut her off. "Sorry to interrupt, but Miss Featherstone's sent a runner, and the boy is most insistent that the lady is dying." Carter's look was all apology, since Miss Featherstone was known to be on the brink of death at least twice a month.

"I'll go." Rowan retrieved his bag from behind his desk, and then gave Gayle an assessing look. "Miss Renshaw will stay here. Have Mrs. Evans draw a hot bath in the second-floor guest bath for the lady."

"I'm fine! Please don't trouble Mrs. Evans on my account."

"It's no trouble. You look like you're about to fall over, Miss Renshaw. So consider this an order. You'll bathe and rest and we'll restart the lab work tomorrow morning with fresh eyes." He leaned closer, the glow in his eyes strong enough to make her heart race as a flutter of restless heat reminded her of the reason the lab work had gone undone. Carter was behind him, so Rowan couldn't touch her or make any overt comments. "Does that sound agreeable to you, Miss Renshaw?"

"Yes, Dr. West." Every thought in her head was about how delicious it might be to torture a man like this—to seduce him if he couldn't move—and it must have telegraphed between them, as his eyes darkened with desire. "A bath sounds perfect."

Mr. Carter nodded. "I'll see to it, doctor, and have Florence fetch you, Miss Renshaw, as soon as it's ready."

"Thank you, Carter." Rowan ground it out, his eyes never leaving hers as the butler backed out of the room.

Gayle heard the door close behind them, but still neither one of them was able to move, caught in the delicious spell of proximity and promise.

"I'll look in on you before I retire."

"Thank you, Dr. West."

I'll be waiting.

"I just come to see to you, miss." Florence stepped inside Gayle's room off the laboratory, holding a small square basket with a hinged lid. "Mrs. Evans said your bath is ready and I wanted to bring you a little something with my thanks for what you did for me."

"That's so dear of you! But you needn't have, Florence. Anyone would have done the same, and I was just glad I was there."

"I wanted to! Dr. West gets gifts all the time from his patients, and I thought—well, I could be your first."

"Thank you, Florence." Gayle bit her lower lip. "You've been kinder than . . . I always look forward to bumping into you in the halls because you greet me, as you did even in the first few days after I'd arrived, and I think of you as a friend."

"I'd love that! If we was friends! Here!" She pressed the basket into Gayle's hands. "I painted it myself! See?"

"It's beautiful, truly beautiful." She held it up to admire

the flowers and scrollwork that decorated the handle. "How is your hand feeling?"

"Better and soon it will be as good as new, I'm sure. Barnaby swears I should be rubbing goose fat on it, but"— Florence crinkled her nose in disgust—"the man once put a snail and mushroom poultice on one of the horses and nearly killed the poor thing! I'm not going to be under Dr. West's roof and ask a footman with no sense of smell for a cure!"

"You're a wise girl, Florence." She retied her robe and stepped into her slippers to finish readying herself. "Are you . . . sweet on Barnaby?"

"Him?" She laughed. "He's mooning over the abigail across the street at Tildon's. They walk out on Saturday mornings sometimes, but she's away with the family for the winter season." Florence reached up to adjust her white mobcap. "I've no beau, presently. But I put a white feather underneath my pillow and I had a dream about a man with ginger hair, so we'll see."

"Do you believe in dreams, Florence?" Gayle asked in surprise.

"Always! But enough of this chatting! The water will be ice if I don't let you get going." She stepped back to let Gayle pass. "I'll walk you down to the guest bath. It's ever so much nicer than yours. I'm sure that's why Dr. West insisted on it."

"Dr. West is . . . very thoughtful."

"Dr. West is the best man that ever was, Miss Renshaw! We all think fondly of him, and you mustn't be too cross with Mr. Carter or Mrs. Evans for it. They thought you were . . ."

"They thought I was what?" she asked, dreading the answer but sure she was about to be accused of prostitution.

"Likely to ruin Dr. West with this apprenticeship business. He's already on the outs with that Dr. Jessop, and mean old Whitfield is even worse! They come regular as a head cold to peck at him because they want him to go back to the Academy and teach like his great-grandfather, *settle in* they call it, and be more respectable instead of traveling off to India and causing a stir with all his newfangled ideas. But Dr. West is too good for those old birds! They try to rattle him, but Dr. West knows better. And I like his new friends!"

"His new friends . . ."

"Since he got back from India, he has a new circle of gentleman friends that pop in from time to time, and I like them! Mrs. Evans was afraid they were bad company for him, but Carter's as soft as peaches about the men now. Why, there's even a lord that comes by and takes a tray now and again! The man stands to be an earl one day! Can you imagine it?"

"An earl. That *is* hard to imagine." Gayle tried to picture her kind and handsome Rowan entertaining some craw-faced earl, and just couldn't. The only earl she'd ever seen was a puffed old gourd of a man who appeared to be allergic to his own upper lip.

"As we see it, Dr. West is doing better than ever—but when you came, well, Mrs. Evans is protective, that's all. 'Cause if the dusty Society gets wind of your skirts walking about in Dr. West's laboratory, they might turn on him faster than you can say *bedlams and bells*. But don't worry. We've all kept mum on the topic, and if Dr. West sees the way clear, well, who's to say it won't come out right as rain?"

"Yes," she echoed in a whisper. "Who's to say?"

"Here we are! Mrs. Evans warmed the towels and I'll leave you to it. When you're finished, just ring the bell and head back upstairs, and I'll see that it's all cleared off with no worries."

"Thank you, Florence."

And she was alone in a grand room with a graceful claw-footed monstrosity that could easily have accommodated two of her. Steam rose from the water's scented surface, and Gayle sighed at the sight. Mrs. Evans had even sprinkled dried flower petals into the bath for a lovely touch.

Her own water closet upstairs provided a washstand and a toilet, but few other amenities. She'd been bathing daily by improvising with a basin of ice-cold water and a sponge, which was well and good for hygiene but was daunting to face in the winter drafts that blew through her rooms.

So this room, this was a slice of paradise with its bright enameled surfaces, ornate brass fixtures, and plush oriental rug. There was even a little fire going in the grate to ensure that there was no chill in the air.

She locked the door and disrobed quickly, sinking into the heated water up to her chin with a heartfelt sigh. She wriggled her toes and closed her eyes to soak in the comforts of a jasmine-scented bath.

I should be upset with the man for not offering a bath before now . . . but I think I'd forgive him anything after this.

The conversation with Florence echoed in her mind, and Gayle sat up to idly soap her arms and elbows as she examined the casual revelations of the day. *Up until now, I've been so worried about my own progress—but I really have selfishly pushed Rowan to the edge of a cliff.*

And how was I planning on pulling him back? Oh, yes. I hadn't planned on it. I was that callous little chit bullying him in his own salon and blackmailing him into getting what I wanted.

Oh, God! What if Rowan is right? If Jessop is keyed up over his lovely bedside manners and concern for his patients, then what am I going to be looked on as?

I insisted that Rowan be open-minded and take this risk.

And all my worries have been about myself. How I would be perceived, how much I would lose if people saw me as little more than his mistress . . .

Now how do I protect him without giving up my dreams?

Because retreat wasn't an option. She'd burned her ships, or at least, most of them. She hadn't worked up the courage to tell her aunt the truth, and was still unsure if she had the strength to forfeit the last living family she possessed by doing so.

I called him a liar, but I'm the one sending ridiculous

letters home every week pretending to be on the Continent buying bonnets and looking at church frescoes.

She stayed in the bath until the water's warmth was gone, and even then, she lingered, distracted by thoughts of Rowan and the future she couldn't see.

* * *

Gayle returned to her room, noting that the house had fallen quiet for the night, and retrieved the case study. She curled up on her bed, tucking her feet under the quilts, and read it all in one pass.

There is something here he wants me to see. But what? It was a contagious fever. He has notes of her symptoms from the doctor in Standish Crossing to confirm it.

High fever. Patient was in a great deal of discomfort, with restless hallucinations accompanying pain. Vomiting bile. Fluid and blood loss immense.

It was a gruesome scene, even in clinical terms.

"Blood loss? From a fever?" Gayle spoke aloud, checking back to see if she'd missed something, but saw in the Standish Crossing doctor's hand on a smaller page his indication that he suspected "bleeding for a remedy," and she wondered if Aunt Jane had tried bleeding Charlotte first to relieve the fever and with an amateur hand and done more damage than good.

Poor Charlotte! So lovely and dear to meet death in such a way . . .

A small handwritten note in the margins caught her eye, and she turned the page sideways to try to discern what Rowan had intended.

Ask D. L. re: appendicitis.

Then nothing.

No indication of cause. It was all about the outcome.

She read it all again, more slowly this time, willing the truth to appear in her hands, but there was only the mystery of one young woman's death.

He'd gone back to Standish Crossing to find the cause, and according to Aunt Jane, he'd ended up practically confessing to murder.

How?

She closed the notebook and set it aside, then blew out her lamplight. In the dark, she felt safe enough to whisper what the study had revealed. "There is no how. He couldn't have done anything. He was well on his way to India when it happened. He's innocent."

Then why did he confess and why do I feel like I've missed something terrible in this account?

Chapter
19

Waking up a short time later, her hair still damp from her bath, Gayle wrapped her blue velvet robe around her and restlessly walked the floor of her room. She lit the lamp on her desk and put the case study away in the back of the drawer, as far as she could, as if it were a snake that might strike her. She wanted to talk to him and send all her fears away. Even an argument was more desirable than being alone with her doubts.

And then it was as if she'd summoned him, as if he'd heard her thoughts.

"You'll catch a cold strolling around like that."

"I'm fine." She smiled at the sight of him leaning against the door frame. He wore only his white linen shirt, un-tucked and unbuttoned to give her a glimpse of his body, and his long black woolen pants. "I didn't hear the bell."

He shrugged. "I came in the back to try not to wake Carter." He walked toward her. "You're not using your dead bolt, Miss Renshaw."

"That would defeat the purpose of deliberately leaving

it open and hoping that you would pay me a call." She held her breath.

"I said I would."

She nodded. "You always do what you promise to do."

"There's a delightful change! Thank you, Gayle."

"I take it that Miss Featherstone isn't dying?"

"Not tonight. Although she did manage to come down with a genuine cold, so it was a nice diversion from her overexcited blood. Naturally, the combination of an imaginary disease and a genuinely sore throat was almost more than the poor creature could manage, but I think it's the recommended treatment that might do her in."

"A new tonic?"

"Warm throat wraps, brandy, and *absolutely no talking for three days.*"

Gayle gasped in delighted horror. "Three days? You're a wicked man, Rowan West."

"Not wicked enough, I fear. Here, come, calm yourself and let's sit for a minute." He pulled her down to sit on the cot and then winced when it squeaked in protest, the rusty frame shifting slightly under his weight. "My God! Tell me this bed isn't as uncomfortable as it sounds!"

"It's worse than it sounds, but I've grown fond of it, so don't insult my dear little room, please."

"I'll ask Carter to get you a new bed."

"Don't! Don't you dare! It's completely inappropriate for you to show any interest or knowledge about my bed, Rowan!"

"I love it when you're prim and impossible, Gayle. But if you prefer, I'll refrain and you can continue to enjoy your dear little room—iron cot and all."

"Thank you."

"Now tell me what has you marching around up here?"

"Did you mean what you said earlier, about having more to lose? Nothing is what I expected on this journey, Rowan, and I can't help but worry that I'm blindly doing more harm than good. But I can't quit. I won't—"

"I spoke out of turn, Gayle." He pulled her close, kissing

her softly behind one of her ears in a tender onslaught that stripped her slowly of her arguments. "Lament the world another day. You and I, we can only control the tiniest little sliver of our existence. The rest of it is out of our hands. But you and this . . . this . . . and this . . ." Each *this* was accented with the touch of his mouth against one of the delicious points of pleasure across her throat and shoulders. "This is all that matters now."

At his touch, all her worries slid away, and she gave in to it. "Yes. I believe you're right, doctor."

She shifted on the bed, tucking one foot underneath her bottom to face him and give her natural curiosity full rein. "Rowan, how am I with you? I mean . . . how does any woman know how to conduct herself when she is with a man?"

He shook his head. "You are yourself. I don't want you conducting yourself, Gayle."

Her cheeks warmed at his words, encouraged in her quest to discover how to please him. In the space of a single heartbeat, suddenly it was all she wanted most in the world—to repay him for his kindness and show him only pleasure. "Rowan, what seduces a man? What do you think a man finds most seductive in a woman?"

"Confidence. A woman who knows what she wants and isn't shy to ask." He sucked in a breath as her teeth grazed the sensitive peaks of his chest, pebbling the flesh. "I—suppose it's different for every man."

She slid her hands up his chest and over his shoulders to push his shirt off him, thrilled at the expanse of bare skin and smooth muscles beneath her touch. She pulled her fingers lightly through the hair on his chest and allowed her hands to roam where they wished, trailing them over his extremities until she pushed him back onto the bed and knelt across his legs to hold him captive. She bent over to concentrate on the buttons and ties at his waist, and unfastened his pants with unhurried hands, all the while watching his handsome face.

He was already hard, his cock jerking up to meet her

hands as she released him. She caressed the velvet-smooth skin, enjoying the delicious textures of corded throbbing power that sprang so jauntily against her palms. The color of it was compelling, the head of him as ripe as any plum, but there the comparison ended as she absorbed with a sigh the masculine beauty that stood so proudly at her attentions. To tease him, she slowly drew the cotton cloth back over him, and then squeezed along the sensitive ridge to elicit a moan of pleasure from Rowan. "I love the way you're formed, Rowan."

"I'm seduced, Miss Renshaw. See how easy that was?" *I don't think I have the self-control this is going to take if I continue to let her—*

Her mouth dropped, latching onto the shape of him through the thin material of his breeches, and he nearly spent himself right then and there. She looked up at him with a wicked smile, his cock straining through the cloth mere inches from her red lips. "One compliment? Truly?"

"Very well. I shall try to present more of a challenge for the sake of education, but—" *Oh, God! So much for bravado. . . .*

She pushed the cloth away, and she brazenly kissed his cock with the sweetest feminine sighs he had ever heard. Her mouth moved up his shaft, only to tease the tip of him, her tongue dipping down to meet the moistened rutting head that begged her for more. When her lips encircled him, and her tongue began to dance across his skin, he had to fight not to buck his hips upward and risk sending them both to the floor.

Rowan moaned and deliberately lifted her up and away from the demands of his cock, determined that this delightful interlude should last more than two minutes. "Here, woman, sit here and smother the poor thing for a bit." He settled her sex onto his, the barrier of her nightgown adding to the sensual promise of the position.

"Rowan." She pouted slightly, but wriggled to find a comfortable perch with his cock pressing up against her. "I wanted to learn how to please you."

He nodded. "And so you are." He grasped her hips, trying to hold her still and slow the pounding of his own heart. "Touch yourself."

She obliged him, tentatively at first, unsure of what could be gained, but she grasped the game almost instantly. The molten desire in his eyes and open approval of her actions was heady. She cupped her breasts, pressing them together for him, encircling them with her hands as his hands had when he'd tasted her in the laboratory.

Without realizing it, she began to writhe and pump her hips as she moved in a primal dance of seduction and satisfaction. Her nipples hardened when her palms passed over them, and her breath caught in her throat at the discovery that her own hands could surprise and seduce.

He never looked away and a new power surged through her.

"Between your legs . . . touch your sex, there, for me."

She nodded, not trusting her voice.

It was a new experience. It had never occurred to her to touch herself, much less to allow someone to watch her when she did. But her nipples were still tingling from her own hands and the ache between her legs was unmistakable.

She dropped one of her hands, fingering the coarse black curls on her mons and then easily found the wet flesh beneath. Slippery and hot, she gasped as her fingers brushed over her clit and slid a little inside her own body. This was a flavor of wicked she hadn't anticipated, and her eyes widened in surprise.

"Go on, Gayle. Touch yourself the way you would like me to touch you."

As before, the nuances of the game came to her very quickly. She imagined that it was his hands pressing the tight little bud between her legs, his finger entering her and stretching her entrance, faster and faster, until her hand was coated with her own arousal and she could smell the sweet musk of her sex.

She was shameless only because he never looked away.

His eyes reflected nothing but desire and approval. She felt more powerful than she ever had in her entire life—a queen in a very small erotic kingdom—but a queen, nonetheless.

Without intending it, the arcs of electricity that began to link her breasts and her clit exploded in a lightning storm of sensation, and Gayle threw her head back to allow her release to take over, wave after wave of shimmering fire pushing her over the edge.

She collapsed on top of him in a graceless, contented heap. "Oh, dear . . . what of your pleasure, Rowan?"

"This is pleasure, Gayle, but perhaps you're right. I don't think I can play the spectator any longer." He sat up suddenly and turned the table on his temptress, pushing her down on the narrow bed, her black hair fanning out beneath her like Ophelia floating on the water. "I'll take my pleasure as I wish."

He'd been in awe of the goddess that had knelt above him and climaxed at his command. That Gayle would trust him and give in to her own passions was a humbling thing, and he hadn't lied about enjoying it. His body craved a release of its own, but he was in no hurry to end this interlude and return to the real world that awaited them both.

He nibbled on her toes and gently bit the inside of her instep, then kissed her ankle and worked his way up her leg, lingering briefly at her knees and then again at the soft curves of her thighs.

She sighed. "This is heaven."

He rolled her over with a wicked smile and leaned over to tongue the crease of her bottom and dip his tongue into the dimples above each rounded cheek. She wiggled at the playful change and gave him a questioning look over her shoulder. "What are you up to?"

"Did you prefer it on your back, then?" Without warning, Rowan flipped her back down into the bedding and spread her legs wide so he could tease the indent between her thighs and her sex. "Is this better?"

"Rowan!" She giggled. "That tickles!"

His delight at her laughter was the herald of all that followed. "You are far too serious, Miss Renshaw. Perhaps that's just what you need before I roger you soundly."

His fingers replaced his tongue, and she was helpless to stop the fantastic torture of his hands tickling her into submission.

Gayle struggled, caught in a merry battle not to scream out in delight, unsure of when she'd last experienced the unmitigated joy of being tickled. It was childlike, but then there was nothing innocent in his touch or the wicked work of his fingers. She bit the inside of her cheek to keep from squealing, kicking out to escape the hands that tormented her with pleasure.

"Enough! Rowan, enough!" she begged.

Never enough. Rowan chuckled but gave in to her pleas for mercy, only to spread her thighs and press his mouth against the swollen flesh of her body. "Here is what I need. To drink you in . . ."

His tongue dipped into the well of her folds, and Rowan lapped up the delicious ambrosia of her essence. He took his time, savoring her, inhaling the sweetness, and fanning her inflamed skin with his cool breath until he knew from her moans and the fever building in her body's frame that she was almost ready for him.

He lifted himself up and covered her body with his, kissing her so that she could taste the salty-sweetness of her own climax on his lips. She began to wrap her legs around his waist to pull him down, but Rowan resisted her to roll her over onto her stomach, one last time, this time lifting her hips so that she was on her knees for him, her sex swollen and glistening with her own crème. His flesh was rock hard and pulsing in a furious rhythm that matched the pace of his heart. He sheathed himself in a condom and prepared to find his own release inside of her.

Gayle lowered herself onto her forearms, pushing her bottom into the air as she spread her knees wide, instinctively wanting to achieve the depth she craved and the access he needed. She was already so sensitive from her own release that, at the first touch of his cock to her slit, she had to cover her own mouth to keep from screaming.

He thrust into her, so hard the iron cot screeched in protest, but she reached back to clutch at his hips, urging him to go on. Again and again, Rowan drove forward, each thrust slower and deeper, in an ancient dance that ground out all logic.

He bent over to encircle her waist with his arms and then leaned back with her head back against his shoulder, her bottom pressed up against his hips. He held her upright, letting her find her balance with her thighs spread wide. She was impaled on his cock, and he filled her completely. Her muscles began to milk him, and there was no need to thrust or make any great movements, as their bodies blended into one passionate organism.

His hands roamed over her body, steadying her but also fondling her breasts and then finding her clit. She trembled against him, thrashing a little as another more powerful orgasm began to gather momentum, and he waited until he was sure she was just on the brink—and then he pushed her over by pinching the ripe red tips of her breasts until she cried out his name and sagged against him in a half faint.

Civilization fell away and Rowan abandoned all pretenses as he went over the precipice, stripped of any façade of tenderness. Her passion had fueled his, and he knew that she was the one with the whip hand. His orgasm jetted from him in scalding spasms that left him shaking.

This was ecstasy so sweet, like falling into an ice green pool of emeralds. . . .

I could meet death with a smile on my face if this were the price.

* * *

Later, Rowan gently pushed the black silk of her hair back from her cheek while she slept and lifted one long, heavy curl to his lips to inhale the floral fragrance of her hair and draw it over his lips.

She's like an orchid—exotic and beautiful, but a man can kill himself trying to keep her.

For the strange courtship of his apprentice, he didn't think there was a source of advice available for the path ahead. He was wary of pressing her too hard on the subject of marriage, for fear of losing her entirely. Miss Gayle Renshaw was a puzzle. For all her reluctance to accept the respectability he was willing to provide, she was equally mortified to be discovered in his bed or looked down on as a mistress. She was caught in the grip of his desires as surely as Rowan was.

A willing captive to desire—for now.

She'd asked for time to get used to it all, and he wanted nothing more than the chance to win her over completely, heart, mind, and body.

But time may be the one thing I don't have.

He held her close and watched her sleep in the illumination provided by a slim ray of moonlight through her windows. It was selfish to keep her close, and he knew he would have to creep out before dawn to his own rooms to ensure that none of the household found him out of bed. But in a week it would be the full moon, and the need to keep her close and safe was as palpable and real as any fear he had ever experienced in his life.

One of us will fall, it said. I suppose I should be worried that it might be me, but all I can think of is Gayle. Should I keep my distance to keep her safe if the threat is against one of us? Or should I ensure that she is at my back to protect her from any outside force?

Damned if I do. Damned if I don't.

Chapter
20

The following day was unnervingly quiet for Rowan. He'd already alerted Carter to be on his guard, hinting that one of his patients had warned of a new rash of burglaries in the area. He'd instructed Barnaby to stay close to the house and to keep an eye on the ladies if they ran any errands. He sincerely doubted that Mrs. Wilson would be in any danger shopping for eels, but he wasn't going to take any chances.

As for Gayle, he'd decided to keep her by his side until the threat passed. As far as she was concerned, it was a normal day in the laboratory as they worked side by side on documenting the latest changes to his testing environments.

When the bell rang in the afternoon, and Carter came to get him, Rowan did his best to look calm as he waited to hear where the hammer had fallen.

Please God. Let it just be Ada Featherstone asking for sugar pills, or even one of Lady Pringley's headaches.

"A runner from Blackwell's." Carter held out the note and Rowan took it with numb fingers.

Rowan, it's Caroline. She fell down the stairs. It's urgent that you come now!

—A

"Miss Renshaw. Come with me. We're needed on a call." He folded the note into his pocket and they were racing for the door. "Carter, tell Theo it's urgent and if the carriage isn't ready by the time I reach the door, tell him to hail a hackney."

Carter rang the bell for Theo, confident that the man would be waiting downstairs, and trailed behind them to hand them coats and finish getting instructions from Rowan. Rowan stopped briefly in the library to pick up his bag and then again at his office on the ground floor to re-pack a few things from the exam room he thought he might need while the house launched into motion at Carter's experienced direction.

A fall down the stairs. It could be a broken bone, an internal injury, a head injury . . . any number of things. He made his selections quickly, and Gayle only watched, no doubt sensing that this was not a good time to ask questions.

Within just a few minutes, they were on their way, and Rowan tried to take a steadying breath. The significance of the date wasn't lost on him, but tripping down stairs inside one's own home didn't sound like the dastardly work of an unseen enemy. Still . . . they would just have to wait and see.

"It's Blackwell's wife. She's fallen down some stairs and Ashe has sent for us saying it's urgent."

Gayle nodded. "They are newly wed, aren't they? When he spoke of her, he was very sweet."

"I'd forgotten you'd met."

"Mr. Blackwell and Mr. Rutherford seemed very nice. You are lucky in your friends."

"Yes." Rowan's eyes dropped to the scars on his wrists. "Extremely lucky."

The ride wasn't fast enough to suit Rowan, but they arrived before long. Rowan jumped out before they'd even pulled to a stop, and then he reached up for Gayle and his bag, only to run up the stairs and go in without waiting on ceremony.

Godwin was at the door. "Dr. West! Thank God!"

Ashe was bounding down the stairs before Rowan had removed his coat. "Where the hell have you been?" The panic on his face was unmistakable.

"Did she break anything?" They were on the move back up the stairs as Rowan tried to understand what he was facing.

"I don't think so, but she's . . . so sick! Godwin sent for me as soon as it happened. He said she was flushed and became dizzy. It was a bad fall, Rowan. Something is terribly wrong!"

"Flushed and dizzy before she fell? Or is that only after?"

"Daisy said it was just before! Could she be—"

Rowan held up his hand as they reached the bedroom door, all too aware that Gayle was on his heels. "I'm not guessing. I'll see her and then we can start ruling things out and get this sorted away, all right?"

Ashe nodded.

"Why don't you wait here, Ashe? Or better yet, downstairs?" Rowan knew what his answer was going to be, but he felt obligated to try.

"No." Ashe's eyes flashed icy resolve, and Rowan glanced at Gayle.

"Stay close." He pushed the door open and prayed that Ashe wouldn't get in the way. Within seconds, it was clear that Caroline was desperately ill. She was writhing in pain, her eyes wild with fear, and it was all she could do to lift her head before the next wave of nausea overtook her.

A hand on her forehead confirmed that she was clammy and cold to the touch, and Rowan did his best to smile and reassure her as he went through the steps of an initial assessment and exam.

He applied pressure to her abdomen and ruled out appendicitis with fleeting relief but dreaded what he was seeing. *Gastric fever.*

Gayle handed him his stethoscope, and Rowan listened with alarm at the rapid pace of her heartbeat and the shallowness of her breathing. *She'll hyperventilate at this rate—or she's going into shock.*

"Gayle, stay here with her. Just do what you can to comfort her. I need to talk to Ashe."

Gayle changed places with him to sit at Caroline's side, capturing one of her hands, and with her free hand smoothing her fingers against Caroline's cheek and forehead.

"Come, let's talk in the hall." Rowan gestured back to the door.

"I'm not stepping one foot outside of this room and leaving her, West. Talk."

Rowan wasted no time in arguing but walked over to the sitting area in the corner of the room. "Fine, we'll stay in the room."

The terror in Ashe's ice blue eyes was unquestionable, and as a friend, he knew that Ashe had to be there with his beloved bride—no matter what was coming. Rowan kept his voice low. "Was she ill earlier? Did she show any symptoms of discomfort?"

"No! We enjoyed . . . a lovely morning." Ashe had to take a deep breath. "She was perfectly fine."

"When did it change?"

"Just a while after lunch, I think. She ate alone in the library—I can barely pry her out of there on some days, Rowan." His words sped up as fear caught up with him. "I went to the sports club this morning with Michael. I should have stayed home! It's Sunday! Threatening letters and I'm off like an idiot playing swords with Rutherford!"

"We all expected the danger to come at us directly, not our loved ones, Ashe! This isn't helping Caroline. Ring for Godwin. I need to know what she ate. I need to see anything that remains of that meal and to know everything we can of its source."

"Poison! Dear God, you think she's been poisoned!"

"Ashe! Ring for Godwin."

Ashe transformed with his mission, a fierce juggernaut who wasted no time in storming down to the kitchens to personally discover the answers and bring Rowan what he'd asked. Godwin and Mrs. Clark trailed after him, each wringing their hands.

"It should have been cleaned and gone by now," Mrs. Clark offered, "but that new scullery maid is as slow as a turtle, and then when Mrs. Blackwell fell—we all dropped what we were doing, sir!"

"A good thing, Mrs. Clark. A good thing." Rowan tried to take it from Ashe's viselike grip. "Ashe, let go."

Ashe came out of the trance he'd been in—clearly his thoughts were elsewhere with Caroline or in a spiral of rage for whoever had done this thing—and let go of the tray's handles.

Rowan walked over to the sideboard and set it down, picking up a knife to poke through the food that had been left. Everything looked innocuous enough, but Rowan spotted the small, pretty box under the napkin, and his heart sank. Two of the three confections had been eaten, and he picked up the chocolate-covered square to break it in half and reveal a white creamy center. "Where did the chocolates come from?"

"I don't know, Dr. West!" Godwin said, then turned to Mrs. Clark. "Did you put them there?"

Mrs. Clark burst into tears. "They c-came this morning without a note. I thought . . . it was a gift . . . from Mr. Blackwell for her! You're always so kind to l-leave little prizes throughout the h-house for her! I told Cook to put them on her tray!"

Rowan held up a hand, trying to think as quickly as he could. *It's gastric fever. It's too sudden and the symptoms are unmistakable. It would be easy enough to hide in the filling. But if I'm wrong and it's something else—and it could be a dozen other things . . . I could waste valuable time or do more harm than good.*

"Rowan," Ashe interrupted, his patience too strained for silence. "Was it the chocolates? Was it poison?"

Gayle looked up at him from across the room as Caroline convulsed on the bed, clutching at Gayle's hand and biting off a muffled cry. Violet eyes met his and an understanding flowed between them.

This is going very badly—and it might already be too late.

Chapter
21

"I think it's arsenic, Ashe. By the looks of it, a potentially fatal dose. But I'm here and I'm going to do everything I can."

Ashe looked like he'd been punched in the midsection, but he held his ground. "You save her, Rowan. You. Save. My. Wife."

Rowan transformed into a general commanding his troops with the firm resolve of a man who could a sense the sea at his back. "Mrs. Clark, I need milk. Fresh, cold milk for your mistress. Godwin, please ask your cook to boil water and then send it up with some cloths. Also, we'll need clean bedding and more bowls.

"Ashe, send a runner to Michael and the others. If there have been any other unmarked deliveries of foodstuffs, we'll need to know. Any sign of the sender will be lost quickly, so the faster we can react, the better our chances of catching them."

Rowan knelt next to the bed and felt Caroline's pulse.

"I'm willing to hazard that this wasn't the lovely day you had planned, Mrs. Blackwell."

Her eyes fluttered open and she tried to smile. "N-not . . . exactly."

"Ashe said you'd do anything to get out of shopping for new clothes, but this is taking it much too far." In one smooth motion, he put a damp cloth on her forehead and handed Gayle the bowl that had been used so that she could fetch an empty one. "As your doctor, I'm going to recommend begging off with a headache next time."

"Easy for you . . . to say," Caroline said.

Gayle smiled as she brought a clean bowl, and anticipating Rowan's next request, brought a clean cloth as well. "Especially since I think Dr. West hates shopping as well."

Caroline doubled over as Ashe returned. It was a few moments before the spell had passed, but Caroline, even in a crisis, was very spirited. "I never . . . thought to have . . . so many people . . . in my bedroom."

Ashe kissed her on her forehead, unabashedly affectionate. "Nor I. You must get better so that we can banish this crowd, my darling. Then we can bar the door and I shall never require you to shop again."

"Now . . . I know . . . it's serious." Caroline gripped his hands before abandoning her efforts to appear courageous. Her suffering was acute, and Rowan knew he would have to add to her misery if he had any hope of curing her.

"Gayle, hand me the oil. We need her to empty her stomach."

Ashe lifted his head, instantly wary. "You can't be serious. She's just stopped vomiting!"

"Ashe, this is why husbands wait downstairs, pacing in libraries and drinking until they can't see straight."

"I'm not going anywhere."

"Then stay out of the way." He took the bottle from Gayle, unwilling to voice the medical argument that any other doctor would have a tube down her throat to pump her stomach, but with Ashe hovering, Rowan knew better and had opted for the "gentler" treatment of using rancid oil to purge the poison from her stomach.

So long as she's strong enough to manage on her own, but if I have to use the tubing, I will—and Ashe is going to lose his mind.

"I have to make sure it's out of her system, as quickly and as extensively as possible." Rowan took the bottle from Gayle, sparing a few seconds to gauge how his apprentice was faring. She was like the calm in the center of the storm, and he fell in love with her for it all over again.

Then he squared his shoulders and proceeded to administer the oil to Caroline. The effect was immediate and dramatic. It was the launch to a miserable journey. After a while, he had to almost fight off Ashe when the treatment took on a life of its own and she couldn't seem to stop.

"She's vomiting up blood, Rowan. You're killing her!"

"*I'm* doing my best to save her. Back up, Ashe, and give me some room, damn it! I'll have you wrestled out of here if I have to! Don't think Godwin won't get every footman and stable boy within two blocks of the house to help me if I tell him to! Now, go stand over there!"

"I swear, I could strangle you, Rowan," Ashe threatened, but took a single step back.

"Later. Kill me, later, Ashe." When Ashe took two more reluctant steps back, Rowan turned his attention back to the crisis at hand. "Gayle, get the crystallized ginger out of my bag and make an infusion."

The infusion helped slightly, along with a mint treatment, and Rowan wasted no time. "Where's the milk?"

Mrs. Clark brought over the tray with a glass of fresh milk. "Here, doctor."

"Gayle, have her drink all of it. Every last drop, do you understand?"

"Every drop," she repeated dutifully, and settled in next to the bedside. "Mrs. Blackwell? You must drink this."

Caroline weakly shook her head, trying to push the glass away. "No." She spotted her husband and began to cry. "I can't, Ashe."

Gayle looked at him, determined to rally his support. "She must, Mr. Blackwell."

"There you have it, darling. You *must*." He returned to take the glass from Gayle's hand and positioned himself to lift Caroline so that she could drink more comfortably. "Rowan's new assistant is, as you see, quite the tyrant and destined to be your dearest friend from what the good doctor has said of her. Now, drink this, my contrary little Quaker, or I'll pinch your nose and force you to do it."

She dutifully choked it down, and two more glasses afterward, even as she struggled to stay awake. Her skin was cold and clammy, and the pain was so intense that it was all she could do to cling to Ashe and cry.

Long hours passed, with Rowan and Gayle working continuously to try to keep her comfortable and warm, reassuring Ashe as best they could, and anxiously fighting each new symptom as it appeared.

As night fell, Ashe pulled Rowan out into the hallway. "She needs something for the pain."

Rowan shook his head. "I'm afraid that would be a mistake. Anything I give her to suppress the pain also slows her heart and breathing and may weaken her ability to fight through this. I don't want to frighten you, Ashe, but—"

"Are you joking? I've never been more terrified in my life, and I'm including the black hell we sat through and that time they took us out one by one and beat us until I was sure it was over. Go ahead, Rowan. Tell me everything."

"Even if I did give her something for the pain, laudanum or morphine, I'm not sure what her system can absorb. The arsenic attacks the stomach and internal organs. If there's too much damage, she could go into shock, suffer paralysis, or worse. Damn it, Ashe! I don't know for certain, but my instincts tell me that the longer she's alive, the better her chances. If we can make it to morning, I think the worst will be over and then it's just a matter of rest and healing."

"Till morning," Ashe echoed the phrase, seizing on the

promise. He returned to his wife's side and resumed his vigil, assisting in whatever he could and tending to Caroline with a ferocious devotion that defied death.

Even so, by midnight, Caroline had suffered a miscarriage of the baby that they'd not yet had a chance to anticipate—a blow that nearly unmanned Ashe. A quiet decision was made to wait to tell Caroline since she was so weak, and Rowan did his best to control the unspeakable sorrow he felt as he watched Ashe kissing his slumbering wife and whispering endless assurances that she was his life, and that so long as he drew breath, he would love her.

"You must live, darling," Ashe spoke softly as he caressed her cheeks, "if not for me, then for your college. Grandfather Walker is going to give you Bellewood, dearest, so you can turn that creaking monolith into the school of your dreams. It was going to be a Christmas present. You can't . . . leave now, Caroline."

Rowan walked away to give Ashe privacy as he implored his wife to live.

Gayle came up behind him. "Here. Mrs. Clark made some hot coffee for us."

He turned, a little surprised. He could tell by the color that it was exactly the way he liked it. "Thank you. That's just what I needed."

Finally, a few minutes after two in the morning, Caroline's pulse was stronger and Rowan was able to look his friend squarely in the eyes and tell him that they'd turned the corner.

Caroline would survive.

Rowan stayed at her side while Ashe went to inform Godwin and the others of the good news, and Gayle sat next to him, watching his face. "You don't look as celebratory as one would expect, Dr. West." She kept her voice low so as not to wake Caroline, covering one of his hands with hers. "Are you all right?"

"It's . . . harder when it's someone you know. And if she'd slipped away, I don't think he would ever have forgiven me." He gave her a dry look. "Yet another in that column, I suppose."

"Is that all that's bothering you?"

"Not entirely." He hesitated but then turned to her to whisper his worst fears. "A violent miscarriage with excessive hemorrhage—the real tragedy may be that there may never be another child. Time might prove me wrong, but . . ." Rowan sighed, lifting one of Gayle's hands to slowly kiss her palm. It was an unguarded gesture. He wanted nothing more than to feel the comfort of her touch. He freed her hand reluctantly but didn't want to embarrass her if Ashe returned suddenly. "I'll say nothing of it, Gayle. They have enough to grieve and recover from for now."

He knew Caroline was as independent and strong a woman as any, but this would be a difficult blow for her. She and Ashe were just beginning their lives together, and he didn't want to be the one to deliver the cruel news that not all their dreams were possible.

The loss of the baby had an even more immediate effect that he didn't discuss with Gayle. Whatever enemy the Jaded had at their heels, the time for defensively waiting for the next attack was over.

The danger would be keeping Ashe from going after them single-handedly once the dust had settled. He knew Blackwell too well—and the others.

Our strategy of quiet evasion and discreet escape just ended.

One way or another, the Jaded will never be the same.

* * *

It was almost four in the morning, and a quiet calm had overtaken the room. Ashe was asleep in the chair by the fire, having given in to exhaustion at last. Gayle surveyed the scene and sighed. It had been a long, horrible day, but a life had been saved and she was still in awe of Rowan's command of the drama that had unfolded.

He was so strong to stand up to Ashe like that, and

*knew just what to do even when everyone around him was
shouting suggestions or reacting in horror. Perhaps that's
why men have had the run of medicine. You have to be a
bit of a bully sometimes—or not worry how you're perceived.*

Rowan was working at the writing desk against the
wall, going over a medical text on gastric conditions, and
making notes. He'd yet to rest, but Gayle knew better than
to ask him to stop.

She turned her attention back to Mrs. Blackwell to
change the cool cloth on her forehead, only to realize that
Caroline was wide awake and making a similar survey of
the room and its occupants.

"You should rest," Gayle whispered.

"I'm too tired to rest," Caroline whispered back with a
weak smile. "Would you keep me company and distract me
for a time?"

"Of course." Gayle lay the cloth aside, clandestinely
checking her patient's temperature with the brush of her
hand. "I only hope I'm good company. I can't remember the
last time I had the leisure of just visiting with another
woman so I may have forgotten how. Here, let me warm
your hands."

"You are . . . just as Ashe described you."

"Am I? Oh, dear!"

"Is it true you wish to become a physician?"

Gayle nodded. "Even more now than when I first started,
I'm afraid. I never realized it would all be so . . . challenging. I am determined to hold my own. Dr. West has been a
very good mentor."

"You care for Rowan, don't you?"

"No!" The protest came too quickly, and she knew it. "I
mean it isn't possible to care for him. I am his assistant and
nothing more."

"I see. It's a bit of an ethical dilemma, then." She put a
hand over her eyes. "Not that the heart ever listens to lectures about the rules."

"Rowan is . . ." Gayle took a deep breath before she

could continue in a whisper that wouldn't carry beyond her patient's hearing. "I don't know why I keep expecting him to disappoint me or hurt me, but I don't think he ever would. If it were possible to love, it would be him."

"I'm not sure I believe that love is ever impossible. Dreams, even ones of independence, have a way of including our passions." She looked over at her husband, her large brown eyes glowing with affection at the sight of him. "You don't lose your dreams. They just expand to include so much more."

"You are a romantic, Mrs. Blackwell." Gayle smiled.

Caroline shook her head. "I am extremely practical and cannot understand why my husband thinks I need so many bonnets."

Gayle laughed softly. "I'm even more practical and cannot understand why anyone thinks I need a husband at all. Bonnets are far more manageable and less trouble."

"You are *not* a romantic, Miss Renshaw."

"And never will be! I will never marry."

Gayle stole a glance at Rowan, who looked a bit uncomfortable with his long legs bent with his knees against the bottom of Caroline's ladies' writing desk. His hand cradled his head as he worked, and his hair was mussed. She realized that his dark physician's coat was missing a button from the cuff and it saddened her. She'd always assumed that Mrs. Evans and the others took care of him, and perhaps they did. But there was so much more that he deserved.

It was hard not to imagine how sweet it would be to have his keeping and permission to fuss as his wife over his buttons and coats. A wife could push the hair from his eyes or see to his headaches and soothe the worries of the day from his brow—and never feel guilty about wanting to be ordinary for doing so.

She'd been sincere talking to Caroline, but not as candid as she could have been. Love wasn't some impossible thing to be kept at bay. She was already in the throes of it and struggling not to lose too much of herself. Because one day, she would complete her education and the choice would come. He would have to let her go.

He'd started to offer her marriage, but she'd stopped him. Even then, with her knees still trembling and the glorious wet between her thighs from their passion, she'd feared the compromises that would come with marriage and the loss of her freedom.

What if I don't have the strength to go?

What if he won't let me go?

She stared down at her hands covering Caroline's pale fingers and knew the answer. *If I keep my feelings to myself, he'll have no choice. He must never know that I love him.*

* * *

"It isn't possible to care for him. I am his assistant." Rowan allowed the words to echo in his head, as he pretended to be engrossed in the pages of his textbook. And then the worst of the conversation. *"I will never marry."*

I'm an idiot. I'm on fire for this woman.

And I'm going to end up alone.

Chapter
22

It was early Monday morning before Rowan indicated that
he felt completely confident to leave. Mrs. Clark had brought
in enough fresh milk to supply an orphanage so that her
mistress could follow her doctor's strict instructions. Godwin had done everything in his power to demonstrate his
gratitude for their services, and every member of Ashe's
household had made an effort to seek them out to say as
much. Like Rowan, Ashe treated his staff like family, and
their love of the new Mrs. Blackwell was evident.

Gayle finished buttoning her coat and waited while the
men spoke privately on the stairs above, out of her hearing.
They were so different, she noted. Ashe was like a gilt lion,
all polish and power, but Rowan was the one she couldn't
stop staring at. There was something humble but princely
about him. He was elegant, without posing, and she loved
the way he was so very still whenever others were speaking.

He drew a woman's eyes with his effortless good looks;
his russet hair was longer in the back than fashion dictated,

but it gave him a wild edge that made her heart beat faster. For all his intellectual pursuits, he held himself like a warrior. Even exhausted, there was a latent energy in the way he moved—as if ready to leap at the next call for help.

At last, he came down to join her, hat in hand, and they left to find Theo at the ready outside. Without a word, Rowan tossed in his bag and then helped her up before climbing inside the carriage to settle back with a ragged sigh.

"What a night!" He stretched his long, lean legs out but carefully kept them off her skirts. "I think I aged ten years. Hell with that! I'm sure of it."

"Who would poison Mrs. Blackwell? Why?"

"They'll be found and made to pay—whoever they are."

There is more to the story than he's saying. He and Mr. Blackwell didn't look completely surprised, and what was that nonsense about knowing it was Sunday? They knew there was danger. Rowan said as much, but has it passed or is the murderer going to try again?

"He truly loves her." Gayle's whisper was quiet but captured his attention completely in the dim confines of the carriage. "I don't think I've ever seen that kind of love before. Not until tonight. Not until—" She stopped herself, horrified to think she'd almost said *you*.

"Gayle, I—"

"Please don't say anything, Rowan. Just kiss me and make me forget everything." She left her seat, shifting over into his arms. Her knees were already trembling from exhaustion, but no lack of rest could inhibit her need for him at that moment. Her fingers framed his face, and she kissed him without waiting for his reply. His cheeks were rough underneath the palms of her hands, the differences between them all the sweeter as they gave her the friction she craved.

As the kiss deepened, there was an emotional edge to it that made her wonder if she'd lost her mind.

Madness. I want him to the point of madness.

She sought a touch that would heal, but demanded no tenderness, drawing his tongue into her mouth and suckling him, as if he alone could give her the sustenance she needed to survive. Bruising kisses flowed into a frantic dance that brought tears to her eyes.

There was not enough time in the ride home to lose any clothing—not enough room to maneuver—and it made every second more potent and strange. She was so tired that her own body felt like an alien machine to be directed but not necessarily controlled.

"Don't be gentle. I need to feel, Rowan."

She wanted to be grounded, tethered to the land of the living and shaken out of the icy lethargy that gripped her heart. Grief and death had dulled her senses. She didn't want to remain in a fog of loss and melancholy.

The heat of his lips to hers was a hint of the purifying fire that Rowan offered.

His hands moved to frame her face, trying to push her tenderly back and slow down the onslaught, but she fought him, biting the sensitive juncture behind his ear, and he stiffened beneath her.

Game on.

It was a rush. This was like a battle of wills, but Rowan wasn't sure where the lines had been drawn. He knew only that Gayle was desperately in need and his own body had thickened without bothering to debate the why or the right or wrong of it. There wasn't time to argue as her fingers slipped under his coat and began digging at his shirt to free it from his pants.

Damn it! Slow, woman, slow!

For Rowan, it was bittersweet. This was the woman he was destined to lose.

The lace attached to the collar of her dress gave way easily, and he was able to tug down on her corset just enough to free the jutting peaks of her breasts. It was the distraction he needed to wrest control away from her. She threw her head back, arching into the attentions of his mouth as he suckled her, circling her nipple with his tongue and laving her in fast tight circles that made her shiver and buck against him.

With his free hand, he lifted her petticoats and found her underneath her skirts, sliding his hand over her already wet flesh. He pushed a finger into the soft silk that coated his touch and dipped it just inside her body to toy with her entrance as his thumb moved across her clit. Faster and faster, he lightly moved over the swollen nub, then waited as the muscles of her body clenched around his finger—only to add another finger and stretch out the sensation.

"Yes! Rowan, yes!"

The speed of his touch increased even more, coaxing her clit until she was bucking against his hand and he had to use all his strength to keep her from falling off his lap.

And then he slowly inserted a third finger, pressing her open as her muscles spasmed to accept the invasion of his touch. Only then did he begin to move his fingers, in and out, a slow counterpoint to the hummingbird-fast touch of his thumb. He was frigging her with his hand and she was helpless to stop him. She began writhing, as if to fight the climax building inside of her, but her thighs widened to give him all the permission he needed.

"I need . . . you . . . inside of me."

"I am inside of you, Gayle." His answer came through gritted teeth as he increased the speed of his fingers, determined to propel her into coming.

"No. You. This. Please." Her hand found his cock through the cloth of his pants, giving it a wicked squeeze as she stroked the outline of his erection. "Rowan, please!"

He shook his head, then teased her throat and nipped at the sensitive juncture of her neck and shoulder. "No, Gayle. I have no protection with me. We cannot."

Rowan was doing anything he could to pleasure her, to taste her and be gratified vicariously by the release she would have—but there was no way under God's vast heaven he was going to put her at risk. His own past experiences provided an icy wall of suffering that left no room for compromise.

This time, my apprentice is going to have to learn to do without.

"Please, Rowan—I want nothing between us. I need to feel you inside of me."

"Come, woman. Just come."

It was a strange declaration of war.

"No." Her voice was like a soft growl in the dark of the carriage, but her breath came faster and faster as the pressure of his fingers lightened and changed—softer, harder, more, less, slower, faster—until there was nothing in the world but the feeling of his hand there, of her breasts pushed up into the chilled air of the night and his mouth suckling her.

"Oh! Oh, Rowan . . ." And then he was there, at the pace and pressure exactly where she needed him to be, and she knew there was no denying the ecstasy that began to flood her spine and arc over skin.

She kicked out with her legs, a frustrated cry escaping her lips, but even as she tried to deny him what he wanted, wave after wave of orgasm ripped through her frame, and she came in a glorious rush that left her tearful and quiet with exhaustion.

The carriage slowed to a stop at the brownstone, and for once, Rowan wasn't quick to open the door and leap out. He waited while she finished adjusting the lace collar of her dress, her eyes averted and her cheeks still stained from the exertion of their coupling.

"Take your time. Theo won't—"

"I'm fine." She opened the door herself and alighted without waiting for him.

Rowan followed, bag in hand, unsure if he could just let her stalk off, but he knew better than to humiliate her in front of Theo by revealing too much.

Carter met them at the door. "Mrs. Evans has a late supper hot and ready for you both."

"That sounds perfect, Carter. We'll—"

"I'll take a tray in my room, if you don't mind," Gayle interrupted him, her demeanor quiet and withdrawn. "I'm a bit too tired to make a good dinner companion."

Rowan was surprised, but he couldn't argue with Carter there. "As you wish. It was a difficult call. I can check with you later if you'd like to go over any notes for—"

"I'll retire early tonight and transcribe everything in the morning, Dr. West." She excused herself, nodding to Carter. "Good night, Carter."

"Was Mrs. Blackwell terribly injured, doctor?" Carter asked anxiously, and Rowan was obliged to reassure him and give what report he could of the ominous event. He omitted the Blackwells' private tragedy but decided that an alerted household was a safer household.

"Poison, you say?" Carter was horrified.

"Be sure to tell Cook that any deliveries she takes, she should take only from a trusted source and face-to-face, if possible. If it shows up on the doorstep, and no one is sure where it came from, I want it out. Now is not the time to assume that a grateful patient has dropped off biscuits!"

Carter shook his head. "Poor Barnaby!"

"Why is Barnaby in a position of sympathy?" Rowan asked, but he could feel the answer coming and began to smile.

"Those women are going to have him tasting everything in there, like some poor medieval page boy, testing for poison. And while he may think it grand at first, I predict you'll have the complaint of a stomach ache before the end of the week, doctor, if she makes him go through the entire larder!"

Rowan laughed, harder than he had in weeks, grateful for the release. But even as he wiped his eyes, he glanced up at the staircase where she'd gone and wished that Gayle had lingered awhile longer to share in the levity.

You need more laughter in your life, Miss Renshaw.

* * *

It was too much. Gayle felt bruised and so uncertain as she made her way to her room. They'd saved Caroline Blackwell's life, but the bittersweet loss of the unborn child weighed heavily on her. But it was about more than grief or sympathy for her new friends that slowed her steps and made her want to crawl into her bed and hug her knees.

What pressed against her hardest was jealousy.

To see the pair of them, so strong and caring of each other, and so united even when they were vulnerable to such random violence—it had been inspiring to watch.

Whenever my mother had so much as a head cold, my father would move into the hunting lodge or come up with some business to take him to Town. For Emily, he stayed, but never for anything or anyone after that.

Gayle shut the laboratory door behind her and leaned against it, as if a horde of angry demons was clamoring on the other side. *Can you hunger for a thing and not starve? Is it just a matter of self-control? Can I set these day-dreams and new desires aside or have I gone too far? Is it my soul that will be consumed instead?*

Rowan's touch in the carriage had promised so much more than carnal release or temporary pleasure. In the impossibly tight confines of a carriage where it shouldn't have been anything but raw, he'd conveyed a regard for her and made her feel cherished somehow. It was as if he took nothing for granted.

I was like a woman possessed. I . . . I was more than wanton. I was wild.

She'd begged him to use her. She'd wanted nothing more than to throw caution to the winds and surrender the battle of wills that was threatening to tear her apart. Instead, he'd kept his promises, almost maddening her with his resolve.

He has more integrity than I do. I'm crumbling in on myself because I want more than I can have and because Rowan deserves so much more. She walked through the lab, trailing her fingers over the tables and glass. *He deserves what Ashe has.*

She knew that Rowan deserved to be loved like that. He deserved that kind of devotion. Because it was obvious that he would give love and devotion in return, without any thought to equal measures. Every fiber in her being recognized that this was no ordinary man to disappoint her or retreat. He made her feel like there was nothing in the world that she couldn't have or accomplish.

But what if Caroline has it wrong? What if you can't preserve your independence and have that kind of love? I've spent a lifetime convincing myself that I didn't need a man to be happy and that once I became a doctor, I wouldn't have any regrets.

There was a soft knock at her door, and she could hear Rowan's muffled voice on the other side. "Gayle? Gayle, are you all right?"

She stood, walked over, and deliberately threw the dead bolt into place. The sound of the metal latch catching was like a cannon going off, and she waited several long seconds before she could hear his footsteps retreating through the laboratory and returning downstairs.

For now, she was awash in regret.

I'm drowning in regret, and if I didn't know better, I'd think I might die of it, Rowan.

Chapter
23

The next morning broke with a thin gray light that subtly invaded her sleep and finally woke her when the sound of a morning drizzle against her windows announced the day's arrival. She sat up abruptly, shocked to discover she'd slept so soundly.

Gayle had anticipated a restless night when she'd fallen asleep in tears, but her body had ignored the troubles of her conscience and seized the sleep it needed to heal. She checked the small clock on her nightstand and was amazed at the hour. It was nearly ten, and she leapt out of bed in a flurry, determined to prove to Rowan that her reliability wasn't in question.

I'll bet he was at breakfast before Mrs. Evans rang the bell and already working on planning his week's appointments and treatments. Rats! Every time I sleep like this, I make it easier for him to think that I'm not strong enough for the work!

With an eye on the gloomy weather outside her window, Gayle chose the dark green cotton wool dress edged in black ribbon. It was one of her more chic work dresses, but she loved the warm mandarin sleeves. She dressed as quickly as she could, her fingers trembling a little as she worked the front tabs of her corset and the ribbons to secure her petticoats. But at last, she was able to hurry out and head downstairs to the library to try to find Rowan and face the day.

But it was Mrs. Evans she met on the stairs. "He's out, Miss Renshaw. He's gone to check on Mrs. Blackwell, and he left strict orders that we were not to bother your rest."

"Oh." Gayle tried not to let her disappointment show. "I was hoping to see Mrs. Blackwell again myself."

"Dr. West said you were an angel through it all! We meant to let you have the morning to recover undisturbed." Mrs. Evans looked at her with a new sincere pride shining in her eyes, as if Gayle were one of the chicks from her nest. "I know I haven't been as understanding . . . but after what happened with Florence, and watching you all this time . . . well, I know you'll do well. I'm still not sure if I want you in there on Wednesdays with those rough river men, but . . ."

"Thank you, Mrs. Evans. I've still a long way to go until— I shall try not to disappoint you."

"Pish! Now, let me send up a tray since I know for absolute fact that you didn't have a bite for dinner and you must be famished!" Mrs. Evans turned without waiting for her reply, cheerfully heading back down the stairs to secure a hearty brunch from Mrs. Wilson.

With a sigh, Gayle returned to the laboratory, wishing she could muster more enthusiasm for the change in plans. There was definitely work to be done, as always, but she truly had hoped to see Caroline again. To reassure herself that she'd continued to improve, but also for the new friendship that she'd begun.

She lit more lamps to improve the light and then began to pull everything she could on gastric conditions and their treatments. It was a daunting bit of research, but Gayle found comfort in the direction of her work and took a copious amount of notes to ensure that she didn't miss anything that might help Mrs. Blackwell to regain her health.

When her brunch tray magically materialized next to her, Gayle smiled and knew that she'd once again managed to happily lose herself in the maze of her studies. She propped up a book with its spine and ate her meal as she continued reading, dismissing the ghostlike voice of her mother saying something about ill-bred women reading at the table.

"*Digestive Diseases and Their Origins*?" Peter James's voice broke in from the doorway as he surveyed the title of her textbook. "I'm not sure that would go with any stew, no matter how delicious!"

Her cheeks grew hot with embarrassment, and she set aside her tray. "I . . . I agree it's not everyone's idea of entertaining reading with egg custard and sausages."

"Not *anyone's* idea, but if I'd caught you reading poetry or a book on fashion, I might have thought to ring for the doctor!" He approached her, his manner as casual as ever. "I apologize for interrupting. It seems that's all I do!"

"No, please don't." It was the first time she'd seen him since he'd sent the note, but she was glad that it wasn't awkward between them. "I'm the one who should apologize. My reply to your offer may have seemed a bit abrupt, but I was—"

"No worries! No worries! You've a right to your days, and I know how few and far between they can be when you're in the employ of someone who has a profession that keeps all hours." He stopped at the medicine cabinet and began his tallies while they spoke. "I don't think I had a day to myself the first year I worked for Mr. Fitzroy."

"That's dreadful!" she said.

He shrugged. "He is one of the best chemists in London and a fierce businessman. There's ten men around every corner that would be happy to take my place."

"I suppose that's true." She closed her book. "But I'm sure Mr. Fitzroy would be quick to say how none of those ten might have your skills or enthusiasm."

"You're too kind!" He wrote down a count and then turned back to her. "Miss Renshaw, I know it's even harder for you. A female assistant. Dr. West doesn't want to see you out on a day off. He's thinking of his reputation—and maybe protecting yours, a bit. I'd a respectable day in mind, but if it's a rule that you're not to step out with any gentleman . . ." He trailed off as if hoping she'd correct his misperception and take back her earlier refusal.

Gayle chose the cowardly way out. "Dr. West is very firm about these matters. I'm so glad you understand. You've been such a good friend to me, I'd hate to think that we couldn't be civil to each other."

"Oh, no fear, Miss Renshaw!" His smile was warm, dismissing the tension between them. "A true friend doesn't abandon you at the first obstacle. Besides, I see you regularly enough with my deliveries, and we can just look forward to those visits."

"Yes, I . . . suppose that's true." Gayle wasn't sure if she should take him at his word or if he meant to imply something more. "Unless Mr. Fitzroy has a miraculous change of heart and allows me to cross his shop's threshold again."

Peter laughed. "We'd be back at the smelling salts!" He made a note on his order sheet and then gave her a more sober look. "Not to fish for gossip, but I heard you went out on a call with Dr. West to the Blackwells'."

"Oh!" *Word does travel fast!*

"He's a favorite of mine, of course," Peter reminded her. "Was everything all right there? Did Mr. Blackwell have an accident?"

"It was Mrs. Blackwell, actually. She . . . suffered a fall." Gayle didn't feel comfortable saying more, and Mr. James looked horrified enough at the report.

"*Mrs.* Blackwell?"

"She'll recover," she added.

"Well, there's a relief! The gossips had it wrong and said it was the man of the house who'd taken ill. That'll teach me to listen to idle chatter!" Peter walked back to the worktable with her books and notes spread out. "Do you mind if I ask you something, Miss Renshaw?"

"Not at all."

"You're not just interested in medicine, are you? I mean, you're not just nosing around the edges or cleaning up the laboratory, are you?"

She shook her head slowly. "No."

"But what will you do with it all? You may have over-prepared yourself if your ambition was to work in a hospital, miss. They won't take you on as a nurse if you know enough to argue with their doctors. . . ."

She held her breath for just a moment. He'd never been unkind or judgmental, and she trusted him. "I was hoping to become a doctor one day. Dr. West has been very supportive and is doing everything he can to see that I'm properly trained."

"Really?" he asked, his entire demeanor suddenly touched with sadness. "Well, then I'll hope for that for you. But between us, Miss Renshaw"—he picked up his order next to the cabinet—"even when a man appears to be helping you, it may be that he's just helping himself."

She gasped in shock, but before she could compose a protest without revealing too much of her relationship with Rowan, Peter James was gone.

*　*　*

The Jaded had gathered again. The early morning impromptu meeting was again at Ashe's home—despite Michael's wish to gather somewhere more clandestine in case they were being watched. But Blackwell had vehemently refused to be more than two floors away from Caroline, and the others had agreed, forcing Michael to concede defeat.

"I meant to thank you again . . . for saving Caroline's life. I was—less than gracious, Rowan."

"You threatened to kill me more than once, but"—Rowan smiled, shaking his hand—"I'm only glad that it's over and you still have your beautiful wife with you."

"I always imagined the healing arts as a bit more delicate, Rowan."

Rowan shook his head. "It's more of a boxing match sometimes than a chess game. But every once in a while, it's miraculous, and so I've come to accept the rougher days to balance it all out."

Galen Hawke, now Lord Winters, stepped forward to welcome Rowan. "I missed your library and our gatherings, friend, but as for this tangle, I'll admit a part of me just wanted to take Haley to Italy and be shut of this."

Ashe held out a warm apple cider to Galen, aware of Hawke's preference to avoid alcohol. "As if she'd let you! But on a serious note, if it is our families that are in danger, then no man here will blink if you wish to take your bride as far away as possible. If I'd been as smart—"

"You aren't gifted with second sight, Ashe," Rowan was quick to intervene to spare his friend an unnecessary bout of guilt over what had happened. "None of us are."

"Did Lady Winters return with you to London?" Josiah asked from his chair by the fireplace.

Hawke shook his head, sitting down with his drink. "I left her there. Her aunt Alice was feeling poorly with a cold, and I didn't want to alarm her. Besides, her father was enjoying the visit, and I knew she'd be in good hands."

"That's for the best, then." Rowan moved to pour himself a measure of brandy. "So it's only Thorne who isn't here."

"Darius sends his regards." Ashe pulled out his letter, setting it on the table in front of them as a courtesy if they wished to read it. "He wrote that he's staying on and thinking he might uncover something there in Edinburgh. We've been doing our gem brokering through the Scottish trade jewelers, and Thorne thinks they may have a better chance of hearing any rumors about the pursuit of a sacred object from India."

Michael hung back a bit, allowing the others to settle in as the men began to catch up on the matter at hand. No other mysterious packages had been delivered. The conversation was a balance between discussing new strategies to keep themselves safe, deciphering the letter and the meaning of *sacred treasure*, and holding Ashe back from running wild with a sword into the East India Trading Company offices. When Josiah quietly pointed out that they still didn't even have a wisp of proof that the Company had anything to do with it, pandemonium broke loose.

"What about Bascombe? He as much as confessed that the Company was behind all of it!" Ashe said.

Rowan tried to defend Hastings. "But if they know that he's babbled, why be so secretive now?"

"Exactly!" Josiah said, but slunk down in his chair. "I mean, it's not exactly Indian assassins with knives, is it?"

Michael held up a hand. "We're getting ahead of ourselves, gentlemen."

"Yes, if the sacred treasure is separate from the rest of the riches, what the hell are they talking about? There were bits and baubles, but I don't remember a damn thing standing out above the others! Hell, it's why it was so easy to parse it all out, remember?" Ashe finished his drink to set it down in frustration.

Michael nodded. "I've been over it in my head a thousand times. We none of us knew much about the cut or quality of a gem, or how it would be valued—any of it."

"Colors," Josiah recalled wistfully. "We'd left so much to fate and chance in order to survive and escape that dungeon in India, it just made sense when we divided the gems and bits of jewelry to do the same. Even then, I remember thinking how remarkable it was. No one was arguing about the size of their share or the value of what we'd taken. We just put them in piles by color on that rough wool blanket spread out over that bunk bed and had Michael hold six stones. And we chose blindly. I never even blinked at how right it all felt. Did any of you?"

They all shook their heads. Ashe smiled. "I thought it was brilliant. Galen chose a ruby and took all the red, I had the sapphires, Darius took the opals, and Rowan, the emeralds. Michael ended up with the diamonds." He ran a hand through his hair. "And for Hastings, there were pearls of every size up to pigeon eggs. I still can't believe it's real."

"And the oath," Michael added. "We just took that oath and we've all stood behind it. We kept our heads and all of us have benefited. No one has made a great ostentatious fool of himself, and unless I missed something, most of us still have our gems tucked away."

Ashe nodded. "Darius brokered only a few gems for each of us through his contacts in Edinburgh for remarkable returns. I'll admit I was surprised at how little we've spent!"

Galen shrugged. "I surprised myself! I made a few improvements of the family estates after I sold just four of my rubies, but then several old investments began to come in, and with my unexpected inheritance, there's been no need."

"I thought the emeralds would be a memory when I wished to get a new carriage and outfit my laboratory, but I sold two—remember, Michael? And then a cousin I'd practically forgotten I had died and left me enough to fund my Wednesday practice for a lifetime. A godsend, but . . ." Rowan's brow furrowed since good fortune had never existed for a West for as long as he could remember.

"We've been extremely lucky, so far."

"Extremely," Ashe echoed grimly, clearly thinking of his beloved Caroline and just how close he'd come to his luck running out.

"What about Hastings?" Rowan asked. "No offense, Josiah, but you don't look like a man with hidden wealth. We've respected your privacy, but have you lost your fortune?"

"Why does everyone always think I'm poor? I've sold one pearl, and Darius acquired a miraculous amount for it, and frankly, I've . . . I haven't needed to make improvements to an estate or buy a carriage."

"It's only because your coat is in worse shape than Rowan's, and *that* is saying something. But I like that you're putting out an aura of starving young artist with paint stains on your clothing," Ashe defended him, then stood to refill his glass with port. "I suspect he does it to draw in the ladies, gentlemen."

"Leave him be." Michael gave Ashe a quelling look. "All right, then. None of us have drawn undue attention to our numbers, but even so, whoever this is not only knows of us, but knows what happened in that dungeon and knows about the treasure."

"How is that possible?" Galen asked. "I know we determined that hiding in plain sight was wiser, but we've never really let down our guard."

Ashe stood slowly, an idea seizing him. "The letter implied that they knew all of us! But what if they don't? What if one of us is still an unknown to them? It may give us an advantage if we want to start asking questions."

"How in the world do you deduct what an unknown person may or may not know? I think you're off the beam slightly." Rowan's criticism was gently given.

"I think Hastings could be the key!"

"Me?" Josiah looked instantly uncomfortable. "The key to what exactly?"

"If I were trying to learn the identity of the Jaded, I would only need one name first. I was the idiot who caught Lady Barrow's eye and earned the nickname *Jaded* in that article, so let's say I'm the start of it. I'm often at Rowan's, as are you, Michael, Darius, and even Galen. Galen would have cemented the connection when he summoned Michael after he was forced to leave London to look after Miss Moreland. And Darius—I'm afraid our connection was similarly established when I dragged him out to that ball last spring and we were publicly seen together right before . . . well, a very memorable scene with Caroline. But where is Josiah?"

"Yes," Josiah echoed sarcastically. "Where is Josiah?"

"We joke among ourselves at how difficult you are to locate, and frankly, no one's gotten you out of your painter's garret for months. I'll bet our writer is having the same trouble. Hastings may be just elusive enough to stand apart.

If he started asking questions in the Company's circles, he might actually get answers." Ashe finished his proposal, a man most satisfied with himself.

"What? Like some sort of Jaded agent, secretly acting on our behalf?" Rowan said.

Josiah shook his head. "No. It's an interesting thought, but no. If anyone is watching, I'm as much in the thick of these meetings as the next man. I was at that same party with you, Ashe, and if you recall, I think *I* was the one who coined the phrase in that misguided conversation! I've been to the sporting club with Ashe, had more than my share of drinks with Michael, and am no stranger to any one of your doorways. While I may have missed the social season this last year, I'm not as invisible as you seem to think."

Rowan leaned back in his chair. "Leave the man be! Michael had the right of it." At Michael's name, Rowan glanced at the man and realized he'd left the circle a bit and was standing at the windows with his back to them. "Michael?"

"I've let all of you down." His voice echoed with defeat as he turned to face them. "I swore to protect you, and for all I've fussed like a mother hen, that's all I've managed. I thought we'd hear from the culprit again, before the full moon as he'd promised, and I was confident that I'd be able to stop him. But this . . ." He shook his head.

Galen approached their friend, reaching up to put a hand on his shoulder. "You're just one man, Michael Rutherford, even if you are the most intimidating man we've ever seen—and you aren't responsible for our safety. It isn't possible."

Rowan seconded the sentiment. "It's too great a burden, Michael."

Rutherford shrugged but rejoined them, taking a seat on the sofa. "Ashe may be casting stones in the wrong direction, but at least he's thinking of ways to stir the pot."

"What are you saying?" Ashe asked.

"I'm saying, if you're going to really stir the pot, you'll

need a bigger spoon." Michael leaned forward as he outlined his plan. "What if we took an advertisement out in the London *Times* and called out this bastard? What if we told him we don't deal with cowards? What if we invited him to step out of the shadows, speak plainly about what he's after, and see what happens?"

Galen sat down next to Michael. "We might gain control of the playing field."

"If the bastard agrees to play along," Ashe said. "Hell, I like it! Call him out. I'll meet him under a bridge somewhere, and we can settle this whole business in a single night's work."

Every member of the Jaded shook their heads or grunted their disapproval in the next instant. Not one of them wanted Ashe to be put in a position where the temptation to seek vengeance could cause him to forfeit his life. "You, Ashe," Rowan spoke for them all, "are going to stay home with Caroline and count your blessings. And *no one* is meeting this dangerous thug under a dark bridge! I think we can be smarter than that, can't we, gentlemen?"

"Penny novels aside, I'm sure we can come up with something better." Michael leaned forward, and before long they were all huddled around the table, quietly trying to plot a plan that ensured that the Jaded wouldn't be caught off guard again.

Chapter
24

Rowan was in a far better mood returning home. Being in the company of the Jaded always made him feel whole, as if the ground beneath him were magically more solid from the camaraderie.

He'd managed a stop of his own before reaching the sanctuary of his brownstone. It was a gift for Gayle that he'd been planning for some time, and one he knew would bring her immense pleasure. He imagined her reaction, indulging in a daydream where she expressed her gratitude with kisses, perhaps even crying at his thoughtfulness and tenderly confessing her secret love for him that his careful token had evoked.

The last is rubbish, but a man can hope for smiles and kisses safely enough!

This time, I won't let her retreat. It's nonsense to leave things unsaid. If I've learned anything in the last seventy-two hours it's that life is precious, and when it comes to love, time even more so.

With his bundle tucked under his arm, Rowan alighted

from the carriage with a determined stride. *A man makes his own luck, they say! And if the gods are—*

Rowan stopped in his tracks at the sight of the man on his doorstep. It was the worst reception Rowan could have imagined. Dr. Horace Whitfield was standing on his doorstep, apparently in the process of ringing the bell.

Damn and hellfire! Nothing to be done but to get it over with!

"Dr. Whitfield! Has Carter left you out in the cold?" he jested, then opened the door to let them both in just in time to startle the poor butler. "I was just on my way in, Mr. Carter. Can you ask Mrs. Evans to send a tray up to the library?"

Carter nodded, retreating to leave Rowan to tend to his guest. Rowan walked the older man upstairs to his study, praying for once that the eternally curious Gayle Renshaw would stay above stairs until he could sort Horace away. "To what do I owe this honor, Dr. Whitfield? I wasn't expecting you until the end of the month."

"I hear that you've hired a nurse."

"Have you?" Rowan did his best to sound nonchalant as he put his bag away and set the wrapped bundle aside.

"Clever man!" Dr. Whitfield stood to move to the sideboard and poured himself a liberal amount of scotch, for his usual medicinal purposes. "It is hard to stay competitive these days, but no doubt your blue bloods are mightily impressed by the idea of you having a nurse on hand for your calls."

Whitfield, you're such a prig! The man had been an acquaintance of his uncle and exactly the kind of man who self-appoints himself a mentor and authority figure. Except the only authority Horace Whitfield wielded was over a dwindling roster of elderly patients in North London and his own liquor cabinet. If he wasn't still tied into the board at the Royal Academy of Medicine and the British Medical Association, Rowan didn't think the man would have a single friend.

"To be honest, I'm exhausted from a long house call.

Was there something you wished from me?" Rowan wanted nothing of the subject, not with a man like Horace poking into things. His relationship with Gayle was still so new and fragile, and every instinct urged him to protect her from the scrutiny of men like Horace. A single misunderstanding could unravel everything she hoped to achieve, and Rowan knew that if the Association caught wind of her efforts, they would deliberately block her.

"Quite a gimmick, to hire a woman like that to hold their hands!"

"I have never invested much in gimmicks. But speaking of investments, I heard you bought a new carriage and matching set of four white-stocking bays to boot. Did you receive a royal appointment that I haven't heard about yet?"

Horace held up his glass. "I'll drink to that delightful dream." After a respectable swallow or two, he gave Rowan a wink. "My new young wife thought I should ride a bit more comfortably and look the part of a well-to-do physician."

"Lucky man."

Horace shrugged. "I'm the luckiest man I know! They say that the number three has its charms, and I must say, the third Mrs. Whitfield's dowry has made her my very favorite wife—may the first two rest in peace."

Rowan wasn't sure what to say and decided to hold his tongue. Horace's lack of sentimentality was more than jarring, and he wondered what the new Mrs. Whitfield thought of her luck.

"I'd also heard she was pretty!" Horace went on cheerfully, and it took Rowan a moment to realize that they had unfortunately left the topic of Mrs. Whitfield behind.

Even so, he attempted ignorance. "Who?"

"Your nurse, of course! You sly thing! I would have thought you'd have been terrified to hire some fresh-faced creature, for fear of upsetting your more matronly patients' sensibilities. But my ears haven't picked up a whisper of complaint! However do you manage it?" Horace snorted another swallow down before going on. "But the answer's in the problem, isn't it? She's far more than pretty, isn't she? Every male patient will perk at the sight of her, and you'll be credited with their miraculous recoveries, and the women—she's pretty enough they'll be charmed by the attentions of an angel. Am I right?"

"*You* should hire a nurse, Horace. Then you could spend more time with that darling new bride of yours."

Horace waved him off. "Only a man without a wife would think that any bride would allow a man to employ a woman like that! It's your bachelorhood that gives you the advantage in this game."

"It's no game, Horace."

"Then what is it, Rowan?" the old man pressed, and Rowan felt cornered.

"It doesn't matter what I say, Horace. You've made up your mind." He tried to pull back as diplomatically as he could. "I'm practically unknown in your lofty circles at the Association, Horace. I can't imagine the addition of one woman to my service would warrant this much attention. Really?"

"You are not unknown, Rowan. Don't patronize me and don't underestimate your own talents. I'm a crass man, and as you know, I don't agree with the way you coddle patients and muddy your hallways with indigent drunks and prostitutes once a week—but your star is rising nonetheless. I just wished to assure myself that it was indeed a nurse you've hired, and that you aren't attempting some strange revolutionary nonsense by secretly including a woman in your practice. Because there was talk of you seeking an apprentice last fall, and now . . ." Horace finished his scotch and set the glass aside. "Reassure me, Dr. West, that everything is aboveboard with this woman."

Damn, it had to come. If ever I needed to be good at lying, here is my moment.

"This truth must stay between us, Horace."

"Of course."

"Everything is completely aboveboard. Miss Renshaw is a headstrong woman with the notion that she is interested in medicine. I imagine her family was distraught and beside themselves at her refusal to even consider suitors and the security of married life. When I saw that she would not be dissuaded and may even put herself into reckless jeopardy, I decided to help her."

"T-to help her?"

"By leading her on a wild goose chase, Horace. I am teaching her, admittedly, because I have no desire to be embarrassed in front of my patients when she is present, but the ultimate lesson will likely be her acceptance of her place and her grateful return to the bosom of her family to prepare for marriage."

"She honestly thinks you're training her?"

"She's useful enough in a crisis, and as talented as any man I have ever encountered. It is a tragedy that her gender will most likely keep her from practicing the art professionally. If she was truly my apprentice and she continued to develop her skills at her current pace, I would be forced to recommend her to a medical school for admittance to their clinical programs, Horace."

"B-but she is not truly your apprentice!"

"Who has ever heard of anything so ridiculous?" Rowan felt like a man dancing on a dagger's point. Telling Horace Whitfield what he wanted to hear without denying anything outright or maligning Gayle was making his head hurt.

"Thank Providence you've not lost your reason! I'm sure her family will be extremely grateful when you've shown her the error of her ways. But her reputation! I certainly hope whatever baker or butcher is lined up to marry your pretty maid won't mind this unorthodox odyssey into Town. But I can't think of a tanner or undertaker that would take a woman with such an unnatural mind! And I'm assuming you've protected yourself in this arrangement. You leave yourself open to all sorts of indecent accusations, Dr. West, by having such a creature in your care."

"My solicitor was extremely thorough in the contract for her education, and Mrs. Evans is as watchful a guardian as Cerberus and a good deal more frightening."

"That's goo—contract? I thought you said there was no official apprenticeship?" Horace looked like a man on the verge of an apoplectic fit.

"I couldn't leave myself open to indecent accusations! You just advised against it, yourself!"

"Yes, that's . . . true." Horace pulled out a handkerchief, mopped his brow, and made a grand show of preparing to leave. "Well, if you don't mind my saying, it's too risky a business! Send her home to her family, Dr. West, before anyone hears of your arrangement and misinterprets your charity for something more. Save yourself the shame and the threat—I will say it!—of being blacklisted for entertaining this girl and her outlandish notions!"

"Horace." Rowan gave him a pat on the shoulder. "What need do I have to worry when I have your friendship and loyalty and you know the truth? I *do* have your friendship and loyalty, do I not?"

"Of course you do, Dr. West, but—"

"I'm not *entertaining* this girl. If anything, why not think of this as a passing experiment that will, in all likelihood, give the Association exactly what they need to prevent any serious attempts from misguided women in the future? How much easier to argue against it when you have a documented example?" *Or argue for it, but we both know you can't even think of a woman succeeding in the medical field, Horace.*

"Yes! Well, you can count on me to avert my gaze while you sort this mess out!" Dr. Whitfield paused in the door for one last parting shot. "Be sure to document everything! If it were me, I'd track her monthly illnesses and be sure to note how it affects her concentration and health. With a delicate constitution so hindered by the feminine inconveniences, you can seize on irrefutable proof of her unsuitability. You might win a medal from the Society, after all, Dr. West!"

Rowan almost cringed but managed a smile. "Yes, good day, Dr. Whitfield!" He closed the door behind him as the old man let himself out and Rowan could hear the muffled voices of Carter helping him with his coat.

He put his forehead against the study door, sighing. *If only Whitfield were the worst of them. . . . Thankfully, Gayle wasn't here to—*

"H-how could you?" Gayle stepped from behind the hidden door behind the curio cabinet, and it was all he could do not to throw something against the wall in frustration.

Today is not my day.

Chapter
25

"This eavesdropping has to stop, Gayle!"

"Is that how you see me? As some jest or passing experiment until I wisely quit and run home begging my aunt to find me a husband?" She was standing in the adjoining doorway to the servants' hall and, quite obviously, had overheard everything.

"I'm entitled to a conversation now and then without you creeping about editing the damn thing!" He knew it was a defensive reaction to be so angry, but there was little he could do. "Do you think I'd tell a man like Horace how I really see you or how I really feel about what you're becoming?" He stood with both hands splayed on his desk, his ire unmistakable. "If you were really listening, most of it was entirely complimentary, Gayle!"

"What? You said I wasn't truly your apprentice! You said that such a thing would be ridiculous! You said you signed that contract only to shield yourself from indecent accusations!"

"I was as truthful as I could be, Gayle, and then allowed

the old goat to fill in the gaps as he wished." He closed his eyes to try to calm himself, then opened them again to address her as carefully as he could. "I *said* that you were as talented as any man I'd ever met and that if you continued, I'd have no choice but to recommend you to the Academy for admittance! But I can't control the world, Gayle, and guarantee you that they'll let you in the doors. What I can do is destroy my standing in the medical community by pushing you under their noses! Would that be enough for you? Do I have to profess to every tight-lipped, overblown physician from here to Kent about your skills or great desire to be a doctor? What satisfies, Miss Renshaw? What requirement would you have me fulfill to prove my feelings for you?"

"Do you truly have feelings for me?"

"Now? You want me to say it now? We're in the midst of yet another delightful argument revolving around my villainous character. I'm exhausted because I've been at a friend's wife's bedside and narrowly escaped watching him become a widower. And while I'd hoped to return home and play out some tender scene of reconciliation, you, Miss Renshaw, are making me question my own sanity! You've pushed and pulled me until I'm not sure where I'm going, Gayle. But *now*? Did you want me to profess my heart now?"

"No! Yes!" She put her hands on her cheeks, horrified. "I don't know what I want anymore! I've forgotten who I am! I want to hear nothing from you! You're so charming and quick! You tell Whitfield what he wants, your patients what they need, and so what's to stop you from telling me whatever sweet lies you think I'm hungry to hear? Don't worry! You don't have to prove anything to me! I'm foolish enough to take you on faith and believe everything you say!"

"You're impossible! Why can't you accept that I'm just trying to protect you?"

"I don't need your protection!"

"Like hell you don't! A lady isn't supposed to go out in

public without wearing gloves, much less
man's hands! How do you think they'll feel
of you running bare hands all over people's l
for a fee, Gayle! Instead of seeing it as a wish to
doctor, they're going to run you out for being some aberration of nature, or worse, just a misguided whore!"

She gasped in shock. "How dare you!"

"Here! Here's the kind of gift that every addle-headed
light-skirt longs for! Here! Take it, Miss Renshaw! Here's
what I apparently think of you! Take the damn thing and
leave me be! For I swear, I cannot win the day!"

He dropped the wrapped bundle on the desk, the weight
of it making an ominous thud that rattled his pens and
lamps. His head was pounding from another one of his
wretched migraines. He grabbed one of the prepared paper
packets from the top drawer of his desk and dropped it into
his pocket.

"I'm going to call on a friend and see if I can't clear my
head. Stay here, Gayle. It's over."

"What are you saying?"

A firm knock at the door reminded her that the world
hadn't disappeared into the cold void that enclosed her
chest.

"A runner, doctor. You're needed." Carter imparted the
news and hesitated just long enough for Rowan's reply.

Rowan read the note quickly. It was a summons from
Lady Pringley, and Rowan hated the taste of the bit in his
mouth. But she was as good an excuse as any to step away.
"Tell Theo. I'll be right down."

Carter closed the door and Gayle sprang forward trying
to stop him. "Rowan, wait!"

"It's fate, the delay of Whitfield arriving and this ridiculous fight. It's better this way." He shook his head. "Good-
bye, Miss Renshaw. Please believe me when I say that I
wish you every happiness and success in your future en-
deavors."

"You have every right to be angry. I shouldn't have—"

"It's over. But I'm a man of my word. I'll find another

...cian with credentials far weightier than mine willing ...take you on and see to it that your education continues without interruption—even if it means shipping you off to Paris or New York. Naturally, I'll return every pound you paid for this adventure, Miss Renshaw. You deserve to be challenged and taught so that that keen mind of yours can flourish. But more important, you deserve to be safe and happy."

"W-what? But I thought . . ."

"First of all, whoever made that threat against my circle and poisoned Caroline Blackwell is still out there, and I'm not willing to put your life at risk. I've fallen in love with you, Miss Renshaw, and that makes a cavalier inclusion in my apparently dangerous existence impossible."

For the first time in her life, words failed her, which unfortunately may have looked like acceptance of his statement as he went on, "Secondly, I cannot be the man who continually makes the same mistakes. I cannot once again be more in love with a woman than she is with me. I cannot sacrifice my livelihood or my honor or live my life in half measures for the joy of another. I had foolish daydreams about how you would come to value me, Gayle. About how you would come to see me as a partner and understand that the passion between us was just a symptom of a greater happiness within our reach. But you don't want me."

He opened his bag and began to make a quick inventory of his tools and supplies, as efficiently and coldly as if he were leaving her with instructions for their next experiment upstairs. "You want your credentials and to be respected. I can't argue against either one of those desires. I'd hoped that they weren't things that would exclude me or eliminate my chances, but . . . You also want your independence. I finally realized that that at least is something I can give you by letting go."

"No."

"I told Whitfield what he wanted to hear, Gayle. But one day, you'll need to tell the truth—to your family, to your peers, and to pompous windbags just like Whitfield. And I love you too much to stand by when they tear you down and vilify you for it. But that's what you want. Someone who will step aside and let you prove yourself. But what kind of man can do that? Raise your hopes only to watch you practically burn at the stake? Another man, Gayle. Not me."

"Rowan, I—"

"Not me, Gayle. I will never be that man." He snapped his bag shut and walked out, the door firmly closing behind him, convinced that hell would never hold more threat of pain or torture than losing the love of his life.

* * *

Tears blinded her as the door shut, and Gayle used the heel of her hand to try to push them away and hold them back. She wasn't even sure what had happened. She'd felt so vulnerable, aware that she was losing her heart and her resolve along with it. She wasn't sure what was possible anymore. The passionate interlude in the carriage had left her shaken. His touch shattered and transformed her into a woman she didn't recognize.

And she'd avoided him like a spoiled child afterward, instead of confessing her feelings and trusting him—she'd hidden in her room behind a dead-bolted door.

Like a coward.

Again.

And when finally she'd heard the bell heralding his return and come downstairs, unwilling to wait, determined to catch him and apologize before he retired or before another night passed without his touch—she'd found herself on the other side of the library door, listening like a thief.

Only to hear him speak to that horrible man Whitfield . . .

She'd overreacted.

Again.

The bundle he'd dropped on his desk caught her eye, and with trembling hands she unwrapped the cloth only to find the anatomy book she'd admired the first morning she was there. It was the one he'd taken from her hands—a book so expensive and beautiful it made her chest ache to look at it. He'd had it rebound and retooled in green leather with her initials on the binding. She opened the book to the first page, and the inscription inside leapt off the paper.

The first words conveyed that it had been first given to him by his father.

Medicine is only a tool, my son, and at the end of the day, all you can ask of yourself is that you did your best to save what could be saved, to let go when required, and to never forget the difference between the two. Use your head.

Under it, in Rowan's familiar and nearly illegible handwriting, she read:

Gayle, as wise as my father may have been, I think I can honestly add: Use your heart. I believe in you, and so long as you follow your instincts, I know that every patient you treat will benefit from your touch.

Ever yours, Rowan

Chapter
26

Lady Pringley's maid escorted him up to her parlor, and Rowan understood immediately that this was not an emergency after all. His usual route to her bedroom was rerouted to a formal and unwelcoming room in drab olive green.

Dear God in Heaven! I cannot win the day.

His patroness didn't have a headache or an attack of her nerves, but she did have a guest. Mrs. Jane Hamilton was sitting to her right, her posture ramrod straight in a gunmetal gray traveling dress. From the grim look on the woman's face and the electric excitement on Lady Pringley's, Rowan knew that whatever venom the woman had been spitting in her own sitting room in Standish Crossing had just arrived in Town.

"Dr. West! You see, I told you he would come quickly enough!" Lady Pringley's color betrayed just how much she was enjoying her role in the unseemly drama. "Dr. West is my most favorite physician and a delightful man, Mrs. Hamilton. When I received your inquiry, I knew immediately that there was some misunderstanding in play, but"—she indicated a chair for Rowan—"I knew Dr. West would appreciate a friendly hand and intervention to help sort things out. Isn't that right, doctor?"

The last of my luck just ran out.

"How fortunate for me that Mrs. Hamilton was able to find such a conscientious and concerned ally in you, Lady Pringley. But there was no need for a third party, Mrs. Hamilton. My door has always been open to you."

"Do not think to charm me now! I'll not have it!" Mrs. Hamilton pulled out a handkerchief, wiping away real tears of frustration. "You're a villain! And I knew there wasn't a soul who would believe me! But I've kept a close watch on you and cut out every article or word I could find on your life here. At the time, I thought it was for my own wretched study, but now, I see that it was Fate! For how else would I have known that Lady Pringley was your patroness?"

"Fate?"

"You have my niece! You've lured her here somehow and corrupted her in some sick game to destroy me."

So much for that imaginary trip to the Continent! Another look at Lady Pringley and he knew she was in gossip heaven at the moment, absorbing every acid-tipped word out of Mrs. Hamilton's mouth. Her ladyship was ready to burst with excitement to hear what he had to say in his defense and unconsciously had leaned forward so as not to miss anything.

"I have no desire to destroy you, Mrs. Hamilton."

"You have my niece, Miss Gayle Renshaw, do you not? Are you denying that she is . . . How can I phrase this, Dr. West, without fainting away from revulsion? Is she a 'guest' in your home?"

"Mrs. Hamilton." He took a slow steadying breath and deliberately kept his eyes on Jane Hamilton's, his voice low and soft. "Come back with me to my brownstone and see for yourself. You and I are bound by the tragic loss of your daughter, Charlotte, and I cannot imagine that you truly wish to discuss all of this here."

"I . . ." She wavered, as if suddenly realizing the unforeseen risks of the scene she'd created. "I thought if your patroness knew you had Gayle . . . I wanted to punish you. . . ."

He nodded. "Of course." He bowed to Lady Pringley before holding out his hand to escort Jane out. "Your ladyship will excuse us. I cannot say how much I will miss being in your service."

The woman sputtered her disappointment at being denied the rest of the story but couldn't prevent their retreat. *Sadly, she's guaranteed to keep me now, if only to try to wheedle the rest of the tale out of me later.*

The ride back to the brownstone was brief enough, but to Rowan it seemed an hour as he sat like a man awaiting his executioner. Mrs. Hamilton refused to even look at him, and he decided it best to wait for the privacy of his study. *There is simply no mercy in this world.*

"Carter, we'll be in the study. Let Miss Renshaw know to come down as her aunt is here." He led Mrs. Hamilton up the stairs and invited her into the private sanctuary of his study to shut the door firmly behind them. "How did you know to look for her in London?" he asked calmly.

She pulled a letter out of her reticule. "She's been writing to me all along. But when she sent this last vague missive full of descriptions of shops and her 'travels,' I recognized the stationery as yours. I'd stared too many hours at your correspondence with Charlotte to not know the paper and spy your initials in the watermark."

"Fair enough."

"How could you, Rowan? Have you some vendetta against my family? Against myself? How many young women would you destroy to achieve your goals?"

Gayle's voice rang out from the doorway, her cheeks flushed with her race down the stairs. "Did he send for you?"

"He most certainly did *not* send for me!" Aunt Jane stomped her foot at the impertinent suggestion. "The demon was perfectly content to keep you without a word to your nearest and dearest and without lifting a finger to persuade you to return to safety or sanity!"

"I am the one who decided to go! I am a grown woman and not some child to be chased after, Aunt Jane!"

"Then act like a grown woman! Mr. Chester made you a decent offer, and thanks to my efforts, the poor man still believes that you're in France picking out wallpaper and china!"

"I'm not marrying Mr. Chester! I'm going to be a doctor! And Dr. West had nothing to do with my departure, Aunt Jane! It was my idea to come to London and—"

"Nothing to do with it, you say? Were you about to protest his innocence in this situation? He killed my poor Charlotte, and now, he's turned you into a whore! You are in no position to defend him, Gayle. He is despicable, and for some reason I cannot fathom, you've *housed* yourself with the worst man living—knowing how I feel!" She started to cry, overwhelmed with unhappiness. "How could you, Gayle? Knowing I hate him more than anyone in the world? Knowing . . ."

"What do I know?" Gayle knelt at her feet. "Say it, please, I beg you. What happened to Charlotte? For you've never said it! I only knew there were secrets and I only knew that I needed the leverage of secrets to get what I wanted. *I* was the villain that put my own desire to become a doctor above everything else. But I have to know what horrible hammer I've been swinging about like a stupid child! I have to know, Aunt Jane!"

Mrs. Hamilton covered her face with her hands but finally looked at Gayle and began to speak. "Sh-she was always an emotional girl. You don't remember, as your visits were so infrequent, but she was . . . beautiful and sweet. *He*"—she bobbed her head in Rowan's direction, clearly unwilling to speak his name—"came to Standish Crossing to stay with a university friend, young Mr. Hedley of the

Briarstone Hedleys, the ones I had always admired. I approved of him by association, and when he showed a great interest in Charlotte . . . it was a nice bit of romance." The last few words were confessed in a whisper. "He was going to India, but Charlotte didn't seem to want to hear of it. She was . . . so in love . . . so desperately in love. I should have seen how unhealthy it was, how unseemly she felt, but I thought it would be good for her to wait for his return. It would temper her nature and teach her patience and the rewards that come with it."

Jane's voice filled with grief and fury. "He must have known! He must have known what state he was leaving her in! He . . . used her. He cruelly used her and sampled her maidenhood, and then he simply . . . left."

Rowan stood with his back to them, his hands pressed against the shelves. Gayle stared at him for a minute, a part of her wishing he would interrupt the tale and change its course, but another part of her was beyond desperate to know the truth at last.

Mrs. Hamilton went on, anger increasing the power of her speech. "I can only imagine her terror and anguish! To be left like a whore with your bastard inside of her and only the promise of your return! Charlotte was too sweet to bear it! She said nothing to any of us but sought out some tinker of a butcher to get rid of it, and . . ."

Jane stood, her hands fisted and wringing her reticule into an unrecognizable mass. "She suffered terribly. The infection and the fever were . . . It was a nightmare and then she was gone. I didn't know what had happened at first, but when the surgeon's wife told me the truth of what her husband had discovered . . . You killed her, Rowan. You did this to my child, and I cursed your name and prayed that God would make you suffer the way my child suffered."

Rowan's head dropped and he was the very image of defeat. "I'm sorry for your loss, Mrs. Hamilton. And while I doubt it will comfort you, your curses worked." He turned back to face them both, raking one hand through his hair with a sigh. "I spent over a year in a dungeon in India in the dark, hungry and tortured. It was . . ." He straightened his shoulders, drawing himself up to his full height. "But it was nothing compared to your suffering, Mrs. Hamilton."

Gayle stood on shaky legs. The physical change he'd undergone was explained by his tale of imprisonment, but where was his protest? Where was his denial? *Could it be true? It explained so much if it was true. His guilt from a distance. His confession. Was the Rowan she'd come to love the kind of man to use a young girl and leave her defenseless?*

"Rowan?"

"I will leave you, ladies, to your conversation. I believe my part in this is concluded."

"Rowan!" Gayle took one step toward him, but the unmistakable pain in his eyes warded her off.

"It's been a long and unbelievably eventful day. I'm going to stay at a friend's." He bowed briefly and withdrew without another word.

"You are on a first-name basis with him, I see." Aunt Jane finished wiping her eyes, and then blew her nose. "Well? What have you to say for yourself?"

Gayle turned back to face her. "I should apologize."

"You *should*? Does that mean that you are going to?" Mrs. Hamilton's sarcasm was unpracticed but potent. "Is it even possible for you to see what you've done?"

"I've lied and deceived you. It was terribly wrong to pretend to go on tour instead of telling you what I intended."

"Is that all? You're only sorry for lying?"

"You told me to act like a grown woman, Aunt Jane. So, yes, I'm sorry that I lied."

"And the rest of it? You disregarded my feelings and my grief and ran off to be with a man that you know I completely despise! And for what? Some nonsensical quest to play at being a doctor? You are delusional if you think anyone will allow it! But for this, you sever ties with your family and throw yourself off the edge of the social world?"

"It isn't nonsense, but yes . . . if you put it in those terms, then, yes. To become a physician, I was willing to give up anything. I love you, Aunt Jane, and so I lied rather than confront you with my dreams. I knew you wouldn't understand. But that was a mistake." Gayle's voice grew stronger as she continued. "I was willing to become cruel and use any means necessary to get what I wanted. But that was a mistake. I was willing to break my own heart—and Rowan's. But that was a mistake."

Mrs. Hamilton stood slowly, staring at her as if she'd transformed into a stranger. "Y-you have your inheritance, Gayle. Come back with me to Standish Crossing. As you said, it was a mistake."

Gayle shook her head. "I'll never go home again."

"You don't mean that."

"Good-bye, Aunt Jane. I'm going to stay and beg Rowan to continue my education. And if he refuses, I'm going to accept his offer to find another doctor who will further my studies, even if I have to leave England to make it happen. I'm going to earn my medical degree and I'm going to become a doctor. As you said, I have my inheritance. I'm not going to hide or lie anymore."

"You would do this? Knowing what he is?"

Gayle nodded. "He's paid for his mistakes. I can't ask him to look back anymore."

Mrs. Hamilton's cheeks reddened, her eyes filling with tears. "I shall wish you well, then. Consider yourself cut off, Gayle. You have no family to speak of and I—I will always feel as if I've failed you."

"You never have failed me. I'm going . . . to miss you, Aunt Jane, but I pray that one day you'll think fondly of me again and understand that I only meant to improve myself and help others. I never wanted to hurt you, but I have. And for that, I will be eternally sorry."

Aunt Jane gathered up her skirts and, without a word, turned her back on Gayle and left the brownstone.

Once she was alone, Gayle felt the tears start falling down her cheeks and she did nothing to stem the tide. *I meant what I said about begging him to continue my education and doing all that I could to become a physician. But I omitted how I intend to beg him to marry me. . . .*

But how exactly do you beg a man to love you again?

Chapter
27

After a night at a hotel, Rowan decided that he would check on Caroline before heading home. Poor Theo had borne the brunt of the excitement yesterday, but he was glad to see a familiar face as they set out for the morning's errand. Rowan's head was pounding again, and he remembered that he'd picked up his headache powders before he'd left yesterday.

"There's a small glimmer of good fortune," he whispered to himself, retrieving the small packet from his inside coat pocket. "Hell, I think I've even got a small bottle of water to mix it with. . . ." Rowan opened his bag to find the vial, but one of the city's infamous potholes caught a carriage wheel and he had to juggle the packet to keep from spilling white powder everywhere.

Bitter almonds. Bitter, spoiled almonds. Acrid.

The smell was distinct and not at all what he expected. He used a gloved hand to brush off the small amount he had managed to upend on his sleeve, and gingerly brought it to his nose for closer inspection.

Not my remedy. Not even close. Looks the same, but the smell . . .

It's cyanide.

"My God, I would have taken enough to kill a man twice over and been dead before we crossed Regent's." Rowan refolded the packet with careful hands, waiting for the fear to pass so that he could think clearly.

For a few fleeting seconds, he wondered if it had been Gayle. But what grudge would she have had against Ashe? He didn't see the connection. So who, then? Fitzroy wasn't even a remote possibility. The man had the integrity of a bishop and would never risk his reputation in such an obvious way.

He used his fist to pound on the carriage wall and alert Theo. "Change of plans! Go to Rutherford's!"

For long minutes, Rowan felt as if the world had frozen into a stillness of time. *Was* Gayle capable of such a thing? She was aware of his headaches and had access to his pharmacy. There was no cyanide in the house, but he'd sent her to the chemists and—

No. As far as we've come, I won't go any further down that road. Gayle is no murderer.

He examined the small white square in his palm. Death in a packet so innocuous and inviting made him marvel at how close he'd really come to losing his life.

One pothole. It all came down to one single pothole.

He was no stranger to death. After India, he'd fully understood just how precarious his own existence was and how things could change in a single breath. But even so, this was different.

It didn't feel like Fate or the hand of God pushing a man one way or another down a path. This was the malign interference of a human being trying to destroy someone else. This was an act of murder that squelched philosophical thoughts of natural order or ethereal loss.

By the time he'd arrived at Michael's rented rooms, Rowan was a man devoid of feeling. He'd lost Gayle, potentially his reputation, and now, nearly, his life.

I have nothing left to lose.

Michael's apartment was uniquely appointed, and there wasn't a delicate curve or breakable object to be found anywhere. He'd bought slightly oversized chairs and rugged tables and even gotten his landlord to provide two large beds to push together so that Michael could sleep across them without his feet hanging off the end. It wasn't so much that Michael was a giant, but being nearly seven feet tall, his friends knew he hated being treated like one. And in his own rooms, he simply *fit* and was allowed to relax.

Rutherford greeted him, openly surprised to have Rowan at his door. "Has something happened?"

"I found poison in my headache medicine." Rowan held out the small packet. "I was on my way to see Caroline. It's almost pure cyanide."

Michael took the offending object and laid it on the table. "Don't you keep your own medication in your study?"

"Yes, or in my bag."

"Then you know I have to ask if you think that Miss Renshaw has anything to do with this?"

"No."

"Rowan." Michael gestured for him to be seated and the men settled in to talk. "She arrived rather suddenly, didn't she? And while I've only gotten bits and pieces from an unreliable source named Blackwell, I take it she wasn't entirely welcome and that you hadn't been getting along."

"Gayle wouldn't poison me."

"Why not?"

Rowan took a deep breath and let it out as slowly as he could. Rutherford was an astute man and a good friend, and Rowan knew that whatever was said between them would be held in the strictest confidence. "The truth is that Miss Renshaw wouldn't have poisoned me because she needs me to teach her everything I know and to assist her in becoming a physician. She's my apprentice and I haven't outlived my usefulness."

"Your apprentice," Michael echoed softly.

"I've ended it. But I'd gathered the packets before yesterday's falling out, so there you have it. She didn't poison me. She might wish she had after everything that's happened, but . . ." It was a depressing revelation. There would be no joyful proclamation of her love in the future. Gayle wasn't going to give in to maudlin nonsense or sacrifice her freedom. He shook his head. "She wasn't going to kill her one and only potential employer and means to achieving her goal of becoming a doctor."

"You're in love. Ashe had it right, didn't he?"

"He did. I'm in love with her, Michael, but it doesn't matter now. It's too complicated to be resolved, and I've told her how I feel so I can set it behind me with a clear conscience." He tried to push it all aside. *It doesn't matter now. Gayle's heard the worst and there's no recovery. I should have thought of it myself. Why waste time spouting on about how much I love her and wish to protect her? She's so contrary, she'd have stayed just to torture me. But Mrs. Hamilton was able to cut the cord, and I should be grateful.* "The most important thing is that she'll be safely away from this mess probably by tomorrow morning. And since we've eliminated her as a suspect . . ."

"Our villain is close," Michael noted, picking up the sealed packet to think. "They'd have to have intimate knowledge of you to know that you have these headaches and that you take your remedies. Your apothecary?"

"It's too obvious, isn't it? Fitzroy's entire professional reputation and career would be over in a single whisper."

"Someone else in your household?" Rutherford probed.

Rowan grew silent. "They're family, Michael. I'm not some blue-blooded thing to push people about because they're in my employ. If any of them had a complaint, I would hope that I would know it."

"You're sure?"

"It's not even a faint possibility. It's a small household, Michael. We live under the same roof, and most of them have been with me since I was a child. I'd give my own life to . . ." Something in him stirred, and Rowan lost his train of thought.

"Rowan?" Michael leaned forward, instantly concerned. "I think I know where we need to go next, and if I'm right"—he stood in one fluid motion—"then we'll have our hands on our poisoner and be one step closer to finding out who's been trying to destroy the Jaded."

Chapter
28

It had been the longest night of her life. Waiting for his return this time was far worse than the evening Gayle had waited in the salon for him that first night. After her aunt had left, she'd gone to her room and given in to her tears.

He'd ended it, but not to the point of throwing her out. He'd offered to find her another position, but her pride was at war with her heart. She'd packed and repacked her bag, sorting and re-sorting her things until she'd lost count of her efforts. She tried to sleep and finally managed a few hours before habit woke her up in time for her daily duties.

After breakfast, Gayle kept watch for him on the ground floor. But after a while, her confidence wavered and she'd restlessly returned back up the stairs to the laboratory to walk about the worktables, wiping down the surfaces and aimlessly inspecting the glass vials and beakers on the shelves.

She refused to leave without speaking to Rowan one last time.

Finally, she passed the time transcribing his notes, marveling at the meticulous care and kindness of her beloved mentor. Every line reflected his character, and she felt stupid to have taken so long to really see it.

Aunt Jane had it all wrong. A man like this . . . Rowan couldn't have known that he'd fathered a child before he left on that journey. If passion had overtaken them just before he departed, it would have been too early for her to show any signs of being with child. If he were concerned, he would have asked, and Charlotte might have assured him that she was fine—perhaps innocently unaware of her condition.

He'd have trusted her judgment. His research was important to him, and he'd have wanted to go urgently enough to accept her at her word.

It made sense to her. She knew what it was to be swept away by his touch, and she couldn't blame Charlotte for succumbing—especially if she had the promise of marriage and no reason to doubt him. *I know what it is to love Rowan West and to want to throw caution to the winds. If Cousin Charlotte did the same, I am the last one to cast blame!*

Gayle wanted to believe the best of Rowan, and she knew from her own experience that he was noble and sincere enough to punish himself by accepting full responsibility for Charlotte's death.

That was why he'd demonstrated such restraint in the carriage. He'd been down that road only to taste guilt and tragedy. He wasn't going to put either one of us through it again.

As for their tangled relationship, she was determined to make it right.

He dismissed me. But he also said he loved me.

There has to be a way to make it right.

He'd bravely taken the brunt of the consequences of his actions. She realized that in comparison, her own less than forthright approach to her apprenticeship, to her goals, and even to him was far different. He'd challenged her to tell the truth, and she had.

Aunt Jane reacted just as I thought she might, but it wasn't the end of the world. And if I'd been honest with her from the start, there might have been a happier outcome. But that's something I'll never know.

It doesn't matter. When he returns, I'm going to promise never to lie again because I do truly want him to love me—and I don't think he can if he can't respect me.

The door opened, and Gayle turned with her heart in her throat, but it was Florence, bobbing a curtsy and coming in with an empty laundry basket. "I know it's not Monday, but the house was . . . the schedule is a bit off, miss. I've come to see to your room, so don't let me interrupt your work."

Gayle nodded, wilting a little. "Thank you, Florence." It was hard to believe that with all the commotion downstairs, the house had missed the dramatic changes and events swirling around them, but she took comfort in the unassuming return to routine that Florence's cheerful announcement heralded.

She looked back at the last note she'd copied after Florence shut her bedroom door behind her for privacy.

A. Featherstone—for all the distractions of our latest invention of "overexcited blood," may genuinely have nervous condition and suffer insomnia. Waiting to hear from L. W. regarding the new litter's development but sure that canine solution is at hand!

"He's going to give the woman a puppy for Christmas." Gayle sighed. *You truly are a hopelessly kindhearted man—so how is it that I could have been so cruel?*

"You work too hard." Peter James's voice interrupted her as he entered the room, moving with his usual familiarity and ease. "But there's no surprise, is there?"

"You're back! I mean . . . so soon."

"After I checked his supplies, I noted that Dr. West was short on a few things." He held up a small brown paper-wrapped package. "See?"

"Oh! Of course." She managed a weak smile. *If one more person comes in that door and isn't Rowan, I think I'm going to faint.* "Here, I'll just take it and put everything away."

"No need, no—"

He was interrupted as the bell rang, jingling merrily on the wall, and they both looked over to note it. Gayle bit her lip in confusion as it was the bell that heralded Rowan's departure. *But how was that possible? I've been waiting for his return! I must have missed it in the night, packing in my room and wailing like a child.*

He recovered with a smile. "No need."

"Please." She reached for the package, gently trying to take it from him. "I need to stay busy and it's no trouble to—"

"No!" He jerked it out of her hands, and they both froze in shock at the force of his outburst and at the sight of the brown paper box hitting the ground between them only to fall open. "It's . . . I'm meant to put it away," he finished lamely.

Gayle was afraid to bend down to get it but was also beginning to feel a miserable awareness of how weightless the package had seemed when she'd held it briefly and how strange Mr. James's eyes appeared. She looked down, and a single glance confirmed that it was nothing more than folded paper, an empty shell. "I-I didn't mean to interfere."

He knelt quickly, gathering it up. "It was stupid of me. But I see the good doctor's just setting out. I expected it would be a busy day and I only wanted to see you again." He stood, putting the paper in his pocket. "A foolish ruse, Miss Renshaw. I apologize for it, but when I thought about what I'd said the other day, I worried I'd stepped off the path a bit too quickly."

Gayle felt a rush of awkward misery flood her stomach. *Please don't make me say it directly, Peter. You've been such a good friend. I don't want to hurt your feelings!* "Mr. James, you've troubled yourself over nothing. But I truly don't want Dr. West to misunderstand your presence here and—"

"It doesn't matter what he thinks. I meant to say as much the other day, but you do have a way of distracting a man, Miss Renshaw. I got so busy trying to demonstrate my good manners, deferring to employers and all that, but that's easy enough when you know the problem is about to solve itself."

"W-what problem?"

"You want to make more of yourself. I understand that, because we're cut from the same cloth, you and I." He took a step toward her. "You don't have to wait for your future, Miss Renshaw. We could walk out of this house together right now. I have money enough now for my apothecary shop, and I won't mind one bit if you'd like to set up your own little medical practice! It can only enhance my business to have a good midwife on hand, you see?"

"Mr. James!"

"Come with me. You don't need these arrogant London pricks to tell you your worth. I knew the first time I saw you that you were a treasure that a man would be a fool to overlook!"

Gayle took a deep breath, her heart pounding in alarm as his language and manners became more and more coarse as he spoke. "I'm flattered, but I'm sorry to disappoint you, Mr. James. I have no desire to leave—"

"I know how it must be." He cut her off, pacing a bit and wringing his hands. "It's sudden, this. And I haven't been able to spend the time I wanted . . . I'd have courted you properly if there'd been time! If West had allowed it! Fitzroy thinks I'm his dog, fetching this and delivering that—grateful for whatever crumbs he throws me. He pays pennies and then talks to me like I'm a fool!"

"I'm sorry. But you cannot think that I—"

"You defend Dr. West and deny it, but I know he's the same to you. And probably worse. Keeping you locked in like a prisoner slaving away for him and doing his best to keep me away from you. But we don't need them. Not any of them. We're not servants to lick their boots. I have three thousand pounds set aside now! Enough to open up my own storefront in a sweet little village somewhere. What do you think?"

"I think you're mad, Mr. James."

"You know I care for you, Miss Renshaw. I'm sure I've made that clear in my letter. And even with *him* dictating your response, I knew you felt the same for me."

"Where did you get three thousand pounds?"

His gaze darted away for an instant to study his shoes before he looked back at her, his eyes glittering with malice. "It doesn't matter! I have it and it's mine."

Three thousand pounds. Not a fortune exactly, but money enough to turn a greedy, ambitious young man's head. Enough to give him a start in some small venture and play on his dreams of being his own man. And who pays such a sum? For what deed?

Poison.

He had access and knew of Rowan's friends. . . .

He must have seen it in her face. "Don't think to tell him. You've no proof of anything. You're speculating now. I can see it in those pretty eyes the way your keen mind is trying to fit all the pieces together."

"Someone paid you three thousand pounds to poison Dr. West's friends. To what end?"

"Why would I ask the man, Gayle? It's nothing to me! Whatever the Jaded have done to deserve their fate, it's naught to do with my life. A bunch of rich blades who don't care anything about anyone but themselves, I'll warrant!"

"You said you liked Blackwell! You spoke so highly of him!"

Peter's face reddened, his expression getting tight and uncomfortable. "I may have admired his horses or envied him his conquests, but it's not like he's pulling up a chair at my dinner table, is he?" He kicked the table in frustration, the glassware rattling and breaking to make her jump. "It wasn't my choice to put him first on the list, Gayle! But as it didn't exactly go as planned, I've set it up so that the way is clear for us to go. No one will look in my direction, miss.

Your doctor's on the blocks next and you're free to leave with me as you like."

"My doctor? What are you saying?"

"There's talk of poisoning, Gayle. I had no choice. And then I realized I'd solve both of our dilemmas in one step. You aren't a slave to be treated like his property, and I knew you'd be glad to see him gone."

"W-what? What have you done to Rowan?"

"Let's just say that the next time the man has a headache, he'll never then have one thereafter. I thought to find the house already draped in black, but these things require patience. He's gone out on another call, so it's only a matter of hours, I'd say." Peter took a step closer, his expression calm, as if he'd gladly solved all her problems. "Don't think on it another minute. Come away with me. It's happiness I'm offering you, Gayle."

Nausea seized her at the threat to Rowan, her memory replaying every furrowed brow and hand through his hair while they'd fought, horrified to think that he might already be gone. . . . *And I've indirectly led to his death!*

She forced herself to breathe, doing her best to match Peter's strange calm so that she could think of a way to stall him or ring for Carter and get help. She consciously didn't look at her own door, all too aware that Florence was probably huddled in terror on the other side.

It was a nightmare.

"Dr. West is . . . a good man, Mr. James. You've been put in a terrible position by this person and you need an ally. Peter, you have to tell him what you've done. They . . . Rowan's friends are determined to find out who is trying to hurt them. You can't—"

"I'm not telling them anything! And you won't, either! I changed the records to make sure it looked like all the poisons were ordered by West. If you push and the police come looking, it'll be your Dr. West who appears to have dirty hands."

"No!"

"And either he's already dead and it looks like he killed

himself from the guilt of poisoning his friends, or he's walking about, and then you mark my words, he'll blame you when they come with a warrant for his arrest. West will point his finger at his new apprentice—so inexperienced and eager, he'll say, a woman too overwhelmed to keep track of the formulas or impatient with her progress and striking out against his patients to have her revenge."

"He would never do that! He's a compassionate person, and if you're in trouble with these people that have paid you—forced you to do this thing—he'll help you!"

"What trouble? I'm paid and it's done! No one even died at Blackwell's, so where's the crime, Miss Renshaw? And if West is gone, then there's no one to say a word."

"And what would they say if I'd shared my headache remedy, Mr. James?" Rowan's voice from the doorway wheeled Peter around, his expression twisting into the snarl of a trapped animal. He grabbed Gayle to viciously hold her in front of him, and picked up one of the largest shards of glass to press it against her throat.

"They'll say . . . you're running mad, Dr. West."

Rowan froze instantly, his eyes locked on only Peter James. "The packet's source seems obvious enough. They'll call you a murderer, because that's what you are."

"I haven't killed anyone!" Peter shook his head vehemently. "If you gave it to a patient, I'd accuse you of burking to please your pretty little apprentice and that would be all the papers would print, Dr. West! You'd need a body or two for her to practice, and there's not a school in the British Isles to give you one, so who's to say that Dr. Rowan West didn't lose sight of his ethics and poison his nearest and dearest in some twisted act of devotion? But you couldn't have given it to anyone! You wouldn't be standing there if you had!"

"Why not let Miss Renshaw go? She's naught to do with this—not really. You don't want to hurt her. She's fond of you, Mr. James."

"You don't deserve her! Locking her up here!" Peter's grip tightened on the glass as the blood from his cut fingers began to flow. Gayle was forced to hang on to his arm to keep herself upright and away from the razor-sharp edge underneath her chin. "I'm a better man than you are," James finished, the arm around her ribs squeezing her so possessively she struggled to breathe.

Rowan held as still as a statue. "You're a clever man, Mr. James. Imaginative and creative for a murderer."

"*No one* has died from any of it! Stop saying that word!"

"You're threatening to cut a young woman's throat, Peter. And I hate to correct you, but someone has died, so that's murder, isn't it?"

"No! I made the delivery to Blackwell's, but don't think I wasn't relieved when I heard that the missus had recovered. Besides, the papers would have shouted it from every rooftop if one of your precious peers had been poisoned and died!"

"Someone did die at Blackwell's, Peter." Rowan's voice was calm and level, and he shifted his weight ever so slightly onto the balls of his feet. "You killed an unborn child. Mrs. Blackwell was pregnant and she miscarried because of the poison *you* gave her. You murdered an innocent soul, Mr. James."

"No!"

"That's a stain on your soul you'll never wipe away. Hell awaits men like you, Mr. James," Rowan went on relentlessly, deliberately trying to upset the man and gain whatever advantage could be had.

"I'm . . . No innocents were to die! I was told . . ."

"What were you told, Mr. James?" Rowan asked softly.

"I was promised that no one who didn't deserve . . . Oh, God! What have I done?"

Gayle whimpered as the glass grazed her throat and Peter's viselike grip began to pull her off her feet, but then it loosened as her assailant's mind absorbed his guilt. Her heels began to kick out as she scrambled for purchase, and she feared that she was one slip away from the jagged point severing her artery. "R-Rowan!"

"Who?" Rowan asked, the intensity of his need to know

was palpable as he moved another step closer, all too aware of Gayle's dilemma. "Who said no innocents were to die? Who paid you to poison the Jaded?"

At the mention of the Jaded's enemy and his unnamed employer, Peter's eyes grew wide with alarm and Rowan sensed that some internal scale had just been tipped. "Gayle! Kneel!"

Rowan lunged for him just as Gayle dropped from Peter's hands, kneeling on the floor and falling out of harm's way. He caught Peter's forearms and they fell together in tandem against the table, the crunch of glass and the grunt of effort the only sound as they fought.

Gayle crawled away only to turn back in horror as the gentle man that she'd known and loved was forced to battle with the maniac that had once posed as Peter James. Rowan couldn't let go of Peter's wrist as the younger man still clutched the treacherous daggerlike shard of glass, and for a few seconds, it was a contest of strength and will as each man tried to wrest control of the deadly edge.

Rowan released his hold on Peter's shoulder, and without warning, swept his arm up to break Peter's grip on him and struck Peter with the heel of his hand underneath the man's chin. Almost simultaneously, he drove Peter's hand down on the table, and the shard went skittering onto the floor where it broke into a hundred pieces. Peter screamed as the debris on the table's surface was pressed into his flesh, and relaunched himself at Rowan—a man possessed.

They fell to the floor together, glass glittering in the lamplight on their coats to give the scene a strange fairy-like quality that belied the violence and blood that was starting to appear in smears and smudges everywhere. Peter struck Rowan with his fist, catching him off guard and gaining the upper hand for a breath or two.

Gayle screamed. "Stop! Please, stop!"

But neither man heeded her, locked in what had become a life-and-death struggle. They rolled across the floor, striking one of the worktables only to send another volley of glass and chemicals to the floor around them.

Then, instead of pushing Peter away, Rowan suddenly pulled him close, as if to embrace him, and whispered in his ear. "That hell . . . for murdering . . . Blackwell's firstborn . . . Your friend who paid you . . . will be the one to send you off to it, Peter . . . when they find out . . . that you've failed."

"No! I can't fail!" Peter James got a hand around Rowan's throat and began to squeeze with all of his might.

Rowan managed to grind out the words, "You . . . already . . . have."

The blood on Peter's hands made them too slippery to hold on for long, and Rowan knocked him off to take in huge healing gulps of air. Peter struggled to his feet, his eyes full of terror, making him look for all the world like a lost child. Rowan glanced to make sure that Gayle was behind him before he went on, determined to strike while he could. "Who hired you, Peter? Betray him and I'll do what I can for you."

"You don't know . . . A man like that . . . I'm dead if I talk."

"A man like that, Peter, who pays for death delivered in neat packages, doesn't appreciate messy delivery boys. He won't let you live. You'd better make you peace with God while you can, because you'll be dead before the police have you to their station. But if you tell . . ."

"I'm dead." Peter's eyes filled with tears, his spirit breaking under the strain. "I'm dead either way." Without warning, he pulled a vial from his pocket, drinking it in a single gulp as he ran to the opposite side of the worktable out of their reach.

"Peter, no!" Gayle watched in horror as he immediately began to gasp for air, his face growing red. She moved toward him, forgetting the danger and only wishing to help if she could.

"Damn it, no!" Rowan raced to reach him as well, but already Peter was wild with convulsions, gyrating in a macabre dance of agony and suffering. Rowan tried to catch at his coat, but Peter began cartwheeling in pain, screaming as the poison truly took hold.

He pulled away from them only to circle back and run toward them, a blood-covered banshee foaming at the mouth. Instinctively, Rowan shifted out of the way, taking Gayle into his arms to shield her as Peter James hurdled himself into the plate glass, shattering one of the great windows, and fell to his death in the narrow paved alley below.

Rowan let go of Gayle to look, battling the fury that came with knowing that no matter how much the man might have earned his end, he'd taken with him the name of their antagonist—and the secrets of the sacred treasure that he'd been after.

He turned back to attempt to say something comforting, praying that Miss Renshaw was none the worse for the excitement, but Gayle had fainted dead away.

Chapter
29

He took off his glass-embedded coat and lifted her gently up into his arms as Michael and several watchmen burst through the door, with Carter on their heels, armed with a fireplace poker. "Are you all right, doctor? You're bleeding!"

"I'm fine, the blood was his mostly. The poisoner is there." He nodded toward the shattered window. "He confessed and then committed suicide before I could stop him."

"Convenient that," one of the policemen commented, openly skeptical of Rowan's story. "Very helpful of your villain to off himself like that and save us the trouble, eh?"

"Wait!" Another policeman hailed them from the other end of the room at Gayle's bedroom door. "There's a girl here!"

A sobbing Florence limped out of Miss Renshaw's room, openly distressed to be the witness. "I . . . I was just straightening up . . . I usually tend to Miss Renshaw's room on Mondays but. . . ." She hiccupped and one of the younger policemen led her into the room and began to pet her hand and speak as soothingly as if she were a child.

"Shhh! There, now. You're a brave lamb, you are!" the ginger-haired policeman crooned, unaware of the glaring look his tenderhearted approach was earning him from his superior officer. But Florence clearly perked up at the attention and became much more coherent.

"I meant, I wouldn't have been up here . . . It's a bit of good luck I was. But I wasn't brave, at all! I was listening like a common gossip when Mr. James came in, I confess it. But when he started talking about how he'd poisoned people but made it look so Dr. West did it—I knew he was going to kill Miss Renshaw!" She started to cry, accepting her new beau's handkerchief with trembling hands. "And I just covered my head! Sh-she saved my life and I . . . I just hid under a bed!" she finished.

Rowan spoke up, still cradling Gayle. "You did the right thing, Florence. Don't trouble yourself. You stayed safe and we're all fine."

Florence sat up straighter and dried her eyes to attempt a weak smile of gratitude. "I never thought Peter James was such a thing! To kill his own sweetheart if she didn't see things his way!"

"Sweetheart?" the captain asked, standing at Rowan's shoulder.

"He was sweet on her, certain. Sending a note and hanging about. I just thought . . . what with him so eager to ask her to walk with him on her days off. N-not that she had any days off as I know of, but . . . he seemed nice enough, didn't he?" She looked directly at the young officer kneeling by her. "If I had a sweetheart, I'd have wished for a nice walk on my days off"—she leaned over to add carefully—"on Fridays."

The pair began to smile and the captain growled, "Ah! Young love!"

Michael mercifully didn't look at Rowan as he did his best to stay composed. But Rowan had had enough for one day. "Sort it out. I'm not going anywhere, but I need to get

Gayle to a bed, unless you'd like to interrogate me while I hold her."

Without waiting for a response, he carried her from the room to his bedroom below stairs.

Chaos unfolded, but it was a strange orderly chaos as he and Michael gave their statements and finally sorted out some of the mess. Carter was beside himself while Mrs. Evans immediately began overseeing the laboratory cleanup, ignoring the police who tried to lecture her about evidence and reports. As far as Mrs. Evans was concerned, justice was all well and good, but broken glass tracked all over her home was not a thing to be tolerated—and if they wished to serve the public good, they could each grab a dustpan.

One of the policemen had been assigned to sit with Gayle so that when she awoke, she could give her own interview without any chance of Rowan's influence or collusion, and Rowan had been asked to wait downstairs in his library until she had finished.

It was maddening.

A small crowd of curiosity seekers had gathered outside, and he could only imagine what the neighbors were thinking now. *Bodies flying out my windows and a small army of policemen tramping in and out of the house—at least Michael was here so I'm not suffering any looks about the loss of our low profile.*

The sting at the end of the barb was when Florence had tossed out that detail of Mr. James's attachment to Gayle. As one-sided as it may have been, he knew how it had sounded. Michael's look had been full of sympathy and it had grated against Rowan's nerves.

He knew that she wasn't romantically involved with anyone else—most especially with Peter James. But he had been jealous of the easy manner she'd had with Peter from the first, sharing her confidences and unguarded smiles. She'd trusted James and thought him kind.

The man was an unscrupulous thing capable of murder—

and not once did she call him a villain or a liar or look at him like he'd contracted leprosy. There's irony!

"You look like hell." Rutherford held out his handkerchief.

"I'm going to take that as a compliment. I'm trying not to think of all the places I'm going to be finding glass over the next few days." Rowan reached up to dig out a small triangle of clear crystal just above his cheekbone. "I feel like I've been peppered with buckshot."

Michael poured them both a whiskey and shut the library door to guarantee their privacy for a few minutes. "Any clues at all as to who hired him?"

Rowan shook his head. "Although, I think a return to Fitzroy's is warranted. Perhaps he'll remember a new customer coming about more recently or seeing James meeting with someone outside of the business."

"In the penny novels, the murderers always make a good speech about why they did what they did before throwing themselves out of windows."

"Are you telling me that you're reading penny novels these days?" Rowan jested, grateful for the levity of the conversation. "That's the second time in less than a week you've mentioned them, Rutherford. I'm buying you books for Christmas. It's settled. We need to improve your library, man."

"Nonsense. I've been in this library dozens of times and there's not a good blood-letting crime story in the lot." Michael glanced around as if assessing Rowan's collection. "No, sadly . . . so if you buy me books for Christmas, Rowan, be prepared for me to do you the same favor!"

"Hmm." He took a sip of the whiskey, letting the burn warm him slowly from the inside and waiting for the numbness to set in. "My grandfather would roll over in his grave. I think I'll put them in my medieval section just to spite him."

"You were quite heroic today, West." Michael downed his drink then refilled the glass. "Miss Renshaw is bound to be grateful for—"

"Don't." Rowan held up his hand, wincing a little as he did. "I know you mean well, Michael, but don't."

"I know. It's complicated." Michael held up his whiskey as if to toast the sentiment. "It always is, Rowan. It always is."

Chapter
30

Waking up in Rowan's bed, it took her a few seconds to realize where she was and absorb that the man sitting on a chair next to the four-poster bed was no one she had ever seen in her life. A police inspector was dutifully waiting for an interview, and Gayle sat up, openly confused at his inquiries. After a few minutes of painfully recounting her last moments with Mr. Peter James, Gayle felt the odd urge to cry.

"Did he say anything else?"

Gayle shook her head. "No." She'd done her best to relay the conversation word for word, praying that it made more sense to the inspector than it did to her. To add insult to injury, it was painfully clear that her interviewer was convinced that she was hysterical with all her babbling about Jaded gentlemen and Rowan's headaches.

"So the bottom line is that someone paid him three thousand pounds to try to poison Mr. Blackwell, and he tried to kill Dr. West . . . because he thought that Dr. West was unkind to you." The man finished his notes and gave her a sympathetic smile. "Honestly, I think it a clear-cut case of a lunatic with access to his employer's bins, but we'll check out everything." He touched his hat and stood to leave. "Thank you, Miss Renshaw."

As soon as he was gone, she groaned in humiliation and buried her face in the pillows. *Rowan is safe. After all of it, I just have to remember that Rowan is safe.*

"How are you feeling?"

She sat up with a squeak, thrilled to see Rowan leaning against the door's frame, his doctor's bag in hand. "I never faint."

"You cannot in good faith make that claim ever again, Miss Renshaw." He crossed over to a nearby reading table, setting his bag down on the floor next to a chair, and came over to retrieve the bedside lamp to improve the light for his apparently makeshift examination room.

"I'm perfectly fine! I don't need—"

He didn't let her finish. "*I* need, Miss Renshaw. *I* need you to get a few glass splinters out of my hands and forearms, and oddly enough, out of the back of my skull. Michael has hands like an overgrown thug, so if you don't mind . . ." He began to lay out a white bandage and place on it some tweezers, a long metal curved wire, and a small scalpel. "Consider it practice."

His expression and tone were neutral enough to catch her attention. She'd longed to see him, all the pent-up anxiety and practiced apologies fell away in the quiet that had fallen between them. No matter what else was about to unfold, for these few minutes, she would be given the chance to care for him and see to his needs.

She slid over to the side of the bed and reordered the tools to suit her reach, adding a saucer to collect the glass in. Then she surveyed the room, leaving him briefly to pour out some water into a basin, and returned with it, determined to do her best. "Would you . . . care to take your shirt off?"

Rowan slowly closed his eyes and shook his head. At last, he opened his eyes and carefully pulled up one bloodied sleeve past his elbow before taking a seat. "Here." He held out his left hand. "If you could start here, it's stinging like I've been swarmed with bees."

"We should use vinegar to clean the wounds, but"—she didn't risk looking up from his hand at his reaction— "perhaps it's better to just flush them all out afterward and then a warm bath." She picked up the tweezers and began the painful process with as gentle a technique as she could manage. His skin was warm beneath her fingers, and Gayle did her best not to smile at the simple pleasure of touching him again. "Try to relax, Rowan."

Rowan held still while she worked and finally began to speak. "The police are finished gathering their statements. It's over and they've taken away your Mr. James."

"He is most certainly not *my* Mr. James!" She looked up through her lashes and realized he was teasing. "You never believed he was."

"No, I never did. I know he's barely an acquaintance. I'm not blind to the knowledge that all those primal urges to strike out at any man between the ages of eighteen and eighty who might wander into your path are misguided."

"No, but it's flattering to think you might." She eyed the growing pile of red-stained bits of glass in the saucer. *All for me, these "stings" as he called them—would that I could kiss him for each one.*

"Very well then, I have to ask, who is Mr. Chester?"

"My parents' solicitor and he's a toad of a man."

Rowan nodded. "Good."

A spark of hope came to life as they fell into a comfortable banter, and Gayle prayed that this demonstration of a lighter mood might bode well. "When Aunt Jane suggested him, that's when I knew just how desperate she'd become for me. Perhaps I should send the unfortunate man a note of thanks."

"And what would you be thanking him for?"

"For being my Rubicon. I knew once I'd turned down Mr. Chester, there would never be any more offers." She poured a little more water over his wrist, and then went on. "Quid pro quo. I owe you a few answers, don't I?"

"I've never pressed you for them. You don't owe me anything, Miss Renshaw."

Gayle looked up at the neutral retreat in his tone, but his eyes were a storm of desire and uncertainty, and she plunged ahead. "Then consider this a gift, freely given, Dr. West. Aunt Jane was my father's sister, and I never understood much of the relationship between them, but they were never close. He left home when he was very young and apprenticed to become an engineer. My father was Richard Renshaw, and he designed a few machines for the textile industry and did very well. My mother was the only daughter of a knight. When my grandfather died, my family received his house and lands in the Lake District, and I remember my father teasing my mother for marrying beneath her. There was no title to pass down, but when I was little, before Emily died, I recall my father calling her Lady Rose to make her smile."

"You come from a good family, Gayle. But then, anyone would have guessed you weren't from South Wales . . . or raised by wolves."

She shook her head, turning to his right hand to continue working as she distracted him with her story. "No, but after they died, Aunt Jane seemed to think I should make a better match than the average girl in Standish Crossing—what with a knight for a grandfather!"

"How did your parents die?"

"I was told my father had cancer, but after studying with you these last few weeks, I'm sure it was something else. Near the end, he retreated to his hunting lodge and died there with an attendant at his side. It must have been something far more shameful than cancer of the stomach, because my mother began showing symptoms of an illness she refused to describe and took her own life a few days after he'd gone." Gayle pushed his sleeve up farther to gently pull the last few slivers from his forearm and elbow. "I've never told anyone, Rowan. Even Aunt Jane was told it was cancer and that my mother simply died of grief. People think I'm odd enough wanting to be a physician, but my mother's suicide would give their arguments a little more bite. So you see, perhaps I'm not from such a good family after all."

"Your secrets are safe with me."

She nodded, secure in his promise, then stood to find the cuts on his head, parting his thick russet hair to meticulously locate the offending pieces of glass that had been embedded into his scalp during his fight with Peter. It was a wicked trick to make sure she stood as close as she dared so that he would feel her warmth at his back, but Gayle was shameless in her campaign to draw him out. "You saved my life, Rowan. But how? How did you know it was Mr. James? I never thought of Mr. James as the kind of man to harm anyone, but somehow you knew. When he appeared and I heard the bell announce that you'd left on call, I had the worst feeling. And then when he started talking about the money and leaving London . . . I feared I'd be found dead on that floor."

"On my way to Blackwell's, I was going to take a headache powder but discovered by accident that it was poison. I went to Rutherford's instead, and Michael pushed me to consider that the poisoner might be a member of the household. And when I refused to believe it could be one of my own, because they're like family, it occurred to me that not everyone feels the same. Lately everyone I know in my field has been harping on how sentimental I am, and indulgent . . . because not everyone is when they run a business. And I thought of Fitzroy, and I knew I had to ask him the same questions that Michael was pressing on me. It started to come together, and when Fitzroy said that James had left for a delivery to my home and was already there and that we could just ask him directly—I just knew. I flew back to the brownstone while Michael went to the police to get help. As for the bells, anyone can trigger them, can't they? So I had Carter pull the bell to signal that I'd left to try to put Peter off his game. Then I came up to try to delay him long enough for the others to arrive and arrest him."

"And it worked. It was mesmerizing, Rowan, to hear you speak."

Reaching over to his bedside table, Rowan poured a glass of warmed cider out of the pitcher that Mrs. Evans had sent up and offered it to her. "I was going to try bribing him next, but that's when it all fell apart."

"No, thank you," she said, changing to the wire for one particularly elusive sliver at the crown of his head. "What was that about the Jaded? How do they come into play with all of this?"

"It's a long story, Miss Renshaw."

"Just this once, Rowan. I-I would very much like to hear you tell a long story."

For a moment, she was sure he would refuse, and that like Charlotte's tale, he would shield her from some truth in his past. But he took a deep breath, crossed his arms defensively, and spoke. "While I was India, my wild notion about tropical fevers had me off in Bengal, and when the Troubles began, I'm sad to say, I was obliviously filling up notebooks and rattling around with bug traps and my medical kit. My guides, however, were happy to deliver an Englishman to some insane raja who had decided to collect them. I never knew why, Gayle, but I spent most of my time in India in a dungeon in the dark wishing I'd stayed in London. There, the unheroic truth!"

"Oh!" Gayle was astonished.

"The other men I met in that hole became my very best companions, and I would not be standing here if it weren't for them. We had had no hope of escape, when suddenly, there was some sort of horrific attack on the place where we were held, and in all of the damage and confusion, the dungeon opened up and we walked out. Of the original eight, only six of us survived."

"The Jaded," she whispered, her brain beginning to spin with the implications of his tale. "But how is surviving such a dreadful experience a thing to make you all fearful of some murderer? Why are you being pursued?"

"Apparently, the treasure rooms weren't far off from

where we were and . . . we picked up a few pocketfuls on our way out the door. At the time, it was simply because we expected to have to bribe our way across the country, and after over a year, it didn't seem outlandish to think the landlord owed us a bit of compensation for our time. Naturally, we've kept all of that secret. I'm telling you only because I trust you with my life, Gayle."

"Thank you," she echoed, amazed. She put down her tools and pressed the cloth against his head, hoping to soothe his cuts. Then she put everything down to sit on the edge of the bed facing him. "Your secrets are safe with me."

"The bad news is that apparently, amidst all the jewels we took, we acquired something that has earned us a terrible enemy."

"What is it?"

"We don't know. If we knew, trust me, we'd be happy to return it to its owner if the price of keeping it is our lives—or the lives of those we love."

She shook her head, smiling sadly. "But, it's . . . so fantastical. I'm trying to picture you like a pirate with a hidden box buried in your garden full of diamonds, and it's—so silly."

"That would be silly. But my share was emeralds, and I've already told you where they're hidden."

"What! You never did!" She fisted her hands at her hips, slightly affronted. "I would have remembered a conversation like that, Rowan!"

"I told you that my fortune was tucked away in the books in my study. I meant it literally. I had the emeralds sewn into the spines of my reference books and favorite novels for safekeeping. Last year when the house was overrun in a search for the jewels, the thieves tore apart my furniture and upended everything. But they never thought to bother with dusty medical tomes or the family Bible."

"Then you really are the first West to make his fortunes on his travels."

"I'm not sure my father would have been proud of the

accomplishment. Stumbling into wealth isn't the same as earning it, Gayle. The Jaded have been wise enough to know it and steer clear of unwanted attention. At least, until recently . . ."

"My! You do lead a life of adventure, don't you?"

"Not always by choice," he conceded. "But now you understand why it's for the best that you've determined to leave."

"I don't want to go."

"Your bags are packed. Women intent on staying don't generally pack their things."

"I didn't . . . know what else to do. You'd left and after Aunt Jane went home, I . . . I don't want to go."

"I don't want you here."

"You don't mean that."

He held his ground, the granite in his eyes unyielding. "I'm not going to argue about this."

"Rowan, there have been so many misunderstandings between us—all of them fall at my feet. You have to accept that I'm so sorry for—"

He stood abruptly and took a step back. "Don't. Don't apologize. You are just as you should be, and if we've clashed, it's because we are each of us dancing over daggers and refusing to look down."

"I want to stay with you, Rowan." She also stood, stubbornly matching his every move.

"Your imaginary tour of the Continent is over, Gayle. For all your talk of independence and a lack of concern about anyone's opinions, you certainly went to great lengths to lie about where you were." He shifted his weight to lean against the bedpost. "Maybe it's time to stop lying and go home to Standish Crossing."

She stomped her foot in frustration. "It was a mistake to lie to Aunt Jane! But I'm not going anywhere, and if there's a gauntlet to be run, I'll do it. I've stood up to her, Rowan. I've made my choice, and it's you."

"And what of Charlotte? Have you decided to forgive me, Gayle, and just put the past aside?"

She started to say yes, but something in his eyes caught her attention and she froze. *I was going to, wasn't I? Because if you were so careless in your youth and so thoughtless, then . . . But Rowan was never careless or thoughtless. If he thought nothing of such things, then why not be careless with me? I was blackmailing him. I was horrible. What better way to keep me from interfering with the male world of medicine than to show me my place. If he truly were that kind of villain . . . he would never have protected me from an unwanted pregnancy.*

But he had.

He'd been careful.

I begged him to use me in that carriage.

Even in the heat of searing passion, Rowan had been careful.

Rowan took a step closer, studying her face. "Yes?"

"You told me once to use my own observations—not to rely on emotional sources to draw my conclusions and . . ."

"Yes?" he asked, the intensity of the question dismissing the last of her fears.

"You didn't overcome Charlotte. You never touched her, did you?"

He shook his head. "I never did."

"You never did. But Aunt Jane . . . It was natural to blame you and *you let her.*"

"I let her."

"Because you *did* love Charlotte and you wanted to protect her mother from the truth."

"Yes. I let it happen because the death of a child is a staggering blow. How could I add to Mrs. Hamilton's agony and smear the good name of her darling girl? To what end? Finger-pointing and some horrible hunt for the heart-broken boy residing somewhere in Standish Crossing? So that his life could be ruined, too?"

"But you'd have been cleared. Your reputation restored."

"It was too high a price to pay. And the shadow of it hadn't touched me here, until . . ."

"Until I arrived and brought all of those troubles to your

doorstep. And you'd come from Lady Pringley's! My God, the gossip that woman will create will ruin you!"

He shook his head. "Hardly. I averted most of it, and Lady Pringley's innate curiosity will keep her tethered to me forever. Women of good breeding have a strange weakness for men with dark and mysterious pasts." His smile was full of painful irony.

"I don't have a weakness for men with dark and mysterious pasts."

"No?"

"I have a weakness for you, but we've already established that you are the furthest thing from a villain imaginable, so my tastes clearly run toward respectable, handsome, kind doctors."

"One ghost banished doesn't solve our problems, Gayle. Whatever enemies I have, they aren't going to give up just because one of their puppets failed. You cannot stay."

"I'm not going anywhere!" She reached out and caught his arm. "If you know anything of me, surely you know that once I've set my mind on something, it's impossible to dissuade me."

"I can't—"

"I have a contract and a teacher. I have a friend and a lover. I have a home and a family. All my dreams, Rowan, are just within my reach, and all I have to do is not let go. I can't let go." Her eyes filled with tears. "I love you, Rowan."

He said nothing, and she seized on her chance.

"I've fought you on every turn. I thought that if I loved you I would be diminished into something or someone else. All my life, I've been *less* because I was a woman and told that I couldn't do what I wanted. But you've never said no. You've never made me feel like I was less of a physician or less of a person. And when you look at me, Rowan, God help me, I feel like I'm *more*."

"It would have been kinder to refuse you that night, Gayle, when you appeared in my home and demanded that I take you on as an apprentice." He ran a hand through his dark russet hair, his expression full of agitation and uncertainty. "A better man would have thought to protect you, even then. I want you to achieve your dream, but I know just how cruel and unyielding the world can be, and I don't know if I can bear to see you hurt."

"I can bear anything if I have you, Rowan." She gently caught his bloodied sleeve in her hand, her fingers moving up his arm above his injuries. "Anything."

"You could have said as much earlier and spared me some pain, Gayle." It was a gentle admonishment and she felt the weight of all her fears disappear like so much smoke.

"There wasn't time." She reached up to touch his face. "It seems when I'm not thinking, the words fly, but when it's truly important, I require preparation."

"And what have you prepared to say at this moment?"

"I was going to say something very eloquent about how you are the man for me and that I couldn't have fashioned a better one. I was going to insist that you marry me even if I do have a terrible temper and a wretched talent for eavesdropping."

"A husband is going to get in the way of your achievements. You told Caroline as much."

"Now who is guilty of eavesdropping? *A husband* might present a problem, but *my husband* will let me use his microscope—and hide under his tables without yelling at me for making tonics that smell like bile."

He smiled and put his hand on the small of her back to pull her closer. "He does sound perfect. Does your husband still have the final word . . . over anything?"

"I am sure to be the meekest and most obedient wife in the world." The lie was as sweet as butter on her tongue, and she couldn't stop the blush that crept across her cheeks at the merriment in his eyes.

"You are the most delicious liar, Miss Renshaw, and the devil's own when it comes to getting your own way—you realize this?"

"But I have the handwriting of an angel," she reminded him softly.

"And what of Whitfield and Jessop and the hundreds of others like them who are going to spit insults when they hear I've married my apprentice?"

"We'll outwit them. You'll casually mention that you've married a wealthy young woman fascinated by medicine and entirely supportive of your research. As a wise man once said, we'll let the old goats fill in the gaps as they wish."

"A wise man said that?"

"The most brilliant man I've ever known."

He pulled her into his arms. "You do know the way to my heart, don't you, Gayle Renshaw?"

Epilogue

The church was glowing with candles set amidst evergreen finery and holly rings, with garlands hanging from every archway to herald the Yule season and the upcoming new year. It was a small gathering of the Jaded and their closest family inside the ancient stone chapel at Bellewood, and the chill of that Christmas morning was forgotten in the warmth and beauty of the occasion.

The bride wore a dress of Lady Winters's clever design, and the groom had deigned to wear a new coat and hat to honor the day. Rowan and Gayle exchanged their vows, and then everyone burst into cheers at the sight of the beaming couple stepping back through the arches out into the daylight. The emerald ring on Gayle's hand gleamed and sparkled with an evergreen fire all its own, and the men exchanged knowing glances at its significance.

The wedding party made their way quickly back to the warm hearth and hospitality of the home of Ashe's grandfather, Mr. Gordon Blackwell, and glasses were immediately raised to toast the doctor and his wife's health and happiness.

The bachelors in their midst made a subdued effort not to roll their eyes or enter into any debates that might draw attention to their dwindling numbers, but dutifully drank after each toast was made. Only Josiah Hastings wasn't present to raise his glass, but they still had numbers enough to hold their own against the growing pro-matrimony faction.

Caroline and Haley pulled Gayle aside to escape the open rivalry and manly camaraderie that was taking over the small party. "We wanted to wish you happy, Mrs. West. And now, naturally, we'll insist that we use our Christian names and become the best of friends."

"I'd like that. I'd like that very much." Gayle's eyes misted at the sincerity of their offer, thrilled to have found two such allies. "Do you think the men have any idea of the coalition forming in their midst?"

The women shook their heads and laughed. It was Haley who answered, "No, and I don't see any reason to enlighten them!"

Ashe came up behind his wife, a glass of wine in hand for her. "Would you like a chair, ladies? Grandfather Walker just pointed out that there are three very comfortable places by the fire. . . ."

"You're hovering again!" Caroline chided, but a blush revealed that she was not unaffected by his attention. "I am well enough to visit in an ice house if I choose, Mr. Blackwell."

"Of course, you are, darling! I can ask Rowan and Gayle to move the party outside if you'd like to prove it since we're expecting snow, but if you indulge me and sit nearer the warmth, then the Old Monster will commend me for my thoughtfulness and stop glaring at me." Ashe's smile was a wanton and wicked thing to behold, and Gayle had to avert her gaze since the pair seemed to have forgotten she and Haley were there.

"Ashe! You rogue! I'll . . . sit by the fire, but only because . . ." Her blush deepened. "You are impossible!"

The women dutifully moved to sit by the fireplace, and Gayle almost laughed as Caroline waved away her overprotective husband. "Ever since—the difficulty—the man has been . . . very attentive," Caroline finished, her color subsiding slowly as Ashe retreated. "I think he'll wrap me in cotton-wool batting and lock me in my room when he finds out we're expecting again."

"Congratulations!" Haley exclaimed.

"Are you?" Gayle asked softly, instantly excited at the wonderful news.

"I believe we are. I'm going to tell him tonight as a Christmas present." She reached out to grasp their hands. "I'm a little nervous, so I've told you for practice just to make sure that when I said it out loud, the world didn't fall away."

"If he locks you up in a garret, just send a note by pigeon, and Rowan and I will rescue you." Gayle squeezed her hand.

Haley nodded. "I can always send Aunt Alice to draw him off so that you can slip out for a visit. She's fearless!"

Gayle looked for Rowan to enjoy the sight of him so relaxed and happy amidst friends. It was the perfect occasion for new beginnings and she couldn't wait to tell Rowan his fears had proven false.

"It's hard to imagine, isn't it?" Caroline asked softly. "Your life without him. But it wasn't long ago when you'd have traded him for a bonnet. . . ."

"Did I say that?" Gayle put a hand on her chest in mock horror. "You must have misunderstood me."

Rowan approached. "I'm sorry to interrupt, but I wish to steal my wife away for just a moment."

Gayle went with him, curious about his purpose as he led her out of the room and down the hall to a quiet alcove overlooking the garden. It had begun to snow, and for a minute, they both just watched it fall and transform the world outside.

"What are you thinking?" he asked, the warmth of his breath against the outside shell of her ear making her shiver with delight.

"I'm thinking that sometimes it's good to be wrong."

"Is it?"

She nodded.

"And what were you wrong about, Mrs. West?" He planted a kiss on the nape of her neck, working his way down in a sizzling trail of fire as he tasted her skin.

"I was wrong to think bonnets were better than husbands."

He nodded, nuzzling the soft indent behind her ear. "So long as you intend to have just one husband, I'll agree."

Gayle sighed, leaning back against him. "And you were wrong about Caroline not having any more babies. . . ."

He stopped and turned her about to face him. "Was I? Did she say anything to you or are you guessing?"

Gayle put her hands on her hips. "She confided it just now and she's going to tell Ashe tonight. It's a miracle, Rowan."

"I don't believe in miracles."

"I forgot. You don't." She tilted her head to one side, assessing the serious cloud overtaking his countenance. "But luckily, you aren't in charge, so it seems they're going to have a baby whether you believe they can or not."

He pulled a hand through his hair, and Gayle recognized his anxiety with new eyes. "It's dangerously soon after her illness. There could be so much damage internally, and arsenic is a known hemorrhagic agent that this—"

"Rowan! The woman is glowing with health and happiness, and from where I am standing, she is young and has every prospect of delivering a very beautiful baby. Your friend is already worried about her every hiccup. You Jaded are not an . . . optimistic club, are you?"

Rowan shook his head. "Not naturally."

She reached up to frame his face with her hands, cherishing him for the care and concern for his friends that made him so serious. "Dr. West, if you don't believe in miracles, then what do you believe in?"

"Fate, my love. I believe in Fate."

And that a man's luck can change!

A Note to Readers

Gayle Renshaw is only a few years ahead of the true-life female pioneers who tried to break into the extremely male world of British medical practice. Elizabeth Blackwell was the first woman to be accepted onto the medical registers in Britain in 1858, but she was educated in the United States and received her medical degree there. After she registered in London thanks to a loophole in the Registry Act, the loophole was promptly "repaired" to prevent the disaster of more women getting any ideas about following in her footsteps. It wasn't until the 1870s that the real battle began, and again, universities would aggressively change their policies to try to prevent women from gaining the credentials they needed to become licensed physicians.

Even Florence Nightingale, who championed the role of the nurse and pushed for higher standards in care, was horrified at the thought of women becoming physicians. She saw women as apt nurses because of the perfect fit of their obedient and submissive natures and nurturing instincts to the sickroom. She was sure that ignorance in medical matters for nurses was a way to guarantee that a doctor's will would reign supreme in diagnosis and provide better patient care (without any debates or silly ideas from the help!).

Women who expressed interest in practicing medicine were seen as an aberration, as though they were going against nature, and they were violently opposed at every turn. (Women who tried to walk into clinical classrooms had filth hurled at them—literally and figuratively—as educated men became abusive bullies defending their turf.)

But as Gayle and Rowan discussed, the more that women were treated as separate beings requiring special medical care different than their male counterparts, ironically, the wider the door became for women to step in and become qualified to provide care for their peers. And once that barrier was down . . . well, the rest is history.

Even if medical history isn't "your thing," I encourage anyone interested in feminism or women's studies to take a look. If the past is a window into our future, then it never hurts to draw back the curtains and see just what we've overcome. ;-)

* * *

For all my medical references, I used: *Health, Medicine, and Society in Victorian England* by Mary Wilson Carpenter, *Anatomy and Physiology*, Second Edition, by William F. Evans, and *The Illustrated Encyclopedia of Healing Remedies* by C. Norman Shealy, MD, PhD. Also, let's not forget the wonderful gift from my dear husband, *Deadly Doses: A Writer's Guide to Poisons* by Serita Deborah Stevens with Anne Klarner.

Keep reading for an excerpt from
the next Jaded Gentleman novel
by Renee Bernard

Passion Wears Pearls

Coming May 2012 from Berkley Sensation!

Chapter
1

As she reached the landing, she saw him standing in front of the fireplace, silhouetted by the orange glow. Broad shouldered and lean, she was struck by the long lines of him and the latent power there. His light brown hair was far too long and tied back in a loose queue with a strip of leather, but the old-world style suited him. It made him look more rugged and otherworldly, just as an artist should, she imagined.

She cleared her throat to alert the man to her presence. "Mr. Hastings," she said. "I've kept you waiting."

"You didn't know I was coming, so how is that possible?" he countered with a smile. "It was only a few minutes."

Eleanor allowed the lie, flattered that he would go to such trouble. "I'm pleased to see you again, Mr. Hastings, if only to thank you once more for your kindness, but also to see if there is some way to rectify the arrangements."

"Is your apartment not comfortable enough? Mrs. Clay has a reputation for being accommodating, but if you're not happy here, I can look for something else."

"No, you misunderstand. It's very comfortable and far too luxurious for what I can afford."

"It costs you nothing. Surely that isn't too taxing for your purse?"

"Mr. Hastings, I cannot allow you to pay for my lodgings. It isn't proper."

His look was pure innocence, as if the concept was new. "Mrs. Clay is simply repaying me for a favor by offering you a room until you're on your feet."

"I do not like to feel cornered, Mr. Hastings."

All playful pretense fell away, and he squared his shoulders like a man facing sentence. "You aren't."

"Let me be frank. I am at my wit's end, sir. My reserves are . . . If I described them as dwindling, it would be kind. I'm not ungrateful for what you've done, for what you're doing for me, but . . ."

"Say it, Miss Beckett."

"I need to know why. Is this some scheme to ensnare me? Have you an ulterior motive for your generosity?"

"I've kept nothing from you. I've never lied about my interests." Josiah sighed. "I only want to paint you; that desire is unchanged. But honestly, after getting to know you and seeing how determined you are to protect your reputation—I'm not sure if I've done you a disservice already. A thousand chaperones wouldn't protect you from the wicked imaginations and cruel tongues of people who will hear only that you modeled for me."

Eleanor couldn't hide her shock at his confession. "You're withdrawing your offer?"

"No." He shook his head. "I'm letting you know that I'm aware of the price you'll pay for agreeing. I'm letting you know that I'm not oblivious to the dilemma I've presented. But if anything, I'm renewing that offer, Miss Beckett. I am more determined than ever not to lose this chance. And as for the cost of your room and board . . ."

"Yes?" she asked.

"If you agree to sit for me, then if you wish, like your

previous employer, I can deduct the cost of a room from your wages."

"And if I don't agree to sit for you?"

"Then you can find something you like better and live wherever you wish at my expense. I'll still insist on helping you, and we can carry on the argument about unwarranted charity and pride later."

There was a long pause as she nervously reached up to try to smooth down a cold, wet curl that had strayed onto her cheek. "I like it here."

"Then you should have your tea while it's still hot, and we can see about a satisfying dinner for us both."

"I have never eaten dinner alone with a man, Mr. Hastings. I'm not sure if it's—"

"Proper?" he completed her sentence. "You have to eat, Miss Beckett. We can ask the server to stay, if that's better."

She shook her head slowly. "No, that was foolish. You've already saved my life and I can't keep insisting that it isn't proper to trust you."

He smiled. "Thank you." He rang the bell for the serving man, who answered the summons almost immediately. Josiah ordered for them both as if to give her time to gird herself for the next debate. Once they were alone, he leaned back in his chair. "May I ask you a personal question, Miss Beckett?"

"I suppose." She was wary, taking new measure of her handsome petitioner. His honesty was disarming and she was struggling to come up with firm objections to a man who offered the solution to all her present difficulties.

"How did you come to work for Madame Claremont?"

"It's a long story and a bit complicated." Eleanor looked away embarrassed, but then lifted her chin. "My father was quite successful in his business until things took a turn for the worse two years ago. He was a chemist and an inventor and came up with an array of new smelling salts that might be vaguely pleasing to the customer."

"Sounds like a clever idea. Not that I've ever been in the market for them, but I can see the appeal."

She gave him a skeptical look, but continued calmly. "He'd invested everything in them, but his partner stole the formulas and patented them as his own to sell to a drug company all too happy with the potential profits."

"Your father must have had some legal recourse."

She nodded. "He did, and the lawyers were also all too happy to take the last of my father's money in the pursuit of his case. He kept most of his troubles from us until near the end, borrowing money from disreputable creditors to shield us from any hardships. But then my mother died of influenza. It was too much for him. His heart failed and he followed her within the week."

"My God," he exclaimed softly. "When did all of this take place?"

"Last summer." She picked up her teacup, the illusion of her cool composure spoiled by her trembling hands. "The solicitors took everything to settle his debts, legal and domestic, and I was literally turned out. I have no relatives to speak of, and I refuse to impose myself on family friends who had made their indifference clear by their silence when it was discovered that my father's fortunes had changed."

"You have no one?"

"I am very resourceful, Mr. Hastings. I've had a superior education, I possess some skills with a needle, and I'm not the sort of woman to sit helplessly on the floor and lament my fate. I'm not afraid of honest work."

"You continually amaze, Miss Beckett."

"Why? Because I sought work in a dress shop and discovered I'm as trusting as my father when it comes to other people and their true intentions?"

"Anyone with a good nature expects to find the same in others. You're no fool, Miss Beckett, and don't think for a moment that I'd mistake you for one."

Her shoulders relaxed and she smiled gratefully. "Thank you, Mr. Hastings."

"But it does make things more challenging if you don't trust your own instincts. I very much want you to sit for me, Miss Beckett. I can't hide my intentions, nor do I want to, but you will have to trust me."

"You really want to paint *me*?" she asked, lowering her voice at the scandalous subject. "You're sure?"

"Is it really so surprising a notion?"

"I am no great beauty, sir, and there is something . . . awkward . . . about presuming that I am worthy of . . . such attention." Her skin warmed at the thought of such a man openly staring and studying her for hours on end. It didn't seem possible to hold anyone's interest for that period of time, but even so, the way he looked at her now, hungry and wary, eager and cautious—as if he feared she would bolt from the room and spoil his plans, made her want nothing more than to let him look his fill. She wanted to do whatever she could to ease the ache in his expression and please him.

And that alone was reason enough to refuse him.

I'm not myself when he looks at me like that. I become another woman who would sit on a dais and preen and hide nothing from him.

"Tell me what you're thinking." His command was soft but compelling.

"I'm wishing I were a stronger person. I'm wishing your offer didn't appeal."

"Why?"

"Because I think saying yes would reveal some great flaw in my character. It will make me less in other people's eyes."

"To hell with what other people think, Miss Beckett." He leaned forward, the intensity of his gaze pinning her in place. "Say yes and become more. Become your own woman, independent again, and unconcerned with the gossip of small minds. You'll have the money you need to create any life you desire. If you never broke another rule again for the rest of your life, so be it. But don't deny me, Eleanor. Help me to achieve this work and I'll spend an eternity in your debt."

Independent again. Any life I desire. It sounds too easy.

She took one deep breath, so aware of the sodden weight of her wet wool skirts, the tight icy feel of her leather boots, and even the confines of her corset and clothing. She felt constricted and cold. To turn him down was to embrace a future without promise, as bleak as an English moor. To accept him was to let go of fear and pride and gamble her very soul for the hope of a life with security and comfort again.

"I am not for sale, Mr. Hastings," she whispered.

"I'm not offering to purchase you, Miss Beckett. I would simply pay for the right to look at you, for as long as I wish—for the sole purpose of capturing your likeness.

And there it was.

The right to look at you, for as long as I wish.

"I'm not taking off my . . ." She swallowed hard, unsure of how a person delicately addressed the subject of nudity with such a man. "I won't pose without . . ."

"I'll not ask you to remove a thing against your will." His brown eyes blazed hotter than the embers of a fire. "And if that was your last objection, I take it that your answer is—"

"Yes."

God help me. Yes.

**From *New York Times* bestselling author
of *Sinful in Satin***

MADELINE HUNTER

Dangerous in Diamonds

Outrageously wealthy, the Duke of Castleford has little incentive to curb his profligate ways—gaming and whoring with equal abandon and enjoying his hedonistic lifestyle to the fullest. When a behest adds a small property to his vast holdings, one that houses a modest flower business known as The Rarest Blooms, Castleford sees little to interest him . . . until he lays eyes on its owner. Daphne Joyes is coolly mysterious, exquisitely beautiful, and utterly scathing toward a man of Castleford's stamp—in short, an object worthy of his most calculated seduction.

Daphne has no reason to entertain Castleford's outrageous advances, and every reason to keep him as far away as possible from her eclectic household. Not only has she been sheltering young ladies who have been victims of misfortune, but she has her own closely guarded secrets. Then Daphne makes a discovery that changes everything. She and Castleford have one thing in common: a profound hatred for the Duke of Becksbridge, who just happens to be Castleford's relative.

Never before were two people less likely to form an alliance—or to fall in love . . .

penguin.com

JOANNA BOURNE

presents her stunning and award-winning debut novel

THE
Spymaster's Lady

She's never met a man she couldn't deceive . . .
until now.

She's braved battlefields. She's stolen dispatches from under the noses of heads of state. She's played the worldly courtesan, the naive virgin, the refined British lady, even a Gypsy boy. But Annique Villiers, the elusive spy known as the Fox Cub, has finally met the one man she can't outwit.

"A FLAT-OUT SPECTACULAR BOOK."
—*All About Romance*

"Love, love, LOVED it!"
—Julia Quinn

Now available in trade paperback

M626T1209

Enter the rich world of
historical romance
with Berkley Books . . .

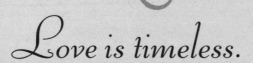

Madeline Hunter

Jennifer Ashley

Joanna Bourne

Lynn Kurland

Jodi Thomas

Anne Gracie

Love is timeless.

berkleyjoveauthors.com

Penguin Group (USA) Online

What will you be reading tomorrow?

Patricia Cornwell, Nora Roberts, Catherine Coulter,
Ken Follett, John Sandford, Clive Cussler,
Tom Clancy, Laurell K. Hamilton, Charlaine Harris,
J. R. Ward, W.E.B. Griffin, William Gibson,
Robin Cook, Brian Jacques, Stephen King,
Dean Koontz, Eric Jerome Dickey, Terry McMillan,
Sue Monk Kidd, Amy Tan, Jayne Ann Krentz,
Daniel Silva, Kate Jacobs...

You'll find them all at
penguin.com

*Read excerpts and newsletters,
find tour schedules and reading group guides,
and enter contests.*

Subscribe to Penguin Group (USA) newsletters
and get an exclusive inside look
at exciting new titles and the authors you love
long before everyone else does.

PENGUIN GROUP (USA)
penguin.com